The
Telltale
Turtle

The
Telltale
Turtle

A Pet Psychic Mystery

Joyce & Jim Lavene

MIDNIGHT INK
WOODBURY, MINNESOTA

First Edition
First Printing, 2008

Book design and format by Donna Burch
Cover design by Lisa Novak
Cover illustration © Robert Lawson
Editing by Connie Hill

Midnight Ink, an imprint of Llewellyn Publications

Library of Congress Cataloging-in-Publication Data
Lavene, Joyce.
   The telltale turtle / Joyce & Jim Lavene. — 1st ed.
      p. cm.
   "A pet psychic mystery."
   ISBN 978-0-7387-1226-0 (alk. paper)
   1. Pet psychics—Fiction. 2. Radio talk shows—Fiction. 3. Human-animal communication—Fiction. I. Lavene, James. II. Title.
   PS3562.A8479T45   2008
   813'.54—dc22
                                                                2008028796

Midnight Ink
Llewellyn Publications
2143 Wooddale Drive, Dept. 978-0-7387-1226-0
Woodbury, MN 55125-2989 USA
www.midnightinkbooks.com

Printed in the United States of America

ONE

"This is Mary Catherine Roberts, the pet psychic. You're live on Lite 102.5 WRSC in Wilmington, North Carolina. Tell me about your pet."

"Hi. My name is Albert. I listen to your show every day, Mary Catherine. I'm calling about my dog, Ginger. She's getting older and has started chewing on things. Her teeth are falling out—that's how bad it is! I'm desperate."

"Well, we know she has a problem, don't we? She wouldn't just pick up that habit. We have to figure out *why* she's chewing. She's trying to tell you something. Dogs want to do what we ask, ordinarily. What does she choose to chew?"

"Mostly my shoes. She won't leave them alone. If I hide them in the closet, she scratches on the door to get at them. If I accidentally leave a pair out, she chews them to shreds."

"I see. Do you walk her often? Besides the obligatory trip to the potty."

"I used to walk her several times a day when I worked for my-self. But my new job keeps me busy for longer hours. I had to cut back. Now I only walk her once in the morning and once when I come home. Just until she goes; you know?"

"Dogs don't like change, Albert. None of us do. If you don't have time to walk her more often, hire someone to do it for you. Your dog needs some exercise. She's chewing your shoes because she knows you have to put them on to take her out. She wants your attention."

"Wow! That makes sense. I'll try it." Albert sounded relieved. "Thanks, Mary Catherine. You're a genius, like always."

"You're welcome. Good luck. Give my best to Ginger."

Mary Catherine looked at WRSC station manager, Colin Jamison, who stood outside the glass sound booth. He looked unusually stressed. That was saying a lot for a man who looked unusual when he *wasn't* stressed.

"Good job," he remarked absently when she stepped out of the glass box. "Your ratings are looking great this month, by the way."

"Thanks." Sometimes she wished she understood humans as well as she understood animals. She wouldn't have to ask ridiculous questions. "Is something wrong, Colin? You look a little under the weather."

He shrugged slender shoulders and adjusted his black wire-rimmed glasses, which seemed to weigh heavily on his thin, sallow face. His curly brown hair was baby-fine above a high forehead and studious brown eyes. "I'm okay. I have a few family problems. But everything will work out. How's the clinic?"

"It's good. Too busy sometimes. But good. You should come down and volunteer for a few hours. You might like it."

He laughed uncomfortably, white teeth as even and straight as his childhood dentist could make them. "Wish I had time! You know my schedule."

"You're digging yourself an early grave." She flung her marmalade-colored Batik shawl flamboyantly across one shoulder. "You should take some time to relax."

"I would. But *someone* has to keep the sponsors happy." He glanced at the man in the sound booth who'd taken Mary Catherine's place at the microphone. "Jimmy won't do restaurant openings, even though he's a food critic. Stacey won't endorse her sponsor's hair-care products on the air even though she gives beauty tips."

"And I won't pitch Meaty Boy dog food. I know." She smiled at him. "I guess we're lucky to have you to keep it all together for us. You're a very talented man."

He tried to return her smile, but his pursed lips wouldn't turn up at the ends and he finally gave up. It made him look like he had a nervous tick. "You could do one *small* endorsement."

The enormous, orange-colored tabby cat who sat on the green vinyl chair meowed loudly and shook his head.

"Quiet, Baylor," she admonished. "Stay out of this. You aren't a dog."

"Wow!" Mindy Evans, Colin's fiancée, looked at the cat as she joined them. "How do you get him to do that anyway? I don't think I've ever seen a cat that's trained like him. I didn't even know you could train a cat. Every time I see it, I'm amazed."

"You mean sit in one place for an hour?" Mary Catherine smoothed Baylor's plush fur with an absent hand. "That's what cats do best. And he wants to be here with me."

"You *tell* him where to sit every day and he sits there." Mindy took Colin's arm and smiled at him. She was a perfect foil for him; pretty, blond, and mostly unconcerned about things. She was good at what she did and kept everyone on an even keel. She'd been at the station since Mary Catherine got there two years ago. "How do you do *that*?"

Before Mary Catherine could answer, a tall, broad-shouldered man in a gray Western-style suit and a matching Stetson pushed his way into the room. "There's my psychic angel! Mary Catherine, you're looking mighty fine today!"

She rolled her expressive, dark-blue eyes. She wasn't sure if it was the terrible cologne he splashed on with a heavy hand, his obnoxiously friendly attitude, or the fact that he'd made his money being the Marlboro man on TV for years. Whatever it was, Clinton "Buck" Maybelle irritated her. Just being in the room with him made her want to hit him with something.

Not a good sign, since most of her intimate relationships with men started out that way. She'd lost her fourth husband, George Roberts, only two years ago, just before she moved to Wilmington, North Carolina. She wasn't ready to go through all that again.

"Mr. Maybelle." Colin shook the older man's hand, sucking up as always. Something *he* did best. "Glad you stopped by."

Buck played a short game of seeing which man could squeeze hardest (Colin *always* lost at this game), only giving up as he saw Mary Catherine head for the elevator. "Say, how 'bout some lunch? I've got my yacht tied up down at River Street. We could take a nice cruise while we're at it."

"I'd love to." Colin cleared his throat. "But I'm tied up in meetings all afternoon. Maybe next week?"

"Not you, squirt! I'm talking to Miss Mary."

"Please don't call me that." Mary Catherine held out her arms and Baylor jumped up into them. He blended in perfectly with her shawl and her shoulder-length hair as he snuggled in close and warily eyed the man in the hat.

"Sorry!" Buck winked at Colin. "The lady is *touchy* today."

She gave him a cold stare. "The lady is touchy every day where *you're* concerned."

"What else can I do to show you how I feel? Isn't it enough I pledge my faith by sponsoring your talk show even though you won't endorse my Meaty Boy dog food on the air?"

"Not really. You manage to sell your dog food without my help. Or should I say because people *think* I'm helping you."

"Now Mary Catherine, we've been over this. I took you to tour the plant. We use prime ingredients. There's nothing wrong with Meaty Boy!"

"Except every dog hates it."

"Dogs eat it!"

"You'd eat swill if you were starving too!"

"Please!" Mindy glanced nervously around the room. "Could you *please* move the discussion outside? I'm afraid you'll be heard on-air."

Mary Catherine ignored Buck. "Of course. Baylor and I were on our way home anyway. I hope things work out for you, Colin. See you tomorrow, Mindy."

The cat meowed again, face alert, whiskers twitching, ignoring everything to watch his prey. His blue eyes never strayed from Buck's florid face as the man followed Mary Catherine into the elevator.

"Meaty Boy is healthy *and* nutritious. I don't get it. Dogs don't care what they eat as long as it has meat in it anyway. What do you have against it?"

"The dogs I've spoken to hate it. They say it tastes like burnt turnips. The only reason you're still sponsoring my show is because you play golf with the station owner! Make a palatable dog food or I'll find a local sponsor who knows how to play golf as well as you do!"

Buck laughed. "You're really something when you're angry! Weehaa! I like a woman with spirit! Why don't you invite your dog friends for a taste test? You know, like people do. They can try different kinds of food and see if they can tell the difference. If they can and they won't eat it, I'll change the formula, even though it's been in my family for a hundred years."

"Oh all right! If I can get any of them to come, I will. But don't blame me if no one trusts you."

He started to move closer to her and the cat on her shoulder hissed, warning him away. "If you can *really* talk to animals, darlin', I suggest you talk to that fur ball there. He's a mite testy!"

"He feels the same about you, Buck. Call me about the taste test later in the week. I'll see what I can line up. Maybe a few of the dogs at the clinic will volunteer. Although it hardly seems fair, since some of them have *already* been abused!"

I'm only doing this for Colin because he looked so out of sorts today. Mary Catherine reminded herself of that fact several times as she left Buck at the Port City Java coffee shop downstairs from the station, grateful that Danny's cab was waiting at the sidewalk outside.

Baylor tossed his big head and looked unimpressed.

"You don't have to deal with him, do you?" she demanded of him. "He only called you a fur ball. He called me Miss Mary and his little psychic angel! How do you think *I* feel?"

"MC!" Danny greeted her as she opened the orange taxi door. "*Buenos tardes! Como esta*? How did the broadcast go?"

"It went fine until Buck showed up." She slid into the back seat. "You know how I feel about him."

"As always," he sympathized. "Where to?"

"Home. Baylor and I both need some lunch."

"We could stop by Raul's café for burritos." He grinned as he hyped his brother's café. His teeth flashed white against his dark skin.

"I don't think I'm up to spicy food today, Danny. Thanks anyway."

"*De nada.*" He shrugged as he pulled out into slow traffic that moved along the river in historic downtown Wilmington. "Baylor, you want a burrito?"

The tabby cat meowed, but Mary Catherine hushed him. "You don't need that either. The last time you sneaked out and got a burrito, we were both sorry. No more beans for you!"

Baylor slid down her lap and slumped on the floor.

"Oh, now he's going to pout!" She shook her head. "It's not enough he's the only animal allowed into the radio station! It's not enough he does whatever he pleases!"

Danny laughed, his agile hands loose on the wheel as he negotiated walking tourists and sightseeing traffic along the narrow street. "Sorry, *amigo*. Maybe some other time."

A large yacht, the name *Blockade Runner* etched on the side, went slowly by, pine deck gleaming in the sun. Artists sat or stood beside easels all along the bank of the Cape Fear River in the old port town. They chalked and pasteled the picturesque river scene with the countless white sails against the warm blue sky. The new summer breeze shuffled through the streets, ruffling the leaves in the oak trees, and the smell of the river drifted across the city.

Gulls followed the ocean-going ships, calling from the sky above them. It was hard to hear anything besides the racket their disordered cries presented. But there was *something* else. A faint small voice steadily called out for help in the midst of the louder shouts of the gulls demanding fish.

Closing her eyes, Mary Catherine focused her concentration on that voice, ignoring all the other sounds that assailed her through the open window. "Danny, we have to stop!"

The young Latino driver immediately put his foot on the brake, the taxi rocking as it squealed to a stop. Other cars behind him pushed on their horns to get him going. "*Que pasa*? Are you okay, MC?"

"I'm fine. But Tommy needs help." Mary Catherine kept her eyes closed but Baylor grimaced, startled by the quick stop.

"Tommy?" Danny looked around, his black hair gleaming in the sunlight that came through the open window. "Who's Tommy?"

"I'm not sure yet." She held on to the sound of the tiny voice in her head. The breeze whipped her thick, tawny blond hair away from her face, blue eyes lost to the world as she stared out at the wide gray stretch of river.

"Do you want to go back to the clinic?"

"No. I need to go *that* way." She pointed toward the rows of large houses on the street above them.

"Do you have an address?"

"No. He's never been outside that he can recall. And such a small thing! Even if he had, how would he have seen an address?"

Danny chewed on his lip. "Okay. Let me get through this traffic so we can turn up Market Street."

She smiled back at him. "Thanks. I'll tell you where to stop."

Not surprised by the request (it happened all the time), Danny drove quickly away from the river, past the old red brick buildings that had lined it for two hundred years and more. Wealthy residents of the city had built on the streets away from the river, turning the backs of their homes away from the water like old ladies. Their owners preferred not to see the sordid alleys and dingy taverns that served the pirates like Blackbeard and Stede Bonnet who came into port after ravaging the coast.

Three- and four-story Queen Anne Victorians and solid Colonials with massive white pillars sat comfortably in their two or three hundred-year grace, happy to lean tired shoulders against soaring oaks and pink crape myrtles. Narrow streets suited the area, even if they didn't keep up with the traffic from more and more tourists every year. The lovely old-lady houses slumbered in the warm June sun, hiding the secrets of the families who lived inside.

"Here!" Mary Catherine stopped him as he would have passed an old house snuggled between two larger ones. The red brick was mellowed to a pink color, half hidden by enormous magnolias whose white flowers swooned in the heat between glossy green leaves.

Danny applied the brakes with a squeal again, turning sharply into the moss-covered brick drive, ignoring the horns that followed his action. "This it?"

9

"I think so. I may need your help. Would you mind coming up with me?"

"Wouldn't miss it!" He grinned, opening the door. "Every day is an adventure with you, MC. Remember last month when you heard that St. Bernard who was staked out at the garage because his owners didn't want to take him with them?"

"Bruno." She nodded, getting out of the taxi quickly. Baylor trotted out behind her. "He's still waiting to be adopted."

"No wonder! He almost ripped my jeans off when I reached for his collar."

"He was scared," she reminded him. "He thought you might hurt him."

"Hurt *him*? *Dios*! He weighs close to three hundred pounds! His teeth are an inch long and ..."

"Shh! I can't hear Tommy."

"Sorry. Got anything to eat?"

She raked through her huge brocade pocketbook, but could only come up with some stale pita bread in a plastic bag and a half-eaten Snicker's bar. "That's about it."

He took the Snickers bar. "*Gracias*. I'm starving."

She glanced up at the house. The pitiful cry coming from inside its lovely façade was enough to break her heart. She hoped it wouldn't take a prolonged discussion with Tommy's owners to help him. She didn't mind explaining who she was and what she did. She hated for any animal to suffer longer than necessary.

The drive and sidewalk were made of the same aged brick as the house. Mary Catherine squinted up at the front door. Black iron letters graced the portal with the address. Ivy grew up the front and side walls. She put Baylor back in the car despite his protests. She didn't know what she'd find in the house and it would be easier without his interference.

Even though they were on one of the main roads through Wilmington, the smell of summer was strong and sweet in her senses with magnolias complementing perfumed roses. Set back at least a block from the street, the house and land gave the appearance of being muffled and sheltered from real life. Mary Catherine could imagine looking out of those wide upstairs windows every day, peering out from the blinds at the world.

When she reached the front door, she stopped. It was a big door, made of strong hardwood, no doubt. An iron post held a lantern to light the way for guests, and there was mail in the fierce-looking black iron box on the wall. A pretty welcome mat with a smiling bumblebee lay on the porch. These were ordinary things people took for granted, like security and warmth. The people who lived in this house probably had no idea what it was like to look for a place to sleep at night or wonder where their next meal was going to come from.

She lifted her hand to knock but the door swung open before she touched it. She blinked, pausing with her hand in mid air. "Hello? Anyone home?"

"Spooky," Danny whispered around the Snickers bar in his mouth as he followed right behind her.

Mary Catherine walked slowly past the pink marble-floored foyer, following the sound of fear and sorrow only she could hear. *Dry. Pale. Bright. Sharp. Pain.* The thoughts were rudimentary, scrambled. Something Tommy didn't understand was keeping him from escaping whatever he was trying to get away from.

11

The sound seemed to be coming from a large sitting room immediately on the right. The instant she stepped on the champagne-colored carpet, she knew she was in the right place. The house seemed deserted, except for one small voice.

"There you are!" She bent down and scooped up the tiny yellow-bellied slider that was trying to push through the plush carpet. "You're hurt. How did this happen to you?" She examined his back leg, a bloody gash leaving a trail behind him.

Fragments of a lovely crystal bowl with a rock and some strewn turtle food came into her line of vision. The glass was shattered. It was probably where Tommy cut his leg. The bright light he saw was a huge chandelier in the ceiling that was turned on, despite the warm sunshine streaming in through the white lace on the front windows.

The thing that wouldn't let him move forward, too large for him to surmount, was the body of a woman in her nightclothes. She appeared to be close to Mary Catherine's age. There were pink curlers in her gray-streaked brown hair and a cut on her neck that looked like it came from her fall against the large, broken piece of the turtle bowl. A pool of blood surrounded her, blooming against the pale carpet like the roses outside the door.

"*Dio!* Is she dead?" Danny asked in a breathless voice.

"I believe she is," Mary Catherine confirmed, taking in the scene. "I think we should call the police."

Besides the turtle bowl on the floor, there was also a potted plant. Dirt was scattered all over the dead woman's slippers. Had she been surprised by a thief in the middle of the night? Was it an accident? All the mess could've been caused by a struggle. Or the woman might've had a heart attack and stumbled across those things. Still, that didn't account for the front door being open.

Compassion for the other woman made Mary Catherine touch her hand. It was cold. "Rest easy now. God provides."

Danny's handsome dark features had turned a terrible pasty shade that looked like old buttermilk. He hurried out of the house to throw up the Snickers bar on the pristine emerald green lawn.

"Oh, dear," Mary Catherine said to the turtle in her hand. "There's a frog out there that wasn't too happy about *that*!"

Hi, Mary Catherine;

My name is Edwin and I live in Perth, Australia. I love your show! A kangaroo saved my life this week! A young kangaroo that I saved from a truck accident three years ago rolled me over to keep me breathing after I was hit in the chest by a tree branch and lost consciousness. She kept jumping up and down and causing a commotion until someone finally came out of the house to see what was wrong.

Do you think I should set her free?

TWO

"WHO FOUND THE BODY?" The detective adjusted his tie several times, in classic body language for frustration. His shirt collar had wilted in the heat and humidity, curling around his throat. There were burrito stains on his pocket and on the notebook he used to take notes. He licked his fingers and smudged it clean.

"I guess we found her together," Mary Catherine told the detective. Danny couldn't come in the room again without being sick. He waited by the front door, chafing his sneaker against the pink marble.

"All right. Detective Angellus will take his statement." He directed the younger man toward the foyer, then turned back to her.

She sighed as she sat and knitted in the far corner of the wide room, trying not to see the detective's furrowed brow. It would have been like not seeing a hurricane coming up from the sea.

"Roberts? Is that right? Mary Catherine Roberts." He looked up from the paper in his hand where the responding police officer

14

had written her name and address. He glanced at Baylor. "Does that animal belong to the deceased?"

"No, he's mine." She put aside her knitting and lifted her head, hoping her chin didn't seem to fold into her neck as it sometimes did. Reaching the ripe age of fifty-plus left little room for vanity; she still didn't want a good-looking man to think badly of her. "Baylor, say hello."

The tabby cat meowed, then tucked himself into the folds of her wide green cotton skirt. He'd insisted on coming inside while she and Danny waited for the police.

"He's feeling a little shy right now."

"Of course he is." The athletic-looking man in the dark brown suit shook his graying blond head. "Okay. I'm Detective Walt Abraham of the Wilmington Police Department. I'll be investigating this case. Do you always bring your cat along when you visit friends?"

She put out her hand to him. This forced Detective Abraham to reach out and shake it. He had good, strong hands. She liked that in a man. It was a sign of character, her mother always said. "Mostly. But I wasn't here on a social call. I don't even know that poor woman."

She shuddered as she glanced at the splash of red that still marked the pale carpet where the woman's body had been. Blue-uniformed people had removed her only a few minutes before. A dozen more police assistants walked around the room, collecting things in plastic bags and taking pictures.

"Oh?" Detective Abraham looked at her in a different light. Mary Catherine looked like a bag lady, or a caricature of a gypsy from the last century. Green skirt, purple vest, and ruffled white blouse seemed to flow around her. Her hair and shawl were almost the color of the tabby cat at her feet. She was roughly middle fifties, five-foot-five, maybe 180 pounds. "What were you doing here then, Mrs. Roberts?"

"The poor thing was screaming out in pain. I heard him and came to help."

Detective Abraham eyed his partner near the door, obviously wishing he'd taken the taxi driver to question. "You heard Mrs. Jamison screaming out when she died. Was this as you went by?"

"Heavens no!" *Jamison? That was a strange coincidence. Was the dead woman related to Colin?* "I came to save her turtle. Of course I didn't *know* it was a turtle at the time. Animals aren't very good at classifying themselves the way humans do. I only knew he was in some kind of trouble and his name was Tommy. I came here to help him."

"Her *turtle?*"

She took the yellow-bellied slider out of her purse. "You can see where he must've been in the bowl when it fell. His front leg was cut by the glass. It pains him but I'm sure he'll be fine. He'll probably need a new home."

"Don't look at me," he said quickly, then checked himself. "Are you for real?"

She sighed and put the turtle back. "That's part of the problem. No one wants to take responsibility. I'll take him in, at least until he mends. Then we'll see if we can find him a good home. Or he might rather be released into the wild again. I believe someone found him near a stream."

"So the turtle talked to you? Was that before or after Mrs. Jamison died? Were you here when he told you he was in pain?"

"No. I was down by the river. That's why Danny's here. He drove me up in his taxi."

"If you weren't here, how did you hear him? I mean, he couldn't talk very loud, could he? He's a pretty small turtle."

"I heard him, but not the way you mean it. They don't really have a language I can understand. I hear his thoughts. They're strange and disjointed. Non-mammals are. But it was clear to me he was in pain and needed help. I'm a pet psychic."

"Pet psychic?"

She handed him her card. "I do a syndicated radio talk show called *Mary Catherine Roberts, The Pet Psychic*, at Lite 102.5. I've been on television a few times. *Life* magazine did a story on me once. I've helped people all across the world with their pets. I lived in California for a while with my second late husband. I worked with several famous movie stars there, although I'm not at liberty to divulge their names. It can be as simple as two dogs fighting because one of the dogs has taken a favorite toy of the other dog. Once he agrees to give it back, everything is fine. Or it can be very complicated. Once—"

"You talk to animals." Abraham scribbled something in his notebook, not concealing his urge to laugh.

She frowned. This wasn't going very well at all. "I know it can be hard to understand, Detective, but I assure you I'm legitimate. I've helped thousands of people with their pet problems. I communicate with animals that need to express something to their owners. It can be about what they're eating, behavior problems, illness. Or in this case, something more tragic."

"And people *pay* you to do this?"

17

"Yes, they do." He'd touched on her sore point. Why was it people thought the worst of someone who made money using their gifts? "But I also run a free clinic where we take in hurt and stray animals and find homes for them. I like to help wherever possible. It's my calling."

"Of course." He smiled at her. "Will you excuse me a moment?"

She watched him speak to the detective at the door. The two men looked at her, then glanced away quickly. She sighed. This was much simpler in Los Angeles. And if George Wilson, her second late husband, hadn't died, she'd still be there with him. He should have told her he was allergic to bees. They shouldn't have been walking through the garden. Unfortunately, she'd never had much luck communicating with insects.

Detective Abraham came back to her. "We'd like you to come with us to the station and make a statement, ma'am, if you wouldn't mind."

Mary Catherine wished she could hear what *he* was thinking. He probably thought she was a flake or worse. She didn't like using parlor tricks to impress people, although she did it when it was necessary. *What was he up to?* "All right. But I hope this won't take long."

"It shouldn't take too long, ma'am." He put his hand under her arm to help her to her feet. "Just a few questions."

As she was gathering her knitting together, Colin walked into the house. "Aunt Ferndelle? Aunt Ferndelle?"

"She's not here." Abraham stood in front of Mary Catherine, long legs spread wide like a pirate on the deck of a ship. "And you are—?"

"Colin Jamison. What's happened? Why are you all here? Where's my aunt?"

Detective Abraham explained that a woman was found dead in the sitting room. Colin sat down hard in one of the upholstered chairs. "I can't believe this! She can't be dead."

Baylor brushed against Mary Catherine's leg and she nodded. "You're too suspicious. Besides, there's no reason to think this wasn't an accident."

A small cry from her purse had a different view. Tommy was sure there was more than one person present when he fell on the floor. There were loud words. One person fell down and stayed on the floor. It was the human who'd taken him from his home in the creek.

Mary Catherine put her hand to her head. Listening to the turtle's random thoughts gave her a headache. "You might be right to be suspicious, Baylor. We have to tell the detective about this!"

———

But no one would listen to her. They took her to the police station, gave her a can of Coke and she waited for three hours in a small gray room before she talked to someone again.

Detective Angellus finally came in and sat down with her at the rickety old table. "I have to tell you, Mrs. Roberts. You pretty much freaked out my partner. The first thing he checked when we got back was to see if anyone had escaped from the state mental hospital. He thought you were Looney Tunes."

Mary Catherine didn't see anything funny about that theory. She didn't like the smirk on the detective's swarthy young face as he glanced through a file with her name on it. "The next thing he checked was to see if you have a record. I see you're originally from Wilmington. Born Mary Catherine Conner. Is Roberts your *real* name or a stage name?"

"I'm surprised that file doesn't answer all your questions. The Internet is a good source of information. I have at least fifty pages about me. It's my real name. My fourth late husband was George Roberts from West Palm Beach. He died two years ago. I moved back here after his accident."

"And George Wilson of Los Angeles? He died from a bee sting. Who was he?"

"My second late husband. And it was *several* bee stings. They were swarming."

"And Andrew Smith of Chicago?"

"My first late husband. He was killed in an unfortunate boating accident on Lake Michigan."

"And Per Van Eppen?"

"My third late husband, from Long Island." She sighed. "Why are you asking me about *my* past? What does this have to do with what happened today?"

Detective Angellus sat back. He made a pyramid of his long hands as he stared at her and smiled. "You're a colorful character, Mrs. Roberts, pet psychic. A widow four times over. Each husband died from something unusual. Long Island. Chicago. LA. You get around, don't you?"

"What do you want from me, Detective? Surely dredging up painful memories for me won't help you solve this case."

"*Is* there a case? Do you think Mrs. Jamison was murdered?"

"I don't know. I'm not a detective. The room was a mess but I suppose that could've been from death throes. Tommy doesn't think it was an accident."

"Tommy?"

"Her turtle." She coaxed the tiny creature out of her bag again, though he protested pitifully. "He saw the whole thing, you know. His field of vision isn't very great but he says there were two people in the room before Mrs. Jamison fell down and broke his bowl. You'd be wise to pay attention to him. The door to the house *was* open when I got there."

"Very observant." He snapped his chewing gum and nodded. "Maybe you should've been with the police. Or maybe you're the other person who was there with her when she died."

"Don't be ridiculous! The woman was stone cold already!"

"You touched her?"

"She was another human being, Detective Angellus. A woman my own age." Her eyes blurred with tears. "How could I *not* touch her?"

"But you didn't know her."

"No. Although I work with her nephew, Colin Jamison, that young man who collapsed at the house. He's the station manager at WRSC."

"He's the man who wandered into the house this morning." Angellus opened another file. His dark eyes were suspicious. "Seems his aunt was worth some money. Did anyone ever mention that to you?"

"I was here when his parents were killed in that boating accident," she replied. "I remember all the press the family got when his aunt inherited the family estate and fortune. I don't think Colin would be involved in something like this. He's not the type."

"What type is he?"

"The kind who waits until his relative dies a natural death. Colin isn't a killer."

"Oh yeah. What does the turtle have to say about that?"

"He has plenty to say, but as you can imagine, his perspective is a little different than ours. He was a wild animal, not raised with humans. They think differently than say a cat or a dog. Sometimes it's hard to understand them."

"So you can talk to animals, but you can't always understand them, and the turtle is telling you about his owner getting killed, but you can't tell us who did it. Does that sum it up?"

"I'm afraid so. Maybe as the shock wears off, he might remember a little more."

"Lucky for you your vet at the clinic verifies where you were last night when we think Mrs. Jamison died." He closed her file and stood up. "Go home and don't get into trouble here in Wilmington, ma'am. We're not like LA or New York. It's a small town. You know that from living here. We tend to remember faces and names. Marry some guy who lives a long time, okay?"

"What about Ferndelle Jamison?" Mary Catherine ignored his ultimatums. "I'm sure her death wasn't an accident. I might be able to coax something more from Tommy."

"We can handle it without the turtle, thanks anyway. Lucky for *you*, the medical examiner thinks it happened about midnight, while you were at your clinic. The taxi driver seems to have a pat alibi for that time as well."

"So she *was* murdered?"

"We don't know for sure yet. But if it was an accident, it was one of those weird ones like your late husbands had. I'll have an officer drive you home, ma'am."

"Thank you, Detective Angellus." She got to her feet slowly after all that time sitting in the hard wooden chair. "I hope it won't be necessary for me to come back again."

"What do you mean?"

"Someone killed that poor woman. I hope you can find out who it was on your own. If not, as I said, Tommy might be some help. I've been involved with police investigations before. In LA, there was a young girl who was kidnapped. The only witness was her dog, Sparky. The police were very happy when I told them Melissa's kidnapper was her uncle, a man Sparky knew well because he frequently brought dog treats with him when he visited. It seems the uncle was setting things up for a while before the incident. People think dogs are only concerned with what they eat, but that's not true." She handed him a business card. "Here's where you can find me."

"The turtle is gonna help us out, right?" He laughed. "Sorry, ma'am. It just got the best of me. I think we can take care of this without the turtle. But tell him thanks for offering."

"I will. Goodbye, Detective."

"Goodbye, Mrs. Roberts. Stay out of trouble, you hear?"

THREE

THE BLACK AND WHITE squad car let Mary Catherine and Baylor out in front of the red brick building that faced River Street. The building leaned slightly backward as though drawn by the sound of the sea coming from that direction. To the front was the Cape Fear River. Lights blossomed across the smooth, dark surface of the water as daylight faded into evening.

Light also illuminated the dozen or so windows that faced her from her home. Around the building were others like it where downtown rejuvenation had created antique shops, bookstores, bars and restaurants. The same spaces had housed taverns, inns, and bawdy houses two hundred years before.

It was this building that brought her home after so many years. Her Aunt Sylvia Caldwell had left it to her. It was a surprise since she didn't even know she *had* an Aunt Sylvia. But everything was in order. Sylvia had been her mother's sister. Mary Catherine's mother had been a Conner, married to Douglas Conner who had left her mother the day after their second daughter was born. Not an auspicious beginning.

The bequest came on the day George Roberts, her fourth late husband, fell off the grandstand at Hialeah. He had a habit of betting on bad horses. It was the first and *only* time she'd given him a tip about what the horses were feeling. She didn't believe horse racing was good for the animals; horses weren't competitive naturally. She hadn't wanted to encourage George either. He was already an inveterate gambler who wouldn't have had a thing if it wasn't for the huge fortune his family had left him.

When he'd won, George was overcome with excitement. He gave out a loud whoop and fell backward, crashing over the rail to the ground below. He'd managed to break his neck on the way down.

Mary Catherine was devastated and vowed never to get married *or* help anyone at the track again. But since George was *only* her fourth husband, the bets were against her. When she'd received the letter from Aunt Sylvia's attorney, it was like a gift from heaven. She'd left Wilmington right after her mother's death when she was eighteen and had never gone back. She'd had a wonderful, exciting life, but she suddenly felt a yearning to go home.

Her aunt's attorney had waited until she'd arrived to tell her the place was in terrible condition. Aunt Sylvia had been sick for years, apparently, and nothing had been done on the property. But with some patience and a large portion of the money she'd managed to save down through the years, she'd brought it back up to livable condition. She'd renovated the upper floors into an apartment for herself and started The Riverfront Free Clinic in the downstairs area that had once been her aunt's sewing shop.

When her agent had approached WRSC about doing the pet psychic show from there, they were happy to have her. She'd settled in and reacquainted herself with the place where she was born by taking long walks along the river and looking out at the Atlantic coast from Carolina Beach. But it wasn't until she'd found Baylor last year that she finally felt she fit in.

He was one of her rescued animals. She'd heard him calling as he was being born to a mother cat that was all but dead after being hit by a car outside her door. He was the only one of the litter to survive. He'd looked into her eyes and they'd fallen in love.

"What happened?" She opened the front door to the clinic after waving to the officer as he left. Danny's worried expression was mirrored by the other two people with him.

"Danny said you were arrested for murder." Jenny Harper, the clinic's official veterinarian, shook her head. "I told him he was crazy."

"They took us both in," Danny elaborated for the sake of the young red-headed volunteer who was there with Jenny. "They let me go right away. I wasn't sure why they kept MC, but sometimes these things are loco."

"I'm sure it was because she was more interesting," Jenny said.

The young volunteer from UNCWilmington smiled at Danny. Mary Catherine wasn't surprised. He was a flirt, but there weren't many girls who didn't like him.

It had been a fortunate day when she'd met him while he was looking for fares along River Street. They'd become good friends through his knowledge of the city as he helped her find hurt and lost animals.

"What *really* happened?" Jenny asked. "The police called and asked me a lot of questions about both of you."

"I told you," Danny answered. "We found a dead woman while we were looking for an injured turtle that MC heard. The woman was murdered. *Muerto*. Someone cut her throat."

"I want to hear it from *her*." Jenny snubbed him, as usual, with a toss of her long gray hair.

Mary Catherine repeated the story with embellishments. "I believe they think she *was* murdered. Poor Colin. I have to call him right away. What a shock for him! Ferndelle Jamison was his aunt."

Baylor nudged her leg with his head.

"Oh, that's right. Tommy said she wasn't alone when she died. Baylor thinks Colin killed her."

Tall and gaunt, Jenny rolled her expressive blue eyes, her gray hair a cloud around her face. "The worried guy who manages the radio station?"

"Yes."

"Who's Tommy?" Jenny wondered.

"Tommy is the turtle." Mary Catherine took the yellow-bellied slider out of her purse. She'd wet him down when she went to the restroom at the police station, but he was still in pain. "Maybe you could take a look at him. I don't think it's serious. I think he might be in shock."

Jenny took the turtle from her. She'd known Mary Catherine since the free clinic opened, and nothing she told her was a surprise anymore. "So this is your only witness to the crime?"

"Yes. And he's obscure about it. He keeps repeating something about his bowl being broken and wanting something to eat."

"Poor thing." Jenny stroked his shell as she spoke to Mary Catherine. "Bruno missed you this afternoon. He acts crazy when you don't come to see him."

"I have to find him a home. He eats like a horse!" Mary Catherine shook her head. "No, Baylor, not with us. He needs a big yard he can romp in and a family to play with."

"It might help if you'd tell him not to bite everyone who comes through the door," Danny added. "I think he only likes *you*, MC."

"He seems to like Bernie," Jenny said.

"The handyman?" Danny's dark eyes looked hurt. "I can't believe it! He doesn't even *know* him."

"We haven't found the right person for him," Mary Catherine agreed. "But not tonight. I'm starving and exhausted. If you'll excuse us, we're going upstairs."

"We haven't exactly had a picnic here waiting for you, either," Jenny assured her. "I'll look at the turtle—then I'm out of here."

"Thank you." Mary Catherine smiled at them. "I appreciate you worrying about me." She sighed. "Yes, Baylor. They were worried about you too."

Jenny and Danny bent down to scratch Baylor's ears and talk to him. Mary Catherine dragged herself upstairs to her apartment, not needing to add to Baylor's already overly large ego. She fell back in one of her red velvet chairs and closed her eyes.

Danny called out to her as he and Jenny left for the night, shutting off the lights and locking the door to the clinic behind them. Baylor slowly crept up the stairs and found a soft place to flex his claws between Mary Catherine and the side of the chair.

———

She didn't realize she'd fallen asleep until a loud knocking at the clinic door brought her to her feet. It was a little after midnight. She'd tried again to call Colin around 9:30, but there was no answer at his condo or his cell phone. She realized he might still be at the police station.

The knocking downstairs continued until she found her pink chenille robe and slippers, touched up her hair and applied a coat of lipstick. She still looked like she'd been asleep.

"I know there's nothing wrong with that since I *was* asleep," she argued with Baylor. "But I have a reputation to protect, you know. What am I saying? You can't *possibly* understand. You lick your fur a few times a day and everyone says you're beautiful! Never mind."

She slid open the peephole in the clinic door. The original iron bolt-and-slab door was still on the building. The carpenter who'd done her remodeling assured her it was once used to keep rowdy pirates out. Her building had been a public house in the late 1700s; closing in the early 1800s to reopen again as a hotel.

A tall, thin man dressed in a tweed jacket with patches on the elbows was standing on the stoop. He reminded her of a young Jimmy Stewart, as he appeared in *Fire Creek,* one of her mother's favorite movies. "Yes?"

"I'm Charlie Dowd. I found this dog in the street. No one else will help him. He's just a pup."

"Our vet has gone home, too. What's wrong with him?"

"I think he was hit by a car."

She bit her lip. The beagle puppy's thoughts of pain and fear filtered through her mind. There was no way she could stand there and *not* help. "Come in." She opened the door. "I'll call our vet and have her come back."

"Thank you." Charlie extended his big, raw-boned hand to her. "I'd be happy to pay, if that helps."

"I'm sure it will." She shook his hand. *Nice hands. Strong and confident.* "I'll call Jenny. You try to make him comfortable over there in the doggy bed. He's in a lot of pain."

"Thanks. I appreciate your help. I saw the car hit him. It just kept on going."

"People don't value a dog's life much," she commiserated as she dialed Jenny's number. The cantankerous old vet wouldn't be happy about being disturbed. "Come to think of it, some people don't overly value *human* life, do they?"

He agreed with her, glancing around the clinic's waiting room. "You're Mary Catherine Roberts, right? The pet psychic? I've seen the ad for your talk show on the sides of buses. I hope I didn't disturb you and your husband."

Her eyes narrowed. *Was this a fishing expedition or was he immediately taken with her?*

It had happened before with her third late husband. Per was immediately in love with her after they'd met at a rooftop party in Manhattan, given by a paranormal magazine publisher she worked for at the time. They were married within the week. He was wealthy, fun-loving, and wanted to take her everywhere.

Unfortunately, he'd died two years later, when a helicopter landed on him as they were about to go to the airport. It was terrible.

"I don't have a husband," she explained, waiting for Jenny to answer. "I'm a widow."

"Oh. Sorry. I didn't mean to pry." He glanced around the room again, then eased his long, lean body into the chair by the bricked-over fireplace as he continued to stroke the beagle puppy's head. "I jog past here a couple of times a week. I noticed when you moved in two years ago and opened the place. You've done a nice job."

"Thanks." She looked at the ugly green walls. "The outside looks all right, but it's been all we could do to get the equipment we need and keep the animals fed. I'm hoping to do some sprucing up on the interior this year. I couldn't have done it without all the wonderful people who've taken an interest and devoted their time and money to help the animals."

Jenny finally answered the phone and Mary Catherine told her the problem. She yawned repeatedly and promised to be there as soon as she got dressed. "Why is it an emergency always happens right after I get home? You know I wanted to see Championship wrestling tonight."

Mary Catherine apologized, thanked her, and hung up. "She's on her way. Can I get you a cup of tea? I know I need some."

"I wouldn't want to put you to any trouble."

"Not at all. I'll be right back." She went upstairs and put on some water for tea, but also threw on an ankle-length, deep purple dress, applied a little more lipstick, ran a brush through her hair again, and spritzed on a little Chanel. It might be ridiculous, but there was no point in missing any opportunities. She didn't *plan* to re-marry, but who knew when husband number five might come her way.

She poured the fragrant green tea into two cups, then went carefully downstairs again. Baylor had stayed with the man, watching him. He reported that he had gone behind the counter and looked at a few things. Bruno barked from the back, starting a storm of howling from the clinic's other patients.

Mary Catherine's eyes narrowed farther as she handed Charlie his tea. It was her fault for being so eager to impress him. She'd have to be more careful who she let into the clinic unsupervised. Who was he? What did he want? She wasn't worried about the clinic. Everything was clean and up to code. But he *could* be a reporter. They were obnoxious at times.

"Thanks." He sipped the tea, patting the beagle's head. "I knew your Aunt Sylvia, you know."

"Really?" Mary Catherine usually wasn't one to put off saying what needed to be said. But this time she wanted to know why he was really there. She hoped he hadn't hurt the dog to get in there at that hour and see her.

"Funny, she never mentioned you."

"We were out of touch for many years because of a stupid feud between her and my mother. I guess she thought of me when she died because she didn't have any other family."

He lifted one brow. "What about her son?"

That was a surprise. "I didn't know she had a son." *He had to be a reporter.* Too bad. He was a distinguished-looking man with his graying brown hair and chestnut eyes. Quite charming. *Too charming*, she agreed with Baylor who flexed his claws then sat very still, glaring at the man. She almost laughed at her *attack* cat.

"I think you should know I'm a private investigator. That's what I do for a living." He pulled out a business card and slid it across the table to her. "One of my clients is Sylvia Caldwell's son."

"Oh?" She sat opposite him on another lime-green vinyl chair. "Is that why you were rifling through my papers while I was upstairs? If you're here to blackmail me or something, Mr. Dowd, you might as well forget it. I have the legal documentation on this building. I'm sorry Aunt Sylvia didn't have a better relationship with her son. And if you hurt this poor dog to get in here—"

32

"I wouldn't do that, Mrs. Roberts." He smiled at her and sipped his tea, apparently not worried about her revelation. "But my client is interested in learning more about you. He'd like to meet to talk about buying this place back from you. For sentimental reasons."

"I'm not interested. As you know, I've put a lot of time and money into restoring this building. It suits me the way it is. I'm not selling."

"I understand. Do you *really* believe you're a pet psychic? Or is it an act?"

Jenny stumbled into the clinic with her princess pajama top on over her jeans, slippers on her feet. "Where's the dog?"

Together they took the puppy into the back office where he could be examined. Mary Catherine was surprised when Charlie waited for her to come back. Baylor sat on the counter watching him, waiting for an excuse to pounce. "If you're really interested in the puppy's welfare, call after ten in the morning and we should know something more about him."

"You didn't answer my question, Mrs. Roberts," he reminded her. "Do you really believe you can talk to animals?"

"How do you think I knew you rifled through my papers?" She smiled as she walked to the door and held it open for him. "Good night, Mr. Dowd."

———

The morning paper brought news of the police investigation into the death of Mrs. Ferndelle Jamison. "Mrs. Jamison was found in her home on Market Street by a taxi driver, Danny Ruiz and Mary Catherine Roberts, a radio talk show host," she read aloud to Tommy and Baylor. "She's survived by her nephew, Colin, whose parents were killed in a boating accident off the coast two years ago."

Baylor looked up from his breakfast and smacked his lips.

"We don't know that, do we?" She chastised the cat. "Just because you don't like him doesn't mean he killed his parents *and* his aunt. You take a dislike to most people when you meet them. Colin is a good man, despite his affectations."

Mary Catherine went on to read about Ferndelle's many charitable contributions to the city. Again, she was touched by the nearness of the death. Somehow it seemed so personal to her. She hadn't known Ferndelle Jamison, yet she felt intimate with her after finding her lying there in her own blood, so helpless in her nightclothes.

"I know you're hungry," she consoled the turtle. "But all I have is a little lettuce. That will have to do until I can get something else."

The funeral arrangements hadn't been announced, according to the paper. "Probably because they're going to do an autopsy on her," she told the cat. "They know something isn't right. I'm sure we're not the only ones to question it."

There was a knock on her private door and she glanced at the clock. It was too early for Jenny or a volunteer to be there. For a moment, she thought it might be that nasty Charlie Dowd again. Her heart fluttered in her chest. She opened the peephole a crack. "Yes?"

Detectives Abraham and Angellus stood outside in the misty morning air. "We have a few more questions, Mrs. Roberts. Could we come in?"

Hi Mary Catherine!

Roger, my terrier, escaped from the garden one day when my son was out visiting a friend's new house three miles away. I was amazed when Roger turned up at the friend's new house. My son went there by car. There is no way he could have left a scent and Roger had never been taken to that address before.

Do you think he's psychic?

FOUR

"You want to arrest Tommy?"

Detective Abraham frowned and looked at the turtle in the bowl on the marble kitchen counter. "We don't want to arrest it... uh... him. We want to do forensic work on it. Him. It might have a fingerprint on it. Him. Damn!"

"You mean you want to cut the poor thing open?"

"No, Mrs. Roberts," Detective Angellus broke into the conversation. "Whoever did this didn't leave much behind to help us. We think there was a struggle between Mrs. Jamison and her assailant. We believe that assailant used the glass from the broken bowl to cut her throat. The turtle was in the glass bowl. It's possible the person who killed her might've touched the turtle. He might have a fingerprint on his back. We could take that off without hurting him at all."

They were sitting at Mary Catherine's kitchen table, a shaft of sunlight from the wide windows illuminating the scene. She poured them each a cup of the chamomile tea she'd received from that wonderful woman in Charlotte whose Great Dane had a problem with ghosts. "I don't like it."

"We can get a court order," Detective Abraham threatened. "The turtle could be an important part of this investigation, as stupid as that sounds."

"That won't be necessary," she decided, "*if* you'll let me be there to make sure he isn't hurt."

Abraham moaned and shook his head.

Detective Angellus shrugged. "What difference does it make?"

"I suppose it doesn't." Abraham frowned at Mary Catherine. "All right. When can you bring him in?"

"I have a show to do this morning," she said. "I can have him there by one."

"That's fine. Thanks." Angellus nudged his partner and sipped his tea. "This stuff is pretty good."

"Please try not to handle him anymore than you have to," Abraham explained. "When you pick him up, use rubber gloves. Put him in a sealed plastic bag—"

"He'll suffocate!" she protested. "He's a living, *breathing* animal."

"Okay. Fine. This is a long shot anyway. It's probably already too late, even if anything was ever there." Abraham drank some of his tea and made a face. "People drink this stuff?"

"It's very soothing," she assured him. "I'll be as careful as I can with Tommy. But you might be right. I had our vet look at him last night. I don't know if you'll find anything useful."

"*Great!*" He glanced at the tea and got to his feet. "Bring him by and we'll take a look. He might be our only clue."

"Don't you mean witness? He told me there was another person there when Mrs. Jamison died. He saw everything that happened, even if he can't adequately describe it. He saw the killer leave when it was over. I hope we won't need police protection for him."

"Police protection?" Angellus finished his tea and got to his feet. "*I'm* not writing up the request for that."

"Don't ask," his partner grunted. "It's a turtle, for God's sake! The DA would laugh us out of his office."

"He knows what he saw," Mary Catherine said. "If you don't think the DA would like to hear it from a turtle and a pet psychic, you'd better get busy finding this other person yourselves."

"Thanks for your help." Abraham went to the door that led downstairs from her apartment. "We'll see you at one."

"I'll be there. Be careful of the loose stair. I'm trying to get my handyman to fix that."

"How desperate are we that we're talking to turtles and psychics?" she heard Abraham ask Angellus as they walked down the stairs together.

"Pretty desperate," Angellus replied. "I can already feel those county commissioner friends of Mrs. Jamison's breathing down my neck to arrest that nephew."

"Just asking," Abraham retorted. "I really didn't need an answer."

Mary Catherine slowly closed the door to her apartment. So they believed Colin was responsible, like Baylor. *Interesting.* She was sure they were all wrong.

First of all, Colin wasn't the kind of person who'd kill someone. "And second," she explained to Baylor as she dressed, "if he *were* going to kill someone, it wouldn't be with a broken bowl! *Please!* He might get blood on himself!"

Baylor rolled on his back and stuck his paws up in the air.

"Yes, his parent's death at sea would be more like him, *if* he were going to kill anyone, which I don't believe. Come on." She tugged on a lightweight marmalade-colored jacket over her pale lavender skirt and blouse. "We're already going to be late."

———

Charlie was downstairs in the clinic. He was holding the beagle puppy that Jenny had pronounced fit to go home that morning. The puppy had sustained some scratches and bruises. Jenny was giving Charlie last-minute care instructions before they left the clinic.

"Mr. Dowd has decided to adopt the puppy he brought in," Jenny told her. "Makes you want to throw a party, doesn't it?"

"Wonderful." Mary Catherine, for once, refused to be impressed. She couldn't imagine what he was up to, but now she knew her cousin wanted to buy the building. Everything he did seemed suspect to her.

"I'm going to name him Sam, for Sam Spade, the private eye."

She waved her hand in dismissal. "He says his name is Baxter. But people rarely know their pet's true names anyway."

"Baxter?" Charlie glanced at the puppy. "He *told* you his name is Baxter?"

"Yes. He also told me what happened to him, so you're in the clear on *that* anyway."

"That's amazing!" He stared at her for a few minutes. "Look, I'm sorry about snooping through your papers. There wasn't anything there anyway. I was just curious."

"Curious?"

"How someplace like this stays in business." He glanced around the clinic. "Now I know. *You* foot the bills."

"Not entirely. We get donations. It works out." She looked at Jenny, who raised her eyebrows and frowned. "I have to go to work. I'll see you later."

"Mary Catherine," Charlie called her name as she walked out of the clinic.

The way he said her name gave her goose bumps. Baylor reminded her that her goose bumps usually led to nasty circumstances that left her with nothing but fond memories. He didn't want to be part of that cycle. She hushed him. She wasn't pleased to notice how Charlie's eyes crinkled at the corners when he smiled or that she liked the sound of his voice. "What is it, Mr. Dowd?"

"Please call me Charlie. Can't we get past the bad start we've had?"

Baylor meowed and walked past her to the car. She knew he was right. It wouldn't do to think of this man in a romantic sense. She wished she was beyond those kinds of thoughts, but clearly one never quite got beyond them. All she could do was try to ignore them and focus on something else. "I don't think that's a good idea."

"Look, I was only doing my job last night. But I came back for the puppy, didn't I? Doesn't that earn me some respect?"

"Not really." She cut him dead. "Excuse me. I'm late for work."

He stood by as she got into her red and black convertible Mini Cooper. Baylor jumped into the back. She didn't look at Charlie, but her hand trembled as she turned the key to start the engine. It made a clicking noise, then nothing. She tried again. Nothing.

"Problem?" he asked as she got out of the car.

"It won't start." She glared at him. "You didn't do something to it, did you?"

He looked hurt. "Why would I?"

"I don't know. But it was fine yesterday." She glanced at her watch. "I'll have to call a taxi."

"Let me take you to the station," he offered.

Her eyes narrowed at the same time that Baylor's did. "That's a *little* coincidental, isn't it?"

"I don't know. But my Suburban is right here. Your car isn't working. I feel like I owe you one. Let me drive you there."

Baylor shook his head, but she accepted. "All right. But if I find out you did something to my car to make this happen—"

"I'll ignore the threat since I'm innocent. Just like last night when you thought I'd hurt the puppy to talk to you." He opened the passenger door on the white Suburban for her. "I happen to be at the right place at the right time a lot. It's my gift. You're a psychic. You must believe in that sort of thing."

Baylor jumped in after her and sat at her feet, hissing when Charlie moved. Ignoring his dire warnings, Mary Catherine settled Tommy's carrying box on her lap while Charlie put Baxter on a blanket in the backseat.

"What's in the box?" he asked after getting behind the steering wheel.

"A turtle."

"You deliver pets too?"

"I'm taking this one to the police. He's part of a murder investigation."

"Really?" He pulled out into traffic on River Street. "The one I read about in the paper today. *You* found the body."

41

"Yes."

"And the police think the *turtle* killed the woman?"

"No." She rolled her eyes. "They think there might be a fingerprint or something on him that will help them *find* the killer. They don't know where else to look. I'm taking him to be sure they don't abuse him."

"I see."

"What does that mean?"

He shrugged. "I don't know. Just making conversation. Ferndelle Jamison was well thought of in Wilmington. She was also loaded. Her family has been here so long, the fortune was probably founded on pirate booty."

"I still don't think that makes her nephew the killer."

"Is that what the police think?"

Mary Catherine knew she'd said too much. "I don't know. Baylor thinks so."

"Your cat, right?" Charlie glanced down at her feet. "I read about you last night on the Internet. You've had a remarkable life."

Not sure if that was a compliment or a criticism, she ignored the remark, looking out of the window at the shops that were opening along the river as they passed. A few doors down from the clinic there was a small bookstore with the most wonderful atmosphere. She loved to go there with Baylor and sit on the floor and read. The other side of the street paralleled the river, where the U.S.S. *Wilmington* battleship laid at anchor as a permanent memorial.

"I've lived here all of my life," he continued. "I worked as a police detective for ten years. But I love having my own business. It's great."

"Looking through other people's windows and snooping through their personal papers?"

"Mostly." He didn't seem embarrassed to admit it. "There's the occasional insurance fraud case or a lost and found kind of thing. Wilmington isn't a big town. We don't get many made-for-TV cases here."

"That sounds *fascinating*."

"I was wondering if you might consider collaborating with me on a case."

She stared at him. "Why would I do that?"

"No reason, I guess. But I know a few people on the job. I might be able to get them to ease up on the turtle."

"I think I can handle that, thanks anyway."

"I'd pay you."

"I don't need your money. I don't know who you think I am, but—"

"You could prove to me that you really *can* talk to animals."

"I don't need to prove *that* to anyone, Mr. Dowd." They reached the radio station and she opened the car door. "Thanks for the ride."

"Mary Catherine!" He jumped out of the SUV and waited for her to come around with Baylor and Tommy. "I'd like to buy you lunch. You could make sure I'm doing a good job taking care of Baxter. I've never had a dog before."

She looked up at him, hating that she was softening toward him with no particular reason whatsoever. Baylor meowed in disgust and left her to stand by the door to the coffee shop. "I don't know why I'm doing this ..."

"Great!" He squeezed her hand. "I'll pick you up after you and the turtle talk to the police. You won't regret it."

She watched the white truck drive away before turning to go into Port City Java. "I don't want to hear it from you," she told the cat, who walked in before her. "You tried to claw your way out through a window to reach that little Siamese who kept calling to you! We *all* have our weaknesses."

She was prepared to explain everything to Colin when she got to the office, but he wasn't there. A large crowd of assistants and talk show hosts were gathered around the TV in the WRSC lobby.

"The police questioned Colin Jamison today in the death of his aunt, Ferndelle Jamison. The well-known society matriarch was found dead in her Market Street home on Tuesday. A large insurance policy and a family fortune with Colin Jamison as the only heir may be the motive. He was released after questioning this morning, with no charges filed against him as yet, but he has been identified as a person of interest in this case. Back to you, Lucinda."

Baylor expressed his satisfaction with the event, but Tommy disagreed. He knew Colin and had seen him often, but Colin wasn't with Ferndelle when she fell on the floor. He wasn't responsible.

Tommy cried again for his lost home and his big rock where he could splash into the water. He wanted real food, not the green stuff Mary Catherine was giving him. He wanted his home and the woman who'd been kind to him.

"I'm sorry, little one." She refrained from stroking his back with her finger, not wanting to smudge any fingerprints that might be there. "I can get you a larger space and a rock, even turtle food. But I can't bring Ferndelle back. Are you sure about Colin?"

He reminded her that he had been there with Ferndelle when she'd died. It definitely wasn't Colin, but he was sure he had seen the other human, the one who held Ferndelle on the floor and hurt her. Mary Catherine asked him if it was a man or a woman. The little turtle wasn't sure. He began mourning his friend and his home again.

Not that she could blame the police for thinking he did it. Baylor did. First there was the open door, which probably meant the person who killed Ferndelle had a key. Then, as the reporter mentioned, there was money involved. Not to mention that business about his parents being killed two years before. Colin had been very angry when everything had gone to his aunt instead of him. It seemed awfully coincidental to *her* and she was on his side.

FIVE

THE NEWS ABOUT COLIN weighed heavily on her heart. Mary Catherine did her show, but it was difficult to drum up the enthusiasm she normally had for it. There were the usual callers asking about things their pets did that they thought were good or bad. The talk show was always a mixed bag of psychic phenomena and pet care ideas.

Just before it was time to finish up, a man called in, saying he had information about Ferndelle's death.

"You should call the police," she told him.

"I will," the caller agreed. "If you can guess my pet's secret by communicating with him psychically."

Pursing her mouth, she agreed. Normally, she would've switched him off as a prank caller. But today, Colin's future might be in the balance. "All right. What do you want to know?"

"You'll have to guess."

"I don't think I can guess randomly. What did you have in mind?"

"I have my pet with me while I'm talking to you, Mary Catherine. Guess what it is first. Then we'll go on."

"An iguana." She shrugged at Mindy as the young woman made a face at her. "I'm sorry. That just popped into my mind."

"Try again. Better make it good this time. I might start to believe you're not really psychic."

Mary Catherine didn't like the sound of the man's voice. But she tried again for Colin's sake. "You have a dog."

"Good guess. What kind?"

She concentrated. "A Dalmatian."

"Wrong." The caller laughed. "I guess Colin goes to jail."

"Wait!" She tried to stop him. But Corey, the engineer, shook his head at her. "The line's dead."

She made herself take a deep breath and finish the show. The last caller was a woman with a dog that was allergic to dog food and would only eat cat food.

"I think he's playing with you," Mary Catherine advised her caller. "He's testing you to see how far you'll go."

"That would make sense, considering we just moved to a new house and I don't think he likes it. He pees on everything."

"Sit him down and have a talk with him. Don't be afraid of looking silly. Look into his eyes. Tell him this is his new home. If he soils it, he'll have to live there anyway. You aren't moving. As to the cat food, switch him back to dog food. He *isn't* a cat. You wouldn't let a child eat pickles all the time either."

The caller laughed. "That's true! Thanks. I'll try that and let you know if it works."

Mary Catherine thanked her for calling. "I'd like to finish up today by reminding all of you that animals are smarter than anyone

47

gives them credit for. They think and feel the way we do. It may be on a different level, more like children than adults, but they get angry, frustrated, and scared. Talk to your pet. Remind him or her that you love them. Try to understand what they're telling you. It might make both your lives better." She said goodbye to her audience, then stepped out of the sound booth.

"That guy who called about Colin was scary. Who do you think that was?" Mindy shivered. "I wish Colin would call. This isn't like him."

"I don't know. But he might have some valuable information about what happened to Colin's aunt." Mary Catherine turned to Corey. "Do we know where that call came from, the phone number?"

"I can try to trace it on the computer."

"Would you?"

"Sure. Do you think he really knows something about Colin's aunt?"

"I don't know. But it's worth finding out."

Corey tracked the phone number and Mary Catherine called it back. There was no answer. Maybe she could get the police to check it out. "Thanks." She said goodbye to Mindy and Corey as she picked up Tommy's carrying box and her shawl. "I'll let you know what happens. Call me if you hear anything else about Colin."

———

She sat and waited in a large room while they dusted Tommy for fingerprints and swabbed him for DNA. She couldn't see where they hurt him, but he was terrified.

After two hours of testing, they came away with nothing. "Unless DNA turns up something, we're back where we were." Detective Abraham brought Tommy back to her.

"I'm sorry. But what he has to *say* is much more interesting." She explained everything the turtle had told her again, including his certainty that Colin was innocent.

"And Colin Jamison is the manager at the station where you work, right?" Abraham scratched his chin. "You think maybe the *turtle* might be prejudiced?"

"No! Tommy doesn't understand any of that. But you might start looking into another motive besides Colin wanting to inherit the family fortune. If Tommy says he's innocent, he probably is. One trait animals don't share with humans—they don't lie!" She explained about the caller that morning and gave him the phone number Corey had traced.

"It wouldn't be hard for him to get that information. He probably looked on the Internet or something and found out Colin works there. He put it together with what he heard about you finding the body. Things like that happen all the time."

"I wish that made me feel better."

"Was the caller threatening to you in any way?" Abraham's bushy blond brows knitted together above his brown eyes.

"No. But if he's withholding evidence that could clear Colin—"

"We'll check into it." The detective smiled at her and patted her shoulder. "I understand you want to help your friend. Let me know if that man calls back again. We'll let you know if the DNA tests turn up anything."

"Do you know where Colin is? No one's heard from him. I *did* come in without making you get a court order. You could help me out some."

"And I'd like to help you out. But we let him go. He's probably at home. He better not leave town until we finish our investigation."

"You don't know Colin, Detective. He's not *that* adventurous."

He frowned. "You'd be surprised how adventurous a murder charge can make a man, Mrs. Roberts. Thank you for coming in with your turtle."

Mary Catherine called Colin as she left the police station, but there was still no answer. She knew they were all wrong about him. She was upset when she couldn't reach him. Mindy told her he still wasn't at WRSC and she hadn't heard from him. They both knew Colin never went anywhere without his cell phone strapped to his hip!

She blinked in the bright sunlight when she stepped outside. There was a white Suburban waiting for her at the sidewalk, outside the police station. "How did you know we were finished?"

Charlie leaned against the hood of the SUV and lazily smiled at her. "I told you I still have a few friends on the job. Lunch?"

Baylor complained as she got in the truck. "Quiet," she scolded. "Or there won't be anything special in your bowl for dinner tonight!"

"I don't think your cat likes me." He stared at the puffed-up ball of fur Baylor had become. "Does he bite?"

"No, of course not." Baylor reminded her that he had sharp teeth and could bite if necessary. She warned him against the action. "Where are we going?"

"You recall that collaboration I asked you about earlier?"

"Yes."

"An opportunity came up that's too good to miss. It'll only take a few minutes. Then we'll have lunch. Are you game?"

"I suppose so," she answered warily. "What did you have in mind?"

———

An hour later, she began to question her judgment. "Where did you say we were going?"

"I thought we'd ride out to the beach for a few minutes. It's a beautiful day. Great company. Why not?"

Baylor growled. Charlie was as charming as he was devious. Mary Catherine was actually enjoying his conversation, totally ignoring what was happening, getting into the truck on the strength of a wink and a smile. She had only herself to blame for her predicament. "It looks like we're going to have a storm. Where *exactly* are we going?"

"The woman I'm investigating is out of town today. Her housekeeper always puts the dog outside while she's gone. I thought maybe you could talk to him. Find out who she's playing around with."

"Oh, Charlie!" She shook her head in disgust. Baylor agreed. This man was sneaky and underhanded.

"It's not a big deal," he assured her. "We pull up close to the fence where they keep the poodle. You talk to it and see if it tells you anything."

"It's not that easy. Just because you can communicate with an animal doesn't mean they always tell you what you want to know."

"You won't be doing any worse than I have. I've been following the wife around for six months trying to find out who she's having the affair with and I have zip. Her husband is starting to get a little upset."

"Did you ever think there might not be *anything* going on? Maybe the woman is innocent. Maybe the husband imagined it."

"*Maybe* doesn't pay the bills." He flipped on the headlights and windshield wipers as it started to rain. "I need evidence one way or another. The best way for me is if she's guilty, but the other way works too."

She looked out at the dark sky as they reached the Atlantic beaches. "I don't use animals to spy on people."

"I learned something interesting about your friend, Colin." He dangled the carrot with a smile. "We could trade."

Mary Catherine knew she was going to do it. But even if it proved to be useful information, she was *never* going to see Charlie again! The man was a menace! "All right. But you tell me what you know about Colin first. *Then* we'll talk to the poodle."

"Fair enough. While I was waiting at the police station, I talked with one of my old buddies. It seems your friend had a big disappointment after his parents were killed. All of the estate passed down to his aunt."

"Everyone knows *that*."

"Did you know he went to court, tried to get his share, but the will was unbreakable? There were hard feelings between them afterward. She was pushing the police to continue the investigation into her brother's death. I also heard Colin should've waited a little longer. Ferndelle only had a few months to live. She was dying from cancer."

"Really? I wonder if Colin knew." Mary Catherine tried to concentrate on what she was saying, but a loud screeching bounced inside her brain and made her want to scream. "Pull over!"

"What's wrong?" Charlie looked at her like she'd gone crazy.

"I don't know. Pull over, *please!*"

He pulled the truck off on the white sandy shoulder. Rain slammed against the windshield pushed by strong winds that added whitecaps to the dark gray sea stretched out to the horizon beyond the last leg of North Carolina. "What do you hear?"

"I don't know. I've never heard anything like it. I don't even know if I can interpret it."

"But you think it's some animal in pain or something?" He paused, his gaze scanning the horizon. "What is it? I don't see anything."

"*Be quiet!*"

"Sure." He shrugged and sat back with his fingers tapping on the steering wheel.

"I don't know what it is, but it's that way." She pointed toward the water.

"This isn't an amphibious truck. I had one of those. Couldn't make the payments."

"Just wait here," she said impatiently. "You too, Baylor."

The cat meowed loudly as the door slammed shut behind her.

53

"She gets worked up over this, doesn't she?" Charlie said to the cat as he tried to stroke the large orange head. Baylor growled low in his throat and showed his teeth, ears flattened back and eyes narrowed. "Do you know what I'm saying? Do you understand English or just hear thoughts?"

Realizing the cat wasn't going to answer, Charlie watched the animal focus on the window, looking in the direction Mary Catherine had disappeared. He got out of the truck, the rain immediately soaking him. It was warm, but the stiff breeze chilled him. He buttoned his sport coat, pulled up the collar, and hunched down inside it for protection against the weather.

He called out her name, but the wind threw it back at him, laughing as it rushed on. Holding one hand above his eyes so he could see through the downpour, he finally spotted her.

She was standing hip deep in a salt marsh by the side of the road. Charlie slogged toward her as she tried to untangle a pelican from some fencing that probably had been put up and forgotten years before. The creature was wild with agitation and fear as thunder hammered and lightning glittered through the dark afternoon sky.

One of the bird's large wings was caught in the wire. Mary Catherine held its head with one hand and tried to untangle its wing with the other. Remarkably, the bird didn't try to peck at her or hurt her in any way, but it wouldn't keep still either and she couldn't get it free.

"Let me help," Charlie offered, his husky voice loud above the roar of the storm washing over the coast.

She turned her head, marmalade-colored hair plastered against her face by the rain. "If you could get her feet out of the way...watch out for her beak!"

But the warning came too late and he yelped when the bird nipped him. "Why isn't he biting *you?* Tell him I want to help too."

"*She* knows it. She's frantic about her baby, that's all." Mary Catherine finally managed to get the mother pelican detached from the wire. "There now!" The bird kicked Charlie, then flew away quickly.

"I hope she said thank you," he said as they sloshed back out of the brine.

"I don't think so. Very few wild animals do. They work on a whole different level than pets we've bred to live with us. Some of them are impossible to understand."

"But they understand you want to help them." He stopped to help her out of the last part of the marsh and his warm hand held hers for a minute as she pushed her wet hair out of her eyes. "You're the genuine article, aren't you? No one is going to pay you for that. You just love animals."

She felt a blush come up in her face. Or it might've been a hot flash. She wasn't sure. Sometimes exertion brought those on. She was soaked and her clothes were probably ruined by the salt water. But it was worth it to see the admiration in Charlie's eyes. She didn't need Baylor's guidance to know what it was either. "Listening to them, knowing how they think, makes me more aware of every living creature, I suppose. You wouldn't pass a child in the pelican's situation. It would be the same way for me with that incredible bird."

"You're shaking." He put her cold hand to his warm face. "No wonder! You're colder than I am. I think we'll have to put off the poodle for today and go change clothes."

"Don't be silly." She tried hard to break free from the spell he was weaving around her. "You can turn the heat on and we'll dry in the car. We've come this far. We might as well get the job done."

She meant to sound competent, but realized she sounded a little gruff when he let go of her hand and started back toward the truck. It was probably just as well. She knew she was vulnerable to this man. She'd been alone too long with only Baylor for intimate company. She wasn't even sure Charlie was a decent man. And she didn't want to get involved with someone because she was needy and he looked at her like she was special. Although that had never stopped her before.

Mary Catherine hobbled across the road after him. She'd lost one of her lavender slingbacks in the marsh. One of her favorites too.

Charlie turned on the heat in the truck. "Are you sure about this?"

She closed the door behind her. "Absolutely. And thank you for your help with the bird. Is your hand all right?"

He held it out and she peered at it closely, holding it in hers until she realized how close they were and quickly dropped it. "The skin isn't broken. You should be fine. She didn't mean to hurt you."

"I know. Were *you* hurt?"

"No. I'm fine." She shivered. "Just cold. Does the poodle live down here on the beach?"

"Yeah." He started the truck moving forward again on the rough, steamy pavement that led out to the tip of the peninsula. The storm was already giving up on trying to push aside the large body of land it had come across. Rain fell fitfully and the wind still raced along the beach, but its fury was spent.

Charlie talked about the couple as they drove toward the house. The husband was a successful stockbroker with little time for his wife. The wife spent her time spending his money and getting a tan. Something had made the husband suspicious and he'd wanted to know if she was cheating. He wouldn't give any other details to be sure Charlie did his job.

"If she's cheating," he concluded, "she's really careful about it. I haven't seen her within ten feet of another man for the last six months. But she's in and out of that spa all the time. I think he might work there. I've checked out the staff. Tom Wilson, the spa owner, seems like my best lead so far. If the poodle's heard anything about Wilson, or any other name, that would be helpful."

"I'll do what I can."

As plans went, it worked fairly well. They pulled up close to the impressive iron fence and Mary Catherine jumped out to see what she could get from the dog. It was a large, black, standard poodle, probably about fifty or sixty pounds.

Luckily, it had stopped raining just before they got there. A light haze hung over the area, imprinting the air with the strong scent of the sea.

"Get anything yet?"

"Not yet." She was too busy thinking about how damp and uncomfortable she was to wonder what the poodle was thinking.

Baylor, on the other hand, was asking why she was standing in the rain, talking to a *dog*. Mary Catherine tried to explain, but the cat fluffed up his tail and hissed at the poodle, who barked back at him.

"What was that?" Charlie asked. "Did you get that?"

"That was ego. Two animals used to being dominant in their households warning each other off. Nothing more, I'm afraid."

"Did you question the dog?"

"I tried. But I need to get on his wavelength first. I have to know how he thinks."

There was nothing from the poodle but thoughts about how handsome and exceptional he was. He cocked his head when she questioned him a little about his life. He made it clear right away that he resented the intrusion into his private thoughts.

"He's going to be difficult," she told Charlie coming back to the truck. "I don't know if he ever thinks in terms of anything except what affects *him*."

"Maybe you could play on that. Maybe this impacted him in some way."

"I'll try." She sighed, already fed up with the animal. Most animals were self-centered but this one was exceptionally so. He couldn't seem to think of anything but what he was going to eat (it was never enough, never as good as he wanted it to be) and what color his nails were going to be painted.

"Hey!" a woman yelled as she ran out to see what was going on. "Are you trying to hurt my dog?"

Tommy cried out as he pushed himself against the side of the box that held him until he finally flipped over on his back and lay there helpless.

"What is it?" Mary Catherine reached through the open window, hearing the scratching in the container. She turned him over and looked into his tiny face.

The turtle repeated over and over again that he knew that voice, while the poodle barked, demanding attention. *He knew that voice.*

Hi Mary Catherine!

My name is Joe and I have a parrot named Jinks. He can look at pictures in magazines and tell me what he sees. And he's right more often than he's wrong. He saw a picture of a dog and made barking noises. He saw a picture of a couple hugging and asked me for a hug. He frequently copies things he sees on television. He saw a man get cookies from the cabinet and flew in there, demanding cookies.

Do you think he's gifted?

SIX

"I asked you a question," the woman inside the fence with the poodle reminded her. "I'm gonna call the police. What were you trying to do to my dog?"

Mary Catherine ignored her, trying to concentrate on what Tommy was trying to tell her. "You know her?"

Tommy was too terrified to respond. He kept flipping his tiny body over and trying to get out of the box. She could tell he believed the woman was a threat.

She looked at Charlie, not sure what to tell him. She wasn't sure she could trust him and didn't want him to realize the case he was investigating might be involved with Ferndelle's death.

She apologized to Tommy as she lifted him from the box, but she had to be sure he was right about the other woman. The turtle reacted immediately. There was no question in her mind that he recognized the woman on the other side of the fence. Animals were very specific about humans. Tommy not only recognized the woman, but said she was there when Ferndelle was killed.

Mary Catherine was stunned, but managed to recover when the woman demanded again to know what she was doing. "I'm sorry. I thought your dog was trying to get out of the fence. That happens to me all the time and I wanted to save you the bother."

"That's very nice of you." The other woman still sounded suspicious. "Don't I know you from somewhere?"

"I'm Mary Catherine Roberts, the Pet Psychic." She put out her wet hand.

"Okay." The tanned woman in the red tank top and shorts reached across the fence and shook it. "I know you! I listen to your show all the time! This makes sense now. Who else would stop during a thunderstorm to save someone's dog? I'm Charlene Tate. It's a pleasure to meet you."

"I'm pleased to meet you too. You have a lovely dog. His name is Jacques, right?"

Charlene giggled. "That's right! You *really* are psychic! I was just telling Colin—"

"Yes?"

"Oh, nothing." Charlene recovered her mistake. "Thanks for stopping. I'm really glad I got to meet you."

Mary Catherine got back in the truck and pushed her hair out of her face. She didn't need an animal for this one. Charlene had given it away by herself. Of course, Tommy's insistence that the woman was on hand when Ferndelle was killed didn't sound good for Colin.

"Did you get anything from the poodle or the woman?" Charlie pulled the Suburban into the street. "I couldn't hear what she was saying."

"The dog was only passing thoughts about his food and his grooming. Some dogs are like that. They don't think much beyond themselves. If his owner had been killed, it might be different."

Charlie watched the turtle continue to flip over in the box. "What's up with him? Is he afraid of the dog? What about Charlene? What did she say?"

Mary Catherine didn't respond. She had to throw him off. Maybe he needed information about Charlene's indiscretion but she had more important things on her mind. She didn't plan to allow Charlie to ask too many questions until she had answers to what had happened when Ferndelle was killed.

"You know something," he accused.

"I know her name is Charlene Tate."

"You know her name? You really *can* talk to animals. I didn't tell you her name, did I? I was careful to keep that from you. I don't know any other way you could've known. Her name isn't on the mailbox. How did you know?"

Mary Catherine clicked her seat belt in place. She could've told him the conventional truth, but she was enjoying his amazement. "You're babbling, Charlie. You already knew I talk to animals. Why are you so surprised?"

"It's one thing to *think* it could be true. It's another thing to *know* it's true."

"I'm sorry. He didn't have much to say except his owner's name. As I explained, you don't always get the answers you want from animals. Charlene thought we were trying to steal Jacques, the poodle."

"Maybe not, but this opens a whole new realm of possibilities. You could talk to animals that have seen bank robberies and col-

62

lect the reward for telling the FBI where to find the people responsible. You could collect rewards for missing jewelry or Brinks trucks."

"I've never considered doing anything like that." She hated to disillusion him, but she'd never stoop low enough to ask animals to help her collect rewards.

"I know it wouldn't work in every case," Charlie continued. "There wouldn't always be an animal that saw what happened. But there could be some kind of animal in a lot of cases. What about mice and rats? Do you talk to spiders and flies?"

"You're getting carried away. I don't talk to insects. They seem to have a different brain function that I can't understand."

"We could go into business together. It would be a great collaboration. We could make some serious money in finder fees."

This conversation was going nowhere, as far as Mary Catherine was concerned. "I think we'll forget about lunch. It's getting late. I need to go home."

Baylor was happy to hear she'd finally come to her senses about Charlie. He couldn't understand her fascination with him. He didn't even have great fur.

Something in the tone of her voice finally penetrated Charlie's ravings. "Sorry. I didn't mean to get carried away."

"Carried away?" She shook her head. "You're way past that. We're talking being swept out to sea by a tidal wave now. I want to go home."

"Let's talk. Let me buy you lunch. It's the least I can do. I'm sorry if I spouted off. I'm just amazed at what you can do."

"You mean you're amazed by the possibilities of what *you* can do with what I can do."

"I've never met a real psychic. I've known a few fakes who claimed to be psychic. It kind of blew me away. But I'm okay now. I won't mention it again. I know a great little seafood place in Wrightsville Beach."

"I'm vegetarian, for obvious reasons."

"I have a cousin who's vegetarian. He eats fish and chicken."

She sighed and rested her head on her hand. "Just take me home, please."

"Okay. That was wrong too. Of course you don't eat anything you can talk to. That makes sense. What about salad? You eat veggies, right? I know a good salad bar. We could go there."

Baylor warned that Charlie was trying to kidnap her. Mary Catherine told him she would handle the situation. "I'm tired and wet, and I've lost my shoe," she said to Charlie. "I want to go home. We can talk later."

Charlie looked at her. "Are you sure? I have a lot of ideas. I think one or two of them could work. Think about your clinic. You could use the extra money to help all the animals."

She was happy to see that, despite his rambling, Charlie had brought her home. As soon as the SUV stopped, she got out, grabbed Tommy, and all but ran for her front door. Baylor trotted quickly behind her, turning back to hiss at Charlie.

"I'll call you," Charlie yelled out, unable to park with all the cars in front of the clinic. "This is going to be fantastic!"

With the door closed behind her, Mary Catherine leaned against it and closed her eyes. She opened them to find Jenny staring at her. "I can't explain right now. But if a man who looks like Jimmy Stewart comes in after me, call the police."

She went up the stairs to her apartment, leaving the vet frowning. "You should be so lucky," Jenny shouted up at her.

———

Mary Catherine showered and changed into a flowing, apricot-colored caftan. She dried her hair, but hid it beneath a flowered turban when she saw it was frizzy. She made a face at herself in the mirror as she put on some eye makeup and a little lipstick. "There. Right as rain."

Baylor, who'd watched her grooming process, disagreed. She never took enough time, according to him. Good grooming took hours and many times required a nap in the sun before finishing.

"That's good for you, since you don't do much of anything else." She opened the door to go back downstairs. "Humans can't lie around all day."

The cat expressed his opinion: *no wonder humans never look as good as cats.*

She was about to answer when Bruno started barking downstairs. His loud bellowing echoed through the building. One of the birds they'd rescued, a toucan named Fred, seemed to be answering the dog's message with one of his own. Jenny was yelling as well. Distracted by the ruckus, Mary Catherine hurried down to see what was wrong.

An older man, dressed in threadbare jeans and a faded flannel shirt, was leading a goat on a rope. He was explaining his situation to Jenny as she tried to quiet the other animals.

Mary Catherine caught part of Bruno's frantic message. Apparently the dog had never seen a goat before and likened it to seeing an alien from another planet. She assured him the goat was from the same world, but Fred wouldn't be pacified. He claimed to have a prior experience with a goat that wasn't very pleasant.

"Can you get Bruno to stop barking?" Jenny asked her.

"I'm doing my best," Mary Catherine responded. "He's afraid we're being invaded."

"Invaded?" Jenny shook her head. "Is that really what you hear from his barking, or are you interpreting that into English?"

"It's one of the curses and blessings of humans raising animals." Mary Catherine patted the goat's head. "They think in the language they hear. Sometimes that's quite a problem, especially if they watch too much TV."

The old man smiled at her and pulled his dirty hat from his balding head. "I'm sorry to have to bring Waldo in like this. I can't afford to feed him anymore and the city doesn't want him grazing in public places. There's not much room around here for either of us."

Mary Catherine shook his hand and introduced herself. "Sit down. Have you had lunch today?"

The man told her he'd eaten breakfast at the homeless shelter that morning. The trouble started there when they told him he couldn't tie Waldo outside to eat the shelter's grass anymore. "I didn't know what to do. I sleep at the shelter and eat breakfast there every morning. After that I take Waldo down to Riverfront Park where he eats enough grass for the day. Now they tell me he can't eat there anymore either. That's why I brought him here to you all."

It was difficult to tell in the small lobby which creature smelled worse. Waldo and his friend both needed a bath. Mary Catherine breathed through her mouth and smiled at them. "I'm sure we have something you and Waldo can eat. There's a little space on the side of the building with some grass, and I'll make you a sandwich. Then we'll see what we can do about your problem."

She looked at Waldo, who calmly stared back at her. The poor thing was confused and frightened. It seemed he believed the man was about to sell him off to a meat packing plant he'd heard about when he was much younger. He thought the smell of the clinic was terrible and could only be explained as the stench of dead animals.

Mary Catherine assured him he wasn't going to be eaten. Everything would be all right. Waldo nodded and went with his friend to find that patch of grass.

Jenny shook her head after they went outside. "You can't go on promising the moon to every animal that walks into this clinic. You can't help everyone."

"That may be true," Mary Catherine half agreed. "But it hasn't happened yet. I'm a Scarlett O'Hara kind of southern Irish lady. I do what I can, and worry about what I can't do later."

"I suppose that's the only reason this clinic got started in the first place." Jenny smoothed Fred's ruffled feathers down with a gentle hand. "I'm always afraid someone is going to come in here and take advantage of you. You have a good heart, Mary Catherine. But people are always looking for someone with a good heart. They're like lions, waiting to tear it out."

"Jenny!" Mary Catherine couldn't believe the vehemence behind the vet's words. "Is there something you'd like to tell me about?"

"No. Everything's fine." Jenny straightened her lab coat and pulled herself together. "I just don't want to see you get hurt."

Mary Catherine watched the older woman walk into the back of the clinic. She didn't know much about her. Jenny had answered an ad for a vet when the clinic first started. She was difficult at times, but animals loved her and she loved them in return. There didn't seem to be anything or anyone else in her life.

Mary Catherine had tried several times to engage Jenny in conversation about her life outside the clinic, but the woman closed up faster than a sea urchin. She didn't know what she'd do without Jenny. Thank goodness her passion kept her from asking for a large salary the clinic couldn't afford.

Jenny went out the back door to check on the goat. She came back inside and immediately went to wash her hands. "I'm never going to get that smell off of me. I'm going to smell like goat and smelly old man for the rest of my life."

"I'm sure you've smelled worse."

Jenny dried her hands. "Please tell me that man isn't going to live here with his goat."

"Of course not. Where would he stay?"

"I don't know. You have this way of adopting people and animals. Maybe you're thinking about hiring him as a night watchman or something. I don't know."

"You know, that's really not a bad idea." Mary Catherine considered Jenny's words as she took out her cell phone. "Maybe you should start reading *human* minds. That way, between the two of us, we'd know what everyone is thinking."

The door to the clinic opened again. It was Colin. Danny followed him into the waiting room. "I found him wandering around outside the station," Danny told Mary Catherine. "I thought you'd want to know. He's a mess. Maybe you can help him."

She urged Colin to sit down in one of the lime-green chairs. "I've been trying to call you all day. Where have you been?"

His glasses were cracked and the frame was bent. There were several bruises on his face and a little blood in his hair from a cut near his eye. His clothes looked like he'd slept in them. He turned his head and stared at her. "Mary Catherine? Is that you?"

"You poor boy," she commiserated. "You've been through hell. Don't worry about a thing. We'll take care of you."

"Someone took my clothes," Colin blurted out. "A man *touched* me. I didn't think they were allowed to do that. Aunt Ferndelle is dead and they think I killed her."

Danny knocked on the bathroom door. "Hey, MC, what's up with Jenny? I just want to *lava mi manos.*"

"She's having some issues," Mary Catherine replied. "Use the sink in the back."

"*Gracias!*" He grinned as he opened the door to the back of the clinic. "I hope she doesn't hurt me while I'm back there. That woman is *mean* to people."

She ignored him and concentrated on helping Colin up the stairs to her apartment. He was so exhausted he could barely walk. She hated to make him climb all those stairs, but it was one place she knew he'd be safe.

"Sit right here." She put him on her red velvet sofa. "I'll run you a bath and we'll find something for you to eat. It might have to be take-out. I don't think I have much here, but I can shop later."

Colin didn't reply. He sat where she put him like a stunned puppet. He stared straight ahead and didn't move. Mary Catherine started the bath, adding a little flower scent since he was smelling like day-old garbage—not as bad as the goat man, but not something she'd want to smell all the time.

She went back into the living room only to find him on his back, snoring. One hand was flung out toward the floor and the other over his face. She sighed and went back to shut off the water. She might have to buy some fabric deodorizer for her sofa when he woke up, but she didn't have the heart to wake him. He obviously needed some sleep.

Before she left him, she covered him with a washable blanket, then went downstairs to figure out what to do with the goat and his friend.

Jenny met her at the foot of the stairs. "Have you lost your mind? Are you trying to make my day even worse?"

Mary Catherine avoided both questions. "What's wrong?"

"You sent Danny back there with me, knowing he thinks every woman is in love with him."

"Surely not *you*." Mary Catherine tried not to laugh. "Where's Danny?"

"I don't know." Jenny stalked away from the stairs. "I hope he's outside with the goat man. Maybe that way he won't bother *me* again."

Danny came back into the clinic and Jenny walked into her office and closed the door. He and Mary Catherine heard the distinct sound of a dead bolt sliding into place. "Has everyone gone crazy around here? I was talking to the goat man. How are you going to help him, MC?"

"I'm not sure yet. Colin passed out on my sofa upstairs. I'm not sure what to do for him either. I was wondering if you would take a look at my Mini Cooper. I had trouble with it starting earlier."

"Sure thing. What are you planning to do to help Colin?"

"I suppose I'll have to follow whatever clues I can get from Tommy." She went outside and told him about Charlene while he checked out her car. "Have you ever heard of a man named Charlie Dowd?"

Danny shook his head under the Cooper's hood. "Nope. This looks *bueno* under here, MC. Try to start it."

Mary Catherine got in the car and turned the key. The engine purred without so much as a sputter. She got out and stared at the car. "Is there something someone *could've* done to the engine that would make it not start this morning, but then it would start now?"

"I don't know since I'm not sure what you're asking. Does this have anything to do with this Dowd guy?"

"He offered me a ride when the car wouldn't start." Her eyes narrowed as she explained.

"*Si.* That sounds bad. No wonder you're suspicious. I don't trust anyone who offers me a ride when my car breaks down. I mean, what's the world coming to?"

"Never mind. You had to be here to understand. He was *very* threatening."

Danny stopped smiling. "Hey, you didn't say he threatened you. You want me to go and rough him up some?"

"No. But if you could ask around about him, maybe you could find out what I'm up against."

"I could do that." He pushed his dark hair out of his face. "This hombre gives you any more trouble, you say the word. Okay?"

"Thanks. Would you do me one more favor?"

He shut the hood on the Mini Cooper. "*Que?*"

"Don't tell anyone Colin's here. If Tommy's right and it wasn't Colin that killed Ferndelle Jamison, he could be a target for the person who killed her."

Danny leaned toward her, crossing his arms over his muscular chest. "Who does the turtle think killed the old lady?"

"He isn't sure about that," she confided. "But I think we may be on our way to finding out."

SEVEN

COLIN WAS AWAKE WHEN Mary Catherine went back upstairs to check on him. She'd used the exercise as an excuse to get out of helping feed the growing pet population at the clinic. She was going to have to find people to adopt the animals that were brought to them. She didn't mind supporting them so much as running out of space to help other animals.

"Mary Catherine?" Colin glanced up at her and adjusted his broken glasses. "I thought I dreamed about coming here. I'm sorry. I didn't realize what I was doing."

"Don't worry about it. I think this is one of the safest places you could be right now. I'm going to send Danny over to your place to get you some clean clothes and toiletries, then we can—"

"No!" Colin jumped to his feet. "I can't take that risk. Someone might mistake Danny for me and kill him instead."

"Kill him?" Mary Catherine sat down in her red velvet chair and picked up her knitting. Baylor jumped on her lap. "What are you talking about? Do you have a head injury?"

"You don't understand." Colin sat down again, wrapping the blanket around him. "I received a death threat. Someone wants to kill me."

She thought back to the strange phone call she'd received during her last show. "Why would someone want to kill you?"

"It was the same person who killed Aunt Ferndelle. He claimed he was responsible for my parents' accident too."

"That sounds like a load of rubbish." Mary Catherine stroked Baylor's soft fur as he considered how many times he'd wanted to scratch Colin for being an annoying suck-up. "I'm sure someone read about what happened in the paper and is having fun with you. People can be very cruel."

Colin shook his head. "No. This is the real deal. Don't you see? I inherit everything now. Whoever did this wants to take away what's rightfully mine."

"I hate to pry, but how much money are we talking about? Is it enough to kill someone for or only enough to threaten them?"

"The estate consists of several properties around the city, including the building I live in. With the money," Colin closed his eyes and counted in his head, "I guess we're talking about ten million dollars."

Baylor meowed loudly and jumped off of Mary Catherine's lap, landing nicely beside Colin. He rubbed his large orange head against him and purred.

"He's not going to share it with you," she told the cat. "It's really a mistake to educate an animal. He watches far too many game shows."

Colin looked at Baylor, who normally hissed and clawed at him. "You mean he likes me now because I have money?"

Mary Catherine watched as Colin put out one hand to stroke Baylor. The cat hissed and bit him. "Apparently, not that much. But I can see where a human with a *real* understanding of money would think that's enough to kill you."

Baylor jumped to the back of her chair, expressing his belief that he possessed a very good understanding of money, thanks to *Wheel of Fortune* and *Jeopardy*. Mary Catherine ignored him and concentrated on Colin.

"I think that's exactly it. I mean, what else could it be? This man knows how much I'll be worth after Aunt Ferndelle's estate is settled. He wants his share."

"Did he ask you for money?"

"Yes! He wants me to sign over everything." Colin got up and started pacing the expensive Persian carpet.

"That sounds like a plan to me. Who stands to inherit if something happens to you?"

"I don't know. Probably one of my cousins. As you know, I'm an only child. Aunt Ferndelle didn't have any children. My family isn't terribly prolific. I'm guessing it would be Cousin Bob. He's a lot older than I am. He probably doesn't want to wait for me to die in case he goes first."

"What about Charlene Tate?"

"What?" He stopped pacing. "What are you talking about?"

"I think you know what I'm talking about." Mary Catherine went to put on the kettle for tea as she explained about Tommy telling her about Charlene. "We met her and her poodle, quite by accident, and Tommy believes she was there when your aunt was killed."

"That's not possible." Colin cleared his throat. "She was with me."

"Tommy already told me you weren't there when your aunt was killed." She nodded toward the turtle that was quiet now in his bowl on the table. "If you're sure she was with you, I guess that clears Charlene. But I wonder how he knew her."

"What does a turtle know anyway?" Colin surged to his feet. "I believe in you, Mary Catherine, but I don't think he knows what he's talking about."

"As I explained to another doubting Thomas earlier today," she began, "animals are pretty explicit about humans. They notice things about them we wouldn't notice. He recognized Charlene's voice."

"That's ridiculous. He's a turtle, for God's sake. You can't even teach a turtle to do tricks."

The kettle whistled and Mary Catherine turned off the stove. "Tommy knew *you* weren't there."

"I guess he *does* know something." Colin stirred sugar into the cup of tea she put in front of him. "Can he describe what the person looks like who killed Aunt Ferndelle?"

"I'm afraid not. But he knows you and Charlene were together and I don't think Mindy was there, was she?"

"Maybe not." He fidgeted with his broken glasses. "I might've told Aunt Ferndelle that Charlene was Mindy. It was only a misunderstanding."

"Misunderstanding? Colin, how could you do something like that? Does Mindy know?"

"I don't know what to say." He sat down abruptly on the sofa, then slid to the floor. "I feel really weird."

Before she could decide if she should call 911 or Danny, there was a knock on the back door. She looked out the peephole and saw Charlie waiting on the stairs. In this case, it became better the devil she sort of knew or at least was familiar with than some devil she didn't know. "Come in quickly." She grabbed his hand and yanked him into the apartment.

Charlie didn't complain, even when she locked the door behind him. "I was hoping you'd had a change of heart. I didn't realize you'd changed *this* much."

"I haven't changed anything," she told him briskly. "I need your help."

Charlie studied the young man on the floor. "You like them young, huh?"

She smirked. "I wouldn't need your help to get him off the floor if that were the case. Could you help me and save the smart remarks for later? I might have a client for you."

"This guy?" He picked Colin up without her help and put him on the sofa. "He *really* needs a bath."

She was surprised and a little thrilled watching him. Charlie was obviously one of those strong, wiry types like her third late husband had been. They could be deceptively strong.

Baylor cautioned her about getting involved with anyone just because he could pick up a human as scrawny as Colin. If he could catch a mouse, that would be a different story.

"This is Colin," she explained to Charlie. "Ferndelle Jamison's nephew."

"Thanks, but no thanks. The Wilmington police and I have an agreement about open cases. They leave me alone to do what I do and I don't mess with their problems. What's he doing here anyway?"

Mary Catherine explained about the threat to Colin's life and his inheritance. "He might've been set up by this Cousin Bob to take the fall for the deaths in his family so Bob can inherit everything."

"Then why would Bob bother threatening him?" Charlie sat down at the kitchen table as he took in everything around the room. "If Colin goes to prison, it would all go to Bob anyway."

She considered what he'd said. "Maybe he doesn't want to wait. Or maybe he's afraid the police will find Ferndelle's real killer and Colin would inherit everything anyway."

"Got any coffee?" Charlie sat back in his chair. "What's your connection to Colin? I know you aren't letting him stay here because you work with him."

"He needed someplace to go. Danny found him wandering around the radio station. I thought he'd be safe here," Mary Catherine said as she poured a cup of tea for Charlie.

"So he's a puppy who needs shelter." He nodded. "I get it now."

"I don't think he's a puppy and you don't have to sound so disparaging. What's so terrible about wanting to help people?"

Colin moaned and Mary Catherine went to him, not noticing as Charlie used his camera phone to take pictures of the room. She wet a washcloth and used it to clean Colin's dirty face. He needed a good dunk in a tub, but that was going to have to wait.

"You can't be right," Colin said. "Charlene can't be involved."

"He knows Charlene Tate?" Charlie put away his phone and paid attention to the conversation.

"Who's he?" Colin struggled to sit up. "Is he a cop?"

"Man, you never lose the look." Charlie went to shake Colin's hand. "I used to be the police. Now I work for myself. Charlie Dowd. Are you by any chance sleeping with Charlene Tate?"

Colin looked up at the older, larger man and passed out again.

"Do you look like Charlene's husband by any chance?" Mary Catherine guessed.

———

Charlie waited around for Colin to wake up. He drank some chamomile tea, but Mary Catherine could see he didn't enjoy it. "How well do you know Colin?" he asked.

"I've worked with him for the last two years." She shrugged. "I guess I know him as well as you can know someone you work with."

"Which means he could've killed his aunt *and* his parents and you wouldn't know the difference."

"I suppose that's true. Do you know something about him that would make you think he *could* kill someone?"

"Not really. At this point, I'm just fishing. He's obviously the man I've been looking for. Funny, I wouldn't have taken him to be Charlene's lover. Tom Wilson at the spa, I could see him. But this guy. What does a woman see in someone like this?"

"My second husband was very sensitive, like Colin. He was a wonderful man. I'm sure Colin is nice to be with. A man like that doesn't take you for granted. He pays attention to what *you* need."

He studied her. "I wouldn't have taken him to be attractive to a woman like *you* either. I guess you never know."

Mary Catherine was dealing with his intent stare, feeling a little lightheaded thinking about what might happen between them. She was almost sorry when she heard Colin moan. Baylor made fun of her for thinking about Charlie that way. She ignored him, wishing their rapport wasn't *quite* so mutual. She'd been able to tell what animals were thinking since she was a child. Baylor was the only animal who could read *her* thoughts as well.

"Maybe you better go over and talk to him," Charlie suggested. "I'd like a chance to get a few answers before I go."

She agreed and sat by Colin's side, holding his smooth, manicured hand. That alone should've told the police something about him. Colin never did *anything* with his hands if he could help it. She wouldn't be surprised if she found out he'd *hired* someone to kill his aunt. But the idea that he physically killed the woman was preposterous.

"Is he gone?" Colin whispered, not opening his eyes. "I didn't know Charlene's husband was so big. I was picturing him short. Maybe with a mustache."

"You mean you've never met him?"

"*No!* Why would I? You usually don't hang out with your lover's husband."

Mary Catherine sighed. She was disappointed in Colin. She'd pictured him dating sweet, intelligent girls like Mindy. She wouldn't have taken him for a cheater. "Charlie isn't Charlene's husband. He's a private detective who was hired to look for her lover. I guess he was looking for *you*."

Colin sat up quickly. "Don't tell him! I'll get dressed and get out of here before he comes back."

Charlie smiled and waved. "Still here. I'm not going anywhere until I've had some questions answered, killer."

"What did you call me?" Colin's face turned redder than Mary Catherine's furniture. "I've taken on men twice your size."

"I'm sure you have." Charlie stood up. "On the polo field, right?"

"I've never played polo. I was captain of my lacrosse team!"

"Whatever. How long have you been banging Tate's wife?"

Mary Catherine winced. "Could we have a *little* civility?"

"Sure," Charlie agreed. "How long have you been boffing Charlene Tate?"

"I don't see where that's any of your business," Colin defended himself. "What Charlene and I do has nothing to do with you."

Charlie shrugged. "That works for me. I'll give her husband, Elmore, a call and *he* can ask the questions."

"*Elmore*?" The name conjured up another man like Colin. Mary Catherine expected Charlene's husband to be named Jack or something with initials. Why would Charlene cheat on her husband with someone just like him?

"He's a stockbroker," Charlie said, as though that explained everything.

"Okay." Colin sat back down with a defeated look on his face. "What do you want to know?"

Charlie took out his notebook. "How long have you been seeing Charlene?"

"About three months. We met at the old Wilmington City Market. I was shopping for some handcrafted slippers for a friend and we bumped into each other. We've seen each other almost every week since then."

"What kind of car do you drive?"

"I have a sweet BMW convertible, if the weather's nice. During the winter, or if we have heavy rain, I have a Cadillac Escalade. I'm thinking about having that one painted. Black is so yesterday."

Charlie put away his notebook. "Okay. That's all I need to know."

Colin's mouth hung open. Mary Catherine shut it with one hand. "Is that all? Don't you want to beat him up or something?"

"This isn't the time to be funny," Colin protested.

"That's not what I was hired to do." Charlie sat down at the table again and drank a big gulp of tea. He made a face as though he'd forgotten what it tasted like. "My job is to give this information to my employer. He'll decide what to do with it. Smile!" He used his cell phone to take Colin's picture.

"Great! Then *he'll* beat me up."

"When you play, sometimes you pay." Charlie pushed the teacup away from him. "Next time, don't sleep with a married woman. Especially one who looks like Charlene. They're *always* married, kid."

"Always young, blond, and gorgeous." Mary Catherine bristled at the hint of testosterone in the air.

"Yeah." Colin and Charlie both agreed at the same time.

"She's awesome," Colin continued. "And you wouldn't believe what she can do with her tongue."

"Clever of you not to bother telling me," Mary Catherine said. "What about Mindy? She's gorgeous."

"Mindy's good looking," Colin agreed. "But she's not *hot*."

"Not like Charlene," Charlie added.

"You know Mindy? *My* Mindy?" Colin demanded.

"Sure. She hired me about six weeks ago to find out who *you* were sleeping with." Charlie smiled. "I love getting a double."

Colin dropped Mary Catherine's blanket on the floor. "Please! You can't tell Mindy about this. It would break her heart. She isn't worldly, you know. And I think she may have a serious medical condition. You wouldn't want to be responsible for killing her."

Mary Catherine waved her hand. "She doesn't have anything wrong with her except for *you*. I'm sure she can take the strain."

"We're supposed to be married next summer. She could tell the station owner. It could mean my job."

Neither Charlie nor Mary Catherine were sympathetic to his plight. "As Charlie said," Mary Catherine quoted, "sometimes you play and you pay."

"I was just kidding anyway, kid. I don't know your fiancée." Charlie laughed. "You should've seen the look on your face!"

"That wasn't funny. I'm a man on the edge. I've been accused of murdering my aunt, and now someone wants to kill me." Colin paced the floor. "Since you're so good at finding people, maybe you could find the killer. It seems like that's the least you could do, considering you tried to ruin my life."

Charlie thought about it. "Sure. Five hundred per day, plus mileage."

Mary Catherine tried to intervene. "I don't think you need to hire him to find out what's going on."

Colin laughed. "At least I can *hear* him, unlike your turtle friend. I need help. Cousin Bob wants that money. I think he'd do anything to get it."

Charlie took out his notebook again. "What's Cousin Bob do? Is his name Jamison too? Where does he live?"

"I think you're going about this the wrong way," Mary Catherine told Colin with a sweep of her apricot caftan as she sat down.

"Maybe Charlene *was* involved with this. I know she was with you when your aunt was killed, Colin. But what if her husband is the one calling you? It's possible she didn't accidentally run into you. She and her husband may have set this whole thing up."

"That would make more sense than Charlene *wanting* to sleep with him." Charlie glanced at Colin. "Maybe they thought they could kill off the old lady, Charlene would find some way to get the money from Colin, then they'd kill him too."

"That could make sense," Mary Catherine agreed. "Except that Colin has already had a death threat. They wouldn't want to tip him off before everything was set up."

"Would the two of you stop talking about me like I'm not here?"

They both looked at Colin in his dirty, smelly clothes. "Maybe Cousin Bob thought he could intimidate Colin into signing over the money. That doesn't necessarily mean he killed the old lady," Charlie surmised.

"I wish you wouldn't call Aunt Ferndelle an old lady," Colin protested.

"It seems to me, even if Colin's parents' deaths were truly an accident," Mary Catherine theorized, "that someone has gone to a lot of trouble for Colin to end up with this money. Otherwise, why not kill him too?"

"*Mary Catherine!*" Colin whined and threw himself on the sofa.

"Who knows he's here?" Charlie asked.

"No one except us and Danny. He won't say anything."

"The taxi driver?" Charlie nodded. "Maybe we should dangle a little bait and see what comes out of the woodwork."

84

"What are you talking about?" Colin demanded. "What wood-work?"

Mary Catherine agreed. "He needs new clothes. He came here just as you see him. We could send him back to his place for a shower and some clean clothes. That should give Cousin Bob or Charlene and her husband enough time to do their worst."

Charlie smiled. "It sounds like a plan to me."

Mary Catherine! Hi! Are we on the air?

My cat, Sythia, always seems to know when I'm going to be home from work. My friend said it was a learned response from coming home at the same time every day. But I came home early one day to trick her. She was still there waiting on the windowsill for me. I believe she and I have a close bond and that she psychically knows when I'll be home.

What do you think?

EIGHT

Mary Catherine was stationed in her car across the street from Colin's apartment. It was dark, but a streetlight close to the doorway illuminated the area. Danny was in his taxi at the corner. Charlie was about to stroll from the corner past the door to the building.

"Are you sure about this?" Colin looked at the scene from the passenger seat. "What if I'm killed or something? He doesn't have to be close to me if he has a gun."

"Oh I think he would've killed you by now if he wanted to make it that easy," Mary Catherine tried to reassure him, but her words didn't have the desired effect.

"Thanks. That makes me feel a *lot* better." Colin sighed and sat back in his seat. "I can't believe Cousin Bob would go to these lengths to get his hands on the family money. It's not like he's poor or something. All of the Jamisons are well off."

"For some people, what they have is never enough. Oh look!" She pointed to Charlie strolling toward the door. "If you're ever going to have any cover until you find out what's going on, this is it."

He nodded. "You're right. I can do this. Charlie has a gun, doesn't he?"

She didn't know but wasn't going to stop the process by saying so. "I'm sure he'll take care of everything."

Colin made his decision. He squared his shoulders and climbed out of the Mini Cooper. Baylor meowed from the back seat, jumping into the front as soon as Colin was gone.

"He's not exactly the heroic type," she said to the cat. "I don't think he's a killer. I can't imagine him not fainting at the sight of blood. Whoever killed Ferndelle was made of stronger stuff."

Baylor disagreed. Humans were not to be trusted, in his opinion. They lied and pretended to be things they weren't all the time.

She glanced at him. "I didn't realize you had such a poor opinion of me."

He pushed his head against her arm and purred loudly.

"Well that's good to know. I was afraid you were basing your judgments of humanity on me." She picked up her binoculars and shushed the cat. "Look! He's almost to the door."

Colin was stepping up on the curb as Charlie reached the side of the building. A few cars had gone by but none of them seemed to have murderous intentions. It all appeared safe and uneventful. Mary Catherine was beginning to wonder if their plan would work after all.

"You see anything, MC?" Danny asked on the other end of the two-way radio he'd given her.

"Not yet. You?"

"Nope. I could take a siesta out here with all this excitement." He yawned. "Hey! What's that? I thought I saw someone."

Mary Catherine scanned the street and sidewalk. There was a small park area on the right side of the old brick building. Like her home, Colin's building was reconstructed from an older space. It was closer to three stories than hers but they were small stories. "I don't see anything besides Charlie and Colin."

Colin had reached the front door by this time. He looked around, then put his key in the door lock. Charlie was continuing to walk past as though he didn't know Colin. Another car crept by on the street and music came from another house with lighted windows and a white picket fence.

Charlie was past the front door and Colin was stepping inside when suddenly, a dark figure came out of the shadows, yelling and throwing himself at Colin.

"This is it!" Danny got out of his taxi and ran to help Charlie grab Cousin Bob.

Mary Catherine exited her car a little more slowly, hoping the event would be over before she got there. She wasn't dressed for tackling someone on a sidewalk. She wasn't sure what that would take, except for Angelina Jolie in *Tomb Raider*, and she didn't have anything that looked like *that* costume.

Charlie had jumped on the shadowed form after it was already on top of Colin. The three of them scrambled on the sidewalk looking like a trapped octopus, all arms and legs. Danny wasted no time jumping into the fray. Mary Catherine wondered how they could tell one from the other as they wrestled through the doorway.

Playing her part, she called Detective Angellus from the number on the card he'd given her. It turned out to be his home number. He answered, sounding as though he was half asleep. "Someone is trying to kill Colin Jamison," she said. "Come quickly. He's at his home. Hurry."

Detective Angellus got out one short query about who was calling before she hung up. She closed her cell phone and waited for another car to pass before she walked across the street. She hoped the detective would come quickly.

It was a sultry night after the early storm, which meant mosquitoes. She shivered. She hated mosquitoes as much as they loved her. Her first late husband, Andrew Smith, always teased her about being mosquito bait. She often missed that dear man, but she had been very young then and didn't really appreciate all that life had given her. If she ever got another man like that, she'd be more careful with him.

She could hear sirens coming their way and urged Charlie and Danny to finish what they were doing and get up. No one seemed to be listening. "You're all going to end up in jail if you don't stop fighting. This isn't part of the plan."

No one responded. She wished she could make out faces and forms better in the dim light. How could such a bright light as the one on the top of the pole lose so much by the time it reached the street? Now if someone could solve *that* problem, think what they could do.

Two Wilmington police cars screeched to a halt in the street and discharged three police officers who ran toward them, calling out for the men on the ground to stop fighting. Mary Catherine tried to explain what was going on, but no one paid any attention.

The police finally broke up the fight by grabbing two of the men and forcibly subduing them. That still left a third man (it appeared to be Cousin Bob) still punching and kicking Colin who was curled in a tight ball, protecting his head and face.

She carefully walked over and hit Cousin Bob in the head with her purse. He looked up long enough to realize what was going on. In that moment, the third police officer grabbed him, pulling him off Colin.

"What's going on out here, anyway?" one of the officers asked the four men.

Colin picked himself up. "He's trying to kill me!" He pointed toward Cousin Bob. "I don't know what I did to him, but he attacked me. These people are my witnesses. I want to press full charges against him."

Mary Catherine smiled, thinking Colin must've been kicked in the head. "Tell them what Cousin Bob said to you about the money."

"Why?" Colin tried to straighten his already trash bound suit and tie. "I just want this man behind bars. Officers, do your job."

"Don't tell us how to do our job, sir." One of the officers shined his flashlight on his face. "Aren't you Colin Jamison?"

"That's right," Colin declared. "You were fast enough to threaten to throw *me* in jail; I think you should do the same with *him*."

The man who'd attacked Colin shook off the officer's grip that held him. "Never mind that! I want *that* man arrested for sleeping with my wife."

Mary Catherine was suddenly feeling confused. "Aren't you Cousin Bob?"

He used his large white handkerchief to wipe his face. "I'm Elmore Tate. I hired a private detective to follow this man and now I know the truth. See here? I have his picture on my cell phone."

Mary Catherine, Danny, and Colin all turned to look at Charlie. He stared back. "I was doing what I was paid to do. I didn't know he'd show up and try to beat Cousin Bob out of his chance to kill Colin. It looks like they need to take a number."

Elmore, free of his restraint, rushed at Colin again. Danny, angry at Charlie, rushed at him. The police officers didn't put up with it this time. "You're all going down to the station."

The police allowed Mary Catherine to follow them to the station. Colin and Charlie rode in the backseat of one car while Danny and Elmore rode in the other.

She supposed it made sense for Charlene's husband to attack Colin when he learned his identity. In all fairness, he *was* sleeping with the man's wife. Maybe the police would be able to tie this attack to Ferndelle's death, as they'd discussed at her apartment.

She was glad none of her husbands had ever cheated on her. It might've been due to the brevity of her relationships, but still she hoped it wouldn't have happened. She dearly loved all of them and trusted they'd loved her in return. She felt sorry for Mindy.

All four men were subdued as they were led into the station. Probably feeling pretty stupid, Mary Catherine supposed. If they'd listened to her, they wouldn't be here.

"*You*," Detective Angellus pointed her way, "in here with me."

She followed him into another tiny interrogation room like the last time she was here. "I wasn't actually involved in this," she denied. "You should ask your officers. I wasn't on the ground fighting when they arrived."

He gestured for her to sit down. "But that was *you* who called me at home, wasn't it?"

"When I saw there was trouble, I called you."

"So you didn't have anything to do with these four guys slugging it out on Water Street. You were an innocent bystander."

"Maybe innocent might not be the best term," she disputed. "But I wasn't fighting."

"Why don't you tell me what happened, Mary Catherine? Then I can decide how innocent you are."

She explained everything, from someone threatening Colin to their plan to bring the man out into the open. Detective Angellus wrote down what she said, then read it back. "Is that about right?"

She nodded. "It seemed like a good idea at the time."

"A good idea would've been to call me when you found out about someone threatening Mr. Jamison. You can't take on something like this by yourself."

"Not to put too fine a point on it, Detective, but I didn't try to do this on my own. Actually my part of calling you at the right moment was fairly small. Charlie Dowd—"

"That old hack?"

"I thought he used to be a police detective?"

Angellus laughed. "Yeah, back when I was in diapers. He was drummed off the job. They said he heard voices that told him where to go when he solved cases. He's a whacko."

Mary Catherine wisely kept her own counsel on hearing voices others couldn't hear. It didn't seem like the best time to remind him that she spoke with animals. She stored away the information about Charlie for future reference. "What about Elmore Tate, the man who attacked Colin?"

"I don't know yet. You stay here and I'll go check on him."

There was no offer of anything to drink this time. She wished she had Baylor with her. She'd left him in the car and now he was sulking by not speaking to her. It would be a more difficult connection anyway, but she felt she'd be able to hear him halfway across the world.

Detective Angellus returned as promised a few minutes later. "You're free to go, Mary Catherine. But I'm warning you, stay out of trouble. My boss doesn't like repeat visitors."

"What about Colin and Mr. Tate?"

"They've come to an agreement, I guess." He shrugged. "As long as they don't press charges against each other, there's not much I can do."

"Is it possible Mr. Tate was involved with Ferndelle's murder and that's why he came after Colin?"

"Not unless he killed her long distance. He was at a sales seminar in Texas."

"And you let Charlie and Danny go?"

"Quit asking questions and go home. If you ever think of doing something stupid like this again, go talk to the turtle or something."

She smiled as she walked past him. "I thought you'd forgotten."

"That you talk to animals?" He grinned. "That doesn't come up around here too often. Actually I heard a repeat of one of your shows on the Internet. People really seem to like you."

"I've been doing this a long time, Detective." With a rare understanding of the human mind, she asked, "Do you have something you wanted to talk to me about? A pet problem?"

Two officers walked toward them and Angellus blew her off. "I don't think I have any problems you can help with, Mary Catherine. Just go home, huh?"

She left him with the sure knowledge that he was lying. Baylor was right for the most part. Humans were deceptive creatures.

Danny, Colin, and Charlie were standing in front of the station, arguing. Tate was nowhere to be seen. She went down the steps quickly when a group of officers turned their heads to listen to the three men argue as they went into the station.

"The three of you better pipe down," she warned. "My car is right over there. I'll take you back to your cars."

"I don't want to ride with this man." Colin pointed a long slender finger at Charlie. "He set me up! Charlene's husband could've killed me!"

"There was no way for me to know he'd come after you," Charlie argued. "I didn't tell him where you lived, just your name and what you looked like."

"That sounds like enough to me." Danny pushed his chest into Charlie. "You're a rotten apple. You need to get out of the barrel."

"That's fine with me." Charlie turned and started to walk away. "You guys are crazy. What did you think was going to happen when Charlene's old man found out who was raiding his henhouse? You better start thinking about that kind of thing."

"Colin?" Mindy called as she got out of her Volkswagen at the curb. "You're not in trouble again, are you?"

"Not if you don't find out." Charlie mumbled the words beneath his breath as he walked by the young woman.

"What?" She ran to Colin's side. "Is everything all right? I got your call. I was so worried after the murder thing and all."

"I didn't call you." Colin looked at Mary Catherine, who quickly denied calling the girl as well. "Was it a man's voice?"

"Yes." Mindy wrapped her arms around her fiancé. "What's going on, Noodles?"

Danny smirked. "Noodles? Is that in reference to his brain or the way he punches?"

"I was thinking lower," Charlie yelled back to the group.

Colin ignored him. "It was probably Uncle Bob. Let's go, Sweet Feet. My car is at the apartment."

When the two had climbed into her car, Danny laughed out loud. "What a pair! Noodles and Sweet Feet! If a *chica* ever called me Noodles, I'd wonder what my problem was."

Mary Catherine watched Charlie's rapidly disappearing back. She would've liked to talk to him about the voices Angellus said he heard. She supposed she'd have to save that for another time. She had no doubt Charlie was far from out of her life. "Let's go. I'm tired and Baylor is hungry."

Danny climbed in on the other side of the Mini Cooper. "Can you imagine the nerve of that guy? He sets up a trap for Colin, knowing that Tate guy was hanging around, waiting to kick his ass. I'm sorry I didn't get another punch in on him."

"He might be telling the truth. Maybe he didn't think Elmore would come after Colin with the information he gave him."

"MC, you always think the best of everyone, but I don't think it's true in this case. You should steer a wide path around that guy if you see him again."

She didn't agree with him, but she was too tired to argue about it. She drove back to Colin's apartment and dropped Danny off at his taxi. "I'll see you tomorrow."

"Yeah. Hey! I almost forgot! How's that handyman working out? He seemed like a nice old guy. I found him wandering around in the street outside the clinic. I knew he must live close by and he'd be perfect for your *curioso* jobs."

"He's doing a good job. Thanks, Danny. I really appreciate all your help."

"*De nada*, MC." He hugged her. "See you later."

The night was softly perfumed around her as she got home and climbed out of the Mini Cooper. The lights on the river seemed as prolific as the stars in the sky above her. The only difference was that many of them on the water were moving as ships headed for the ocean and boats returned to their berths. The river scent was heavy in the air tonight, pungent with the smell of diesel from a big ship going by.

Mary Catherine sat outside with Baylor beneath a spreading oak tree that had probably seen its fair share of duels between pirates and gentlemen as it grew along the Cape Fear River. She and the cat both loved to sit outside at night and listen to the owls call and the doves murmur softly in the shadows. Frogs and crickets added their own symphony punctuated by horns tooting on large and small river vessels.

"I know you're hungry." She stroked Baylor. "You said you wanted to sit outside for a while too."

The only sound audible to most human ears was the rush of the breeze from the river and the raucous cries of a few pesky gulls. But she heard the cat as he thought about the food that awaited him upstairs in their apartment and the softness of the red velvet chair beneath his claws.

"All right. Let's go up. I've heard enough complaining out here anyway. Those river rats never get enough to eat!"

Mary Catherine got up slowly, easing out the kinks in her legs as she moved. Baylor dropped to the ground at her feet, waiting impatiently for her to get to the door. She felt around in her pocket and found the key. There was a scratching sound on the building wall close by and Baylor hissed, turning to face the sound. He couldn't identify the perceived threat and she couldn't make out anything except the shadows.

"It's just the old tree branches," she said out loud for her benefit as well as the cat's. "We've stayed outside so long we're getting spooked."

But her pleasant conversation avoided the slight edge of fear that tugged at her heart as Baylor hissed and growled in the direction of the strange sound. Mary Catherine managed to get the key in the lock and open the door, but her hands were shaking. She urged Baylor to get in the building, but he'd gone into some kind of defensive mode. He still couldn't tell her what the problem was, even though he definitely saw it as a threat.

She looked out into the darkness and wished she had the cat's keen night vision. Many times he could make something out in the blackness she could never see. It was too bad he couldn't always tell her what he saw. Baylor was as close as any animal she'd ever known to articulating human thoughts, but he still saw things as a cat.

Mary Catherine reached down to pick up Baylor and bring him inside when he darted away from her and disappeared into the night. Her heart stopped for an instant then picked up a rapid, uncomfortable beat. "Stop playing games," she said for the sake of hearing her own voice. She could certainly tell the cat in a much more efficient manner to get his butt in the building. But just then, she needed to hear another human voice and hers was the only one available.

The cat didn't appear. She wasn't sure if she should go out after him or if she should let him find his own way back. She certainly couldn't follow him into all the nooks and crannies his agile body could find. If it hadn't been for the way he'd left her, she wouldn't even consider it. They were as close as a human and a cat could be, but she tried to give him his space when she could.

"Baylor?" She peered out into the night. "I'm going to bed. If you don't come in now, there won't be any food until breakfast."

There was a loud hissing and sudden howl she had no trouble identifying as his. She put down her purse and picked up the broom that was near the door to the clinic. Baylor was in trouble and she was going to find him.

NINE

MARY CATHERINE HELD HER broom out in front of her like a sword. She could hear Baylor's frantic yowls with her ears and his angry thoughts in her mind. Something was definitely wrong. Behind the anger, she sensed his fear of what he didn't understand. He couldn't get free of something; she had to find him.

She tried counseling him to calm down so he could help her, but there was no reasoning with him. Animals reached a point where there was no rationalizing their fears, like humans, and they panicked to the point of mindlessness. She tried to get him to consider where he was, but it was no use. He was beyond understanding her.

"Baylor!" she whispered his name as she skulked along the edges of the building in the shadows. "Stop fighting and answer me!"

His silence was more unnerving than his howls for help. Where was he? What was wrong with him?

She wished she'd brought a flashlight. She wished she'd called the police. Neither one of those luxuries belonged to her at that moment. Her back was starting to ache from leaning over looking for the cat.

Her broom handle hit the metal structure of the outside stairs to her apartment. She saw a shadow move across the stairs, too big to be Baylor, and swung at it as hard as she could. The shadow yelped and swore. This was a human animal.

"Watch it with that thing!" Charlie yelled as she lifted the handle to swing it again.

"What are you doing out here? Where's Baylor?"

"I was going up to your apartment to talk to you. I don't know where Baylor is. I thought you could communicate with animals."

She held the handle like a baseball bat. "Don't get cute with me! What have you done with my cat?"

"Nothing. Really. I just got here. I wanted to apologize again for what happened tonight."

Mary Catherine didn't know if she believed him or not. It was much harder to tell with people than with animals. In any case, he was standing close enough that she could tell he wasn't holding Baylor. "He's trapped out here somewhere. I have to find him."

"Let me help you. I'm a private detective. That's what I do, find lost things."

Something in his tone of voice distracted her from Baylor's plight for a moment. "That *is* what you do, isn't it?"

"I don't know what you mean."

"Detective Angellus told me you were kicked off the force because you said you heard voices that helped you solve your cases. You find things because they call to you. You're psychic too."

"I don't know what he's talking about," he argued. "Angellus can kiss my—"

"Shh! Did you hear that?"

He looked around. "Hear what?"

"That scratching sound."

"All these old buildings have rats." He took a step toward her. "Look, I've never had a cat but I've known plenty of cat ladies. Sometimes cats go off on their own. I'm sure Baylor will be fine."

"I think it's over here." She brushed past him with her broomstick in the lead again. He followed behind her until she reached the other side of the metal stairway. Mary Catherine's broomstick hit something metal that didn't resound like the heavy stairs. She knelt down in the rabbit grass and gravel, feeling around until her hands came in contact with a cage.

"Baylor!" She tried to find some way to open the cage, but without a light, it was impossible. Her hands were bruised and cut from trying to force the lightweight metal mesh open. "We have to get him inside. He's trapped in this cage."

Leaving the broomstick where she dropped it, she picked the cage up in both arms. Baylor made no response to her calls. Terrified that he was dead, she rushed back into the clinic, ignoring Charlie as he followed her and closed the front door behind them.

In the overhead fluorescent lights, Mary Catherine could see Baylor in the cage. She couldn't tell if he was unconscious or dead. She fought with the cage again, trying to force the door open. It was wired shut.

"Let me in there!" Charlie brandished a pair of pliers that came out of his Swiss Army knife. "You're never going to get it open with your hands."

"Hurry!" she urged. "I think he may be dead. Why would anyone want to kill my cat?"

Charlie cut the wire that kept the cage door from opening and pulled the cat's inert body out of the cage. "He's still warm. I think his heart's beating."

Mary Catherine gathered Baylor in her arms and rocked him like a baby, her tears falling on him. "I think you're right. I think he's alive. I don't understand how this happened."

Charlie picked up a small colored dart from the cage floor. "I think someone tranquilized him. This looks like one of those darts zookeepers use."

She looked at the projectile. "Someone shot that into Baylor? They wanted to trap him out there?"

Charlie's brown eyes narrowed as he watched her. "Maybe they were trying to trap someone else."

"What are you talking about?"

"What's a surefire way to lure you outside?"

"Why would anyone *want* to lure me outside?"

He shrugged. "I don't know."

She stroked Baylor's fur and considered the possibilities. "The only person out there besides me was you. Is that why you came? To trap Baylor and lure me outside?"

"Yeah. Sure." He laughed. "Good police work, Mary Catherine, but no deal. I probably didn't get here until *after* this happened. And I don't have any reason to lure you anywhere."

"I think you should go now."

"Be reasonable. The real catnapper might still be out there."

She took out her cell phone. "Go now or I'll call the police."

"All right. I'm going. Call me if you need me."

She took a deep breath as he walked out the door.

"But *I* didn't trap your cat," he said before he closed the door. "Think about *that*."

She slammed the door hard in his face and locked the dead bolt. She didn't know what had possessed him to trap Baylor, if that was what happened. It didn't make any sense, but sometimes you couldn't see the whole picture right away. Maybe there was something more going on that hadn't shown itself yet.

Baylor's rough tongue licked her hand as she stroked him, and he reminded her that no one should trust humans.

Happy he seemed to be recovering, she still questioned him ruthlessly. He had no idea what happened to him or who was responsible. He followed the sounds they'd heard until something sharp hit him in the side. He'd tried to warn her, then blacked out.

Bruno was barking loud enough at this point to rattle the bricks in the building. Fred the toucan was yelling dire warnings and Waldo the goat was worried about what he was going to eat.

Mary Catherine took Baylor back to see the St. Bernard, to let him know everything was fine. Bruno was unimpressed with her safeguards and offered to patrol the building for her. She declined his offer of help, but promised she'd call him if she needed him.

She and Baylor went upstairs, where the cat continued to recover with a bowl of food in front of him while he flexed his claws on the red velvet furniture.

Mary Catherine tried not to think bad things about people, but Charlie was proving to be a mistake. She'd taken him into her confidence and he'd betrayed Colin and possibly tried to betray her. He'd never told her the name of her relative whom he said he was working for that first day when he'd searched the clinic office.

She recalled his story about her cousin and that he wanted to buy her building. Now it seemed it might have been a ruse to get in and nose around. She should never have trusted him. "We won't make that mistake again, will we?" She smiled at the orange tabby cat as she ran her hand through his thick fur.

Baylor purred, but doubted her good intentions.

———

"This is Mary Catherine Roberts, the Pet Psychic, and you are live on WRSC Lite 102.5. Do you have a problem with your pet?"

"Hello, Mary Catherine. My name is Seth. I'd like to tell you how much I enjoy your show. You always give such good advice."

"Thank you, Seth. What can I do for you?"

"I was wondering if you've ever talked to dolphins? I live on the coast in the Mobile, Alabama, area, and I frequently feel like I understand the sounds dolphins are making."

"I've spoken with a few dolphins. I hate to say it, but the dolphins at Sea World are much easier to talk to because they've been around humans. I'm sure you've heard me say a hundred times on this show that domesticated animals understand and respond to humans better than creatures in the wild. I'm sure that makes sense on some level. They learn our speech patterns, I think, and that makes it simpler."

"I think I understand how that happens," Seth agreed. "My question is: do you think it's possible to keep a dolphin as a pet? I have a large swimming pool and I feel sure that this one particular dolphin would like to spend time with me."

"I guess my first question would be: how do you know it's the same dolphin?" Mary Catherine looked at Mindy who held her thumb up, approving of the question.

"The dolphin has a black spot on his nose. He comes up to the shore where I sit every day. I can tell we have something between us."

"Are you sure this is a *boy* dolphin?"

Her question was met by silence before Seth replied, "N-not exactly. Why? Are female dolphins attracted to human men?"

"I'm not sure about dolphins, but other species are attracted to the opposite sex in humans. I don't know if they'd ever do anything about it, but—"

"Maybe I should start with some fish," Seth said. "Thanks for your help, Mary Catherine."

"You're welcome. I hope it works out for you." Mindy was gesturing that the next call would be the last one. "Hello! This is Mary Catherine. Do you have a pet question?"

"Yes. I was wondering how long you think it would take to smother a cat?"

She sometimes received strange calls like this. She usually hung up and went on to the next call. But before she could respond, the caller continued, "I think it would only take a minute or two. You just didn't give me enough time with Baylor last night."

Mindy was making slicing motions across her throat to Cory, the engineer in the sound booth, to cut the call. Normally Mary Catherine would've agreed, but this was different. She wanted this man on tape and she wanted to keep him talking in case there was anything the police could use to identify him. She was definitely calling Angellus as soon as she got off the air.

"You're the same person who called in about Colin Jamison, aren't you? Why would you want to hurt Baylor? He doesn't even *like* Colin. What possible reason would you have to call me like this?"

"You don't know?" The caller laughed. "If you think about it, I'm sure you'll understand. Or maybe you can get your little turtle friend to help you out. You've butted in where you don't belong. Get out now, or I won't be responsible for the consequences."

The line went dead and Mary Catherine sagged forward to lay her head on the table. The sound booth door opened and Mindy rushed in to see if she was okay. "That was terrible! I can't believe you kept him on the air after that first bit."

Mary Catherine picked up the phone and called Angellus. "That's why I kept him going. I think he's involved with this thing Colin is going through. I'm sure he's the same caller we had before. He probably read about me being involved with Ferndelle's death and thinks I'm coming too close to catching up with him."

Angellus' voice mail picked up and Mary Catherine explained why she needed him at the radio station.

Mindy's mouth opened wide and her eyes narrowed. "You think it was Cousin Bob? Colin ranted about him all night last night. I've been nervous all morning that he tried to go after the man by himself."

Mary Catherine smiled, thinking about how she almost had to pry Colin out of her car last night with three of them there to protect him. "I don't think you have to worry about that. But it could've been Cousin Bob. The police need to hear this tape and pay Cousin Bob a visit."

"Do we know where he is? Colin didn't seem very sure."

"I don't know but the police should be able to find him." Mary Catherine took Baylor and her purse outside the sound booth to the lobby. Baylor had insisted on coming with her even though he was a little woozy from last night. Now he was all claws and teeth, at least in his thoughts, hoping they'd catch the person responsible for trapping him.

She reminded him that if he hadn't run out like some common street cat, nothing would've happened. "We'll wait out here until Angellus arrives."

Mindy nodded. "I wish there was another producer here today. I'd like to hear what they have to say. I'm really worried about Colin. He's so depressed and unlike himself."

"I'm sure he'll be fine, once all this is over." Mary Catherine looked at the pretty, young woman and wondered if Colin had bared his soul to her. It wasn't anything to do with her, but she thought the girl deserved to know the truth about his "fling" before she married him. Marriage was a difficult enough proposition with the tiny lies couples told each other, without dealing with a large, pre-wedding lie.

Buck Maybelle picked that moment to get off the elevator, all smiles under his Stetson when he saw Mary Catherine. "Just the lady I've been looking for!"

"Not now, Buck. I'm waiting to speak to the police. I'm sure you won't want to be here when they come. I've heard they're looking for manufacturers of bad dog food."

"That's not funny." He unbuttoned his suit jacket and sat down beside her on the orange plastic sofa. "Besides, you agreed to the challenge. I'm ready."

She'd totally forgotten about the Meaty Boy taste test. She'd had far more important things on her mind, but a promise was a promise, no matter how obnoxious. She didn't want to alienate the station owner and she had no doubt Buck had already told him about the taste test.

"All right. When is it set for?" She hushed Baylor who was hissing at the man.

"I was thinking three PM today. Does that work for you?" He laughed as he crossed one leg over the other and swung one long arm along the back of the sofa behind her. "All of the TV stations will be there. I think your own reporter, Diana Wilson, will be there too."

"It's your funeral," she told him. "The dogs aren't going to like it. They didn't like it before. Why would that change now?"

"Humor me, my little psychic angel. I think you'll see this taste test will settle everything. Then you'll do my commercials. That was the agreement."

She sighed. "Yes it was. I'll be there. But the dogs are *my* choice."

"That's right. You bring 'em and I'll feed 'em." He leaned toward her as though he meant to kiss her, but before his mouth could connect with her face, he jumped up, screeching. "Where's that damn cat?"

Baylor yawned and posed on the back of the sofa behind Mary Catherine where he'd scratched Buck's hand. He looked at the man in smug satisfaction while she scolded him, at least out loud. "Baylor! You bad cat. Tell Buck you're sorry."

Baylor's thoughts were everything contrary to telling Buck he was sorry but Mary Catherine made it up for him. "He's really sorry, Buck. I don't know what got into him."

The Meaty Boy mogul sucked on the inch-long scratch on his hand. "I know what got into him! He's a sneaky little devil."

Detective Angellus got off the elevator at that point. He smiled when he saw Mary Catherine, then sobered as he approached. "This is getting to be a habit."

"Can't you do something about that cat?" Buck asked him. "Security in this building isn't what it used to be, I can tell you that. Why are animals allowed in here at all?"

Angellus flashed his ID. "I'm afraid I'm not qualified to answer that question, sir. I'm here about information pertaining to my homicide case. I'm assuming that's coming from you, Mary Catherine."

"Yes, it is." She stood up, taking Baylor with her. "I think it might be better if we go down to the coffee shop to talk. It can get a little loud up here."

"That's fine with me." Angellus looked at Baylor. "Will they let the cat in there?"

She smirked. "Of course. It's Baylor. They know him."

"Don't forget about my taste test," Buck reminded her, still nursing his scratched hand. "It's at the Meaty Boy plant at three PM. Don't forget your dogs. But leave that miserable cat at home."

"I won't forget." The elevator doors closed. "That man is so obnoxious," she told Angellus as they rode down to the ground floor. "I don't know what he thinks he's trying to pull off, but no *normal* dog would choose his dog food over almost anything else."

"Does this figure in with Ferndelle Jamison's death in some way?" Angellus responded. "This better not be a wild goose chase, Mary Catherine."

"Believe me, Buck Maybelle has nothing to do with this. But I might know who does."

They went into Port City Java, Mary Catherine smiling at Angellus' gallantry as he offered to pay for both their drinks. He brought his latte to the table with her iced mocha and they sat down together, facing the busy street.

She didn't wait for an invitation to tell him what had happened at the station, as well as what had happened to Baylor last night. "If I hadn't found him, I believe the man would have harmed him."

Angellus took out his notebook. "And this is the second time the man called you?"

"We get some crazies, don't get me wrong. But I think this man knows something about Colin's aunt and he definitely knew about Baylor."

"Why do you think he'd come after your cat? I mean, why not go after Colin?"

Mary Catherine checked her lipstick, then smiled. "I'm sure it has something to do with my reputation. This isn't the first murder investigation I've been involved in. Once in awhile, animals are the only witness to a tragedy like the one with Ferndelle. I've consulted with police departments in several other states. I think the killer knows I can find him."

Angellus sipped his latte as he tried to hide a smile. "You're something else. So you think the killer is worried about you using the turtle to find him so he came after Baylor?"

"That's what I think."

"Why not come after *you*? I think the chances are pretty good that with you out of the way no one else would talk to the turtle."

110

She considered his point. "It's possible he meant to hold Baylor hostage until this is over. Maybe the threat on the phone today was another effort to keep me quiet."

Angellus put away his pen and notebook. "I don't think anybody else is going to buy that, Mary Catherine. But no matter what, a phone threat, even to your cat, should be taken seriously. I'll have someone go over the tapes and see what we can find."

"Thank you, Detective. I know this is hard for you to believe."

"You could say that." He finished his latte and glanced around the crowded coffee house. "But I have a question for you. This may seem unimportant."

"No!" She leaned forward, trying to sound surprised. "What is it?"

He looked uncomfortable. "My wife is a big fan of yours. She made me promise if I saw you again I'd ask about our hermit crab. He doesn't ever come out of his shell, you know? What do you think we should do?"

Hello Mary Catherine!

I'm a researcher in Tokyo. I've had many strange encounters with animals, particularly dogs, during the course of my two-year study into animal behavior before earthquakes. All animals react strangely just before an earthquake hits. If we can learn to understand their behavior, I believe we can use their ability to sense these things before they happen and save many human lives.

Have you ever had a dog predict an earthquake?

TEN

Mary Catherine wasn't sure what to say. She didn't know any therapies for hermit crabs. "I could try to talk to the poor thing, if you like."

Detective Angellus nodded. "That would be great. My wife gets home about five. Any time after that would be fine. I'll draw you a map while you get those tapes."

The irony of the request wasn't lost on Mary Catherine. Angellus had made fun of her ability to communicate with animals. Now he wanted her help. It didn't surprise her.

She didn't mind, especially since he was going to try to help her. She went back upstairs to the radio station with him to get copies of the tapes from Mindy. "When do you think you'll know something? Should I stay away from my apartment until this is sorted out?"

"I don't know how long it will take to ID the man on the tapes." He shrugged. "It could be anyone. I don't think you have to worry about him trying to hurt you. I think this guy is probably just mouthing off. If he was that close to you last night and wanted to hurt you, he would have. Just make sure you don't give any statements to the police or any media. We don't want to draw this guy out again until we figure out who he is."

"What about Cousin Bob? Are you going to check him out?"

"As soon as I figure out who Cousin Bob is. In the meantime, take it easy. Lay low."

She agreed. "You don't have to worry about that. And I think Baylor and I might check into a hotel for a few nights."

"Okay. Let me know when you're set up." Angellus sniffed and ran his hand across his forehead. "Don't forget about my wife's hermit crab, huh?"

"I'll be there after five," she promised as her cell phone rang. He mouthed his goodbyes as she took the call. It was Danny calling from the clinic. He thought he had a family who might be interested in adopting Bruno and wanted to know when she'd be back.

She told him she was leaving the studio and would be there in a few minutes. She thanked Mindy for copying the tapes and left with Baylor in her arms. She took the elevator downstairs, considering which local hotels allowed pets and wondering if she could sneak in with Baylor if she couldn't find one that did. She didn't know if she should leave her house, but she didn't feel safe there, either.

She looked up as someone opened the door that led outside. Her head snapped up when she recognized Charlie. "What are *you* doing here?"

"You're psychic. You tell me."

"If you don't leave, I'll call the police."

"You can't really believe I'd hurt Baylor, can you?" He put his hand out quickly and ruffled Baylor's tawny fur. "We're buddies."

She was surprised when Baylor didn't scratch him. The cat answered her question with a clear response: this wasn't the human who'd trapped him.

She wondered how he could be so sure. The cat responded with a yawn, flexing on her arm. The scent was different. He would've recognized Charlie's cologne since he'd smelled it before. It definitely *wasn't* Charlie.

You could've told me before I made an idiot of myself. Baylor didn't apologize, refusing to take the blame for Mary Catherine jumping to conclusions.

"I'm sorry," she finally said to Charlie. "I was wrong about you last night. Baylor tells me it wasn't you outside the building."

"Of course it wasn't me!" Charlie scratched Baylor's ears. "I wouldn't hurt an animal."

"I jumped to conclusions." She couldn't believe Baylor was allowing Charlie to touch him without pulling back a bloody finger. "I was upset."

"That's okay." He looked at the door behind her. "I saw Angellus come out. What's up?"

A little stirring of self protection made her shy of answering his question completely. No matter what, he'd sent Colin's name and picture to Elmore Tate. She was having a little trouble totally trusting him. "It wasn't much. He had a few questions to ask me."

"Did it have anything to do with what happened to your cat last night?"

"Of course I told him about what happened."

"And you told him about the guy on the radio today?" He held open the door to her Mini Cooper after she'd unlocked it.

"You were listening?"

"I was. He sounded like a psycho to me. Was Angellus going to pick him up?"

So much for not telling him. "He's going to research it."

"In other words, no. You're on your own."

"He'll be in touch. I'm going to help him with his hermit crab."

Charlie closed the car door, but leaned against it. "Hire me. I'll protect you and catch the crazy guy."

She stared at him with her mouth open until she realized it and brought her lips together. "You have more nerve—"

"I'm not that expensive and you may need an extra set of eyes."

"We'll be just fine, Mr. Dowd. Thank you for your generous offer. Baylor and I always manage to get by." She started the car and began moving forward before Charlie stepped back from the door.

"Honestly," she stared back at him in the rearview mirror as she spoke to Baylor. "I can't even imagine him offering to help if I pay him. Especially after what happened with Colin last night."

Baylor meowed and lay back against the seat.

"That's funny coming from you. You never like *anyone*, but you were letting him scratch your ears. You hate having your ears scratched. I can't believe you trust him."

Mary Catherine approached the stoplight on Water Street going toward home. The light had just turned red, but one last car made it through the intersection on the yellow light. She put her foot down on the brake to stop the car, but nothing happened.

She tried again, looking down at the brake pedal to see what was wrong. She pushed her foot up and down on the pedal but nothing happened. She was sailing through the intersection without slowing down.

Baylor jumped up when he realized her dilemma. He meowed and hissed at traffic headed their way from driveways and the other streets.

"That's not going to do much good." She pulled up the hand brake but nothing happened. "I don't know what else to do. We either go on this way and risk hitting someone or pull up over the curb and hope it stops us before we hit a building."

She switched off the engine but the car kept rolling. Trucks honked their horns and drivers swore at her as they got out of her way. "It's no good. I thought we might slow down enough, but we're picking up speed. We have to take our chances with the building. Maybe the curb will stop us."

Mary Catherine veered sharply to the left. The curb was there beside her, but her turn managed to find a driveway. There were construction scaffolds with workers on them in her path, with nowhere to turn away from them.

The men in yellow hard hats started yelling and urging her to veer away. She tried to take the car to the right again but it was going too fast. Even though the Mini Cooper was close to the ground, the imbalance was too much. The little car flipped on its side. She didn't knock the men from the scaffolding.

She didn't move for a moment, taking stock of where she was and trying to figure out if she was okay. Baylor meowed angrily that he was fine, if anyone cared. He vowed never to get in a car with her again.

Mary Catherine looked out the window, not sure how to get out with the car lying on its right side. She was only being held in place by her seat belt. If she released it, she'd be flung down on top of Baylor on the other seat.

"Are you okay?" Charlie looked in through the open window. "Is Baylor all right?"

"We're fine. Can you help us out of here? I'm afraid to release the seat belt."

"Stay right there. I'll get some help."

——

Two burly firemen helped Mary Catherine out of the wrecked car while a third fireman got Baylor out. The cat was playing up the accident as much as possible. He lay on his side, barely moving, pitifully meowing.

"He's fine," she told the distressed fireman who held the cat. "He's faking it for attention."

The fireman looked at her, then looked at Baylor. "He seems injured to me, ma'am. Maybe we should call a vet."

"Maybe. I hope the vet brings a *big* needle to give him a shot." Mary Catherine mocked her pet's fear of needles.

Baylor pulled his head up quickly and looked around at the crowd that had gathered at the scene. He stopped meowing and jumped down to the ground at the fireman's feet.

"You're such a whiner," she told the cat. "I might really be hurt, but you barely moved in the car."

A paramedic approached her and offered to take her to the hospital. "You may be injured and not realize it," the young woman told her.

"No, thank you. I'll be fine. It was more a surprise than anything else. I'm sure I'm not hurt."

They had her sign a statement releasing them from responsibility, then the young paramedic got in her van and drove away. Mary Catherine was more worried about her own little car. It had obviously born the brunt of the misdeed. "It looks like we'll need a doctor for the car," she told the cat who was sniffing it. "At least *she* protected us."

"I think there may be something more to this than meets the eye," Charlie said. "Look here."

Mary Catherine stood beside him and stared at the car. Because it was flipped on its side, she could see the large, oily patch on the bottom. "What is that?"

"I think someone may have cut your brake line. I noticed something was wrong after you pulled out at the radio station. You left behind some brake fluid. That's why I followed you."

"You mean someone did this on purpose?"

"It wouldn't just cut itself," he assured her. "Maybe you should give Angellus a call. Trying to snatch your cat is one thing; trying to kill you is another."

"I'm not sure he'd agree with you on that." She pulled out her cell phone just as two uniformed police officers approached her for a statement.

Charlie told them what he'd seen and pointed out the spot on the car. The officers nodded and wrote down what he said. Mary Catherine quickly switched her call to Danny's cell phone, asking if he could come and get her. She also needed the name of a good tow truck driver.

When she got off the phone, the officers wanted to speak to her. "Is there someone in particular you think might want to hurt you?"

"No one that I know of, although I'm part of an ongoing murder investigation. I think it's possible that may have made me a target."

The officers wrote down what she said and they seemed polite enough, but she could tell they thought she was a silly, middle-aged woman. She would've insisted they check her story, but a news van came up and started filming the wreck. She remembered what Angellus had said about staying out of the limelight. It would be better to call him herself later.

"Can I offer you a ride home?" Charlie asked.

"No, that's all right. Danny's coming. But thank you for following me. It was nice to see a familiar face." Mary Catherine looked at him and felt the absurd urge to cry. She brushed it aside and recalled that she wasn't quite sure about trusting him.

Baylor reassured her Charlie was trustworthy. She picked up the cat and told him he could be wrong. "You chase mice and half eat them even though you know you're going to get worms and Jenny will have to stick that big probe up your butt. You're not exactly a font of wisdom, my friend."

She waved to Danny when she saw him, excusing herself from Charlie, and hurrying to the side of the old taxi.

"MC! *Como esta*? How did this happen? Is Baylor all right?"

"We're both fine," she answered as she got into the bright orange car. "As to how it happened, Charlie seems to think someone cut the brake line."

Danny got in behind the steering wheel and made a face at the mention of Charlie's name. "That guy! I don't trust him as far as I can throw him. He ratted Colin out, MC. What were you doing with him, anyway?"

"Nothing, really. He came looking for me and followed me from the radio station when he saw the car was leaking something."

"Yeah. Right. He probably cut the line himself. Let's think about this; he was there last night when Baylor was trapped and now he's here today when something happens to your car."

She considered his words. Hadn't she thought something was odd that day at the apartment when her car wouldn't start and Charlie was conveniently there to offer her a ride to work? Maybe he was responsible for that problem too. "Why would he do anything like that? He's not involved in the murder."

Danny shrugged as he negotiated the taxi through the onlooker traffic. "Maybe he's involved. He knew right where to find that *mujer* Tommy says was there when Ferndelle was killed. Maybe there's more to this than we're seeing. What do we know about this guy anyway?"

Mary Catherine thought about that as they drove toward her apartment. "Baylor says he's trustworthy. He said the man who trapped him wore a different cologne."

"What about Tommy? Does he recognize Charlie?"

"He didn't seem to, not like when he saw Charlene." Danny pulled into the drive beside the building. The goat man, in jeans and a faded Margaritaville T-shirt with a broad rimmed straw hat on his gray hair, was sitting outside the clinic on a bench.

"What are you gonna do about that guy?" Danny smiled and waved at the old man who was watching his goat eat grass.

She shrugged, noticing a sore spot on the side of her neck that hadn't been there before the accident. She hoped she wasn't too hasty sending the paramedic away. But maybe a hot bath was all she needed. "I don't know. He's not in the way. He just wants to hang out with his goat."

"I wouldn't want to be you explaining that to Jenny. She's already unhappy with that nice old dude I found to do the handyman stuff around here. What's up with her anyway?"

"Jenny just likes to complain, but as long as she's willing to work here for almost nothing, I can take it. I'm going upstairs to take it easy for a while before the Meaty Boy taste test."

"Si, that's right. I've been hearing about that all day on the radio. I can't wait to find out if Meaty Boy is as bad as you say it is."

"I'm taking Bruno with me and you know he can be terribly honest. I thought Jenny's dog, Candy, would be a good bet because she's very particular."

"Hey! You should take Bubba! He only eats table scraps. If Meaty Boy can win him over, it must not be too bad."

Mary Catherine accepted Danny's offer, even though she wasn't sure his bassett hound, Bubba, could tell the difference between *any* food in his mouth. The stories that animal could tell about wild beer parties with Danny were enough to make her shudder.

"That would be excellent." She was pushed for time she didn't have after the accident. Three dogs would have to be enough. She couldn't be picky which three at this point. She'd never talked to a dog who could stand Meaty Boy. She had no reason to think this would be any different.

"*Bueno*! I'll pick you up here at two thirty. Think it would be okay if I come in and watch?"

"I don't see why not. Thanks for coming to get me. I'll see you later." She smiled and waved to Bernie the handyman who was working on the loose stair outside. The goat man smiled and waved to her as well. She hated to admit it but even that exertion was painful. She was beginning to feel like she'd run a marathon.

"Are you okay?" Jenny asked from the clinic door. "Danny told us about your accident. Is Baylor all right?"

Baylor, sensing a sympathetic ear, immediately lapsed into meowing and holding one paw up as Mary Catherine set him down on the tile floor. Jenny picked him up and stroked him. "Poor thing. I'll just take a look at you and make sure everything is all right. After what you went through last night and then the accident today, I'd be surprised if your nerves aren't completely frazzled."

"Well if you keep feeling sorry for him, he'll let you test him for anything that isn't painful," Mary Catherine told her. "He's the biggest showoff in the world when it comes to something like that."

"What about you?" Jenny looked at her through her thick spectacles. "You probably need some attention yourself."

"That's okay. I'll be fine." Mary Catherine began to ease her way up what had become an incredibly long staircase. "I know you have some medical background, but if something is wrong, I'd rather call a people doctor, if you don't mind. I'm going upstairs to take a hot bath. I may need a good massage after this. I think my whole body is bruised."

It took her a few extra minutes to reach her apartment, but Mary Catherine finally walked into the living room and sank down in her red velvet chair. She looked at the bathroom door but didn't know if she could make it. What had seemed like nothing was very painful now. She began hoping nothing was broken or out of joint. Surely she wouldn't be able to walk if she had a broken bone.

Her cell phone startled her. She looked at the number. It was Colin. "He called again, Mary Catherine. Detective Angellus was barely out the door when Cousin Bob called and threatened me again. He said if I don't do what he asked me to do, I won't live to see the morning. I don't know what to do."

"Pack something and get out of town for a few days," she advised. "If he can't find you, he can't hurt you. Detective Angellus is going to pay him a visit that might end this whole problem."

"But I can't leave town. The police said I have to stay in Wilmington. If I leave, they might arrest me."

"You have money, Colin. Hire a bodyguard. My second late husband was never without his bodyguard, except in the bedroom. You can do the same thing."

He thought it over for a moment. "I suppose you're right. I wish this would be over so I could have my life back."

Mary Catherine was almost too sore to commiserate with him. "It'll all be over soon, I'm sure. In the meantime, protect yourself. Maybe Detective Angellus will have some answers for us today or tomorrow."

"Thanks. I guess it won't be too bad to hole up here with Mindy."

"I hope you plan to tell her about Charlene."

"No! Why should I? It'd only hurt her feelings. It only happened this one time. It won't ever happen again."

Mary Catherine doubted that. From what she could tell, men who fooled around always fooled around. And that was a rule of thumb for *married* men. A man who cheated on his fiancée— where would you go from there? "I guess that's your business, but it was really hard to look at her today and not say anything."

"I appreciate you not telling her," Colin said. "Hang on a minute. There's a knock at the door."

Mary Catherine waited impatiently since she had only a couple of hours to drag her body into a hot bath, change clothes, and then go to the Meaty Boy taste test. She wasn't looking forward to that event before the accident, now she was sorry she'd ever agreed to it.

She was holding on to her cell phone and trying to ease herself out of the chair when she heard Colin yelling on the other end. "No! Get back! Leave me alone!"

"Colin? Are you there? Is everything okay?" Mary Catherine waited for an answer until the phone went dead in her hand.

ELEVEN

Mary Catherine was about to speed-dial 911 when there was a knock on her outside door. She forced herself up and out of the chair even though her poor body felt as though it was coming apart. "Just a minute," she called out, limping to the door.

It was the handyman; *what was his name?* She smiled and frantically searched her memory. "Yes?"

"I fixed the loose stair, ma'am." He pulled at the brim of his hat in respect. "What would you like me to start on next?"

She tried to remember anything on the long list of problems she'd had with the building. Nothing came to mind. And she still couldn't think of his name. "I guess that's all for today. Maybe you could come back tomorrow and we could work on a to-do list for you."

"Thanks. I'll be back tomorrow then." He turned away and started back down the stairs.

"Thank you. I appreciate your work." She suddenly recalled his name. "Thanks, Bernie."

"No problem." He waved without looking back. "See you tomorrow."

Mary Catherine closed the door and dialed Colin's cell phone number. There was no response; only his voice mail answered. She hated to call Detective Angellus again but this seemed to be part of the same case. She justified it that way and punched in his cell phone number.

"Angellus here."

She told him about Colin's phone call after apologizing for calling him again. "I know he's at Mindy's apartment. Should I call the police to go over there? Are you close by?"

"I'll have an officer swing by," he promised. "I'm out at Bob Jamison's house on Bald Head Island. I don't think he has anything to do with what's happening to Colin or Ferndelle Jamison's death."

"What could he possibly have said to you that made you believe that?"

"The man had a stroke a few months back, Mary Catherine. He can't get out of bed much less go around murdering people. From what I can tell, he can't even use the phone to threaten Colin."

"That doesn't make any sense," she argued. "There has to be another answer."

"There is. Colin killed his aunt for the money and has spent all this time trying to convince you he's innocent so you can bug me into looking for another suspect. I'd say that's worked pretty well. Up until now anyway."

"Well, in case this isn't made up and Colin *is* in trouble, would you call an officer to go by Mindy's apartment on Second Street? We can debate his guilt or innocence later, *if* he's still alive. I'd go myself but I don't have a car, and Danny is at the airport."

"I'll take care of it. Don't forget my wife's hermit crab."

Mary Catherine promised not to forget and closed her cell phone. She dragged herself into the bathroom, thankful she'd put in a whirlpool bath when she'd remodeled the apartment. Gutted it was more like it, she considered, as she turned on the hot water and added relaxing bath crystals that turned the water Caribbean blue.

The building had sat empty for a few years and the repairs had been massive before she could even think of moving in. The first floor had rats and burn spots where homeless people had made fires, surprisingly not burning the whole building down. The upstairs floor was large but had been used for storage. Her aunt had left boxes there that Mary Catherine had transferred to the basement after the entire building was restored.

It had been an expensive project, but well worthwhile. She'd been lucky that her last husband hadn't insisted on a pre-nup so she got an equal share of his wealth along with his three children from his various other marriages. Between that and her signing bonus with the radio station, she'd managed to set up the clinic as well as her beautiful apartment.

Soaking in the tub, she thought about the mess Colin was in. She wasn't a private detective, even though she'd helped the police with several investigations. Maybe Charlie was right and she should hire him to help find out what was going on.

Baylor was still downstairs being pampered by Jenny, but he reminded her she didn't especially trust Charlie and no good could come from spending too much time with him.

She was surprised, since Baylor admitted to trusting Charlie. Apparently he meant in a friendly-stranger type of way. He didn't want her to get personally involved with the man. She laughed and told him she had no intention of anything but a business relationship with Charlie. Baylor heavily stressed his doubt.

Removing herself from the cat's random thoughts, she thought about Charlie and her feelings for him. She wasn't sure what it was about him she found attractive. Goodness knew, he didn't seem to have any money and he had a knack for turning up at difficult moments, which could be construed as either good or bad. She didn't know if she'd want to spend time with a man whose presence was constantly linked with bad things happening. Still, it had been very nice to see his face right after the accident.

Her little clock went off on the side of the tub. It hardly seemed any time at all. Her poor, abused body wasn't ready to leave the warm, relaxing water. She'd kept her cell phone on the edge of the tub in case Angellus or Colin called, but she hadn't heard from anyone. She hoped Colin was all right. It was frustrating to be in such a helpless position.

She tried to focus on something else. Her reputation and name were on the line with the Meaty Boy taste test. She didn't want to form a totally negative opinion of the dog food, but it was difficult. For Colin's sake and the sake of revenue dollars for her pet psychic talk show, she had to give Buck a chance.

She groaned as she got out of the tub and dried off. Tommy was complaining from the next room. She padded in there, wrapped in her towel, to comfort him. She never realized turtles became so attached to their owners. She didn't think of a reptile as being so personable. Tommy was the first turtle she'd run across who cared what happened, as long as he was fed.

"You poor little thing. I know this is hard for you. I don't know what to tell you. I can't look for a new home for you until this thing with Ferndelle's death is settled. I know it's hard for you to understand, but the police sort of feel like you're evidence."

The turtle didn't understand what she was talking about. He missed Ferndelle and the large bowl with his rock. He didn't like the food Jenny had sent up for him. He wanted to go back to his old life.

Mary Catherine stroked his shell and sighed. She'd never make him understand what was going on. His little mind couldn't fathom the complexity that surrounded a human death. Even a dog or cat would have trouble with that, and they were very good at understanding what went on in the human world.

She put him back in his tank and added a bowl that she hoped he would use as a rock. Jenny had told her how important rocks were to turtles, but so far every rock they'd tried to give him was rejected. She put him on top of the overturned bowl and encouraged him to use it. He stared back at her, telling her again how much he missed Ferndelle.

She wished he had some other knowledge that would help them find Ferndelle's killer. The only thing he could actually recall was Charlene being present at the time. Since Colin swore she was with him all night, that seemed to be a dead end. Nothing he could tell her seemed to help the investigation.

Now that Cousin Bob had been ruled off the suspect list by Detective Angellus, she was afraid they were back to Colin being the only one who could have murdered the old lady. He had motive (the family money being held up by Ferndelle) and no alibi for the time when she was killed (except for Charlene's word, and Tommy disputed that).

Slowly and carefully, Mary Catherine put on a pale lavender ankle-length skirt with a matching blouse and jacket. She was a little liberal with her makeup and included pale lavender eye shadow since she knew that TV cameras would be at the taste test. She brushed out her naturally thick blond hair and topped it with a large lavender hat she'd bought at Macy's ten years before.

Jenny brought Baylor upstairs as Mary Catherine was limping out of the bedroom to retrieve her purse. "You look pretty good for an old lady," the vet told her.

"Thanks, I think. Not to split hairs, but I think you might be a few years too old to call *me* an old lady."

Jenny laughed as she put Baylor on the carpet, her long, gray naturally curly hair fanning out around her. "I can call anybody whatever I like. That's how old I am."

"Okay." Mary Catherine changed the subject. She didn't want to get into an argument with Jenny. "How's Baylor doing?"

"He's fine. A little tense and I think he might have sprained his paw. But he'll be okay."

"I think he's in better shape than I'm in." Mary Catherine took everything out of her white purse and put it into her matching lavender purse. "I might go see a chiropractor later."

"Those quacks? You might as well roll yourself down the stairs. It would do you as much good."

"You know, your people bedside manner could use some polishing."

"I'm not here for people." Jenny opened the door to go back downstairs to the clinic. "And don't take Baylor out anymore without getting him a proper pet seat so you can strap him in for the next time you decide to roll your car."

Mary Catherine opened her mouth to say something scathing about Jenny criticizing her driving when the vet never drove a car, but before she could formulate the words, Jenny was gone. She looked at Baylor. "You certainly snowed her."

Baylor ignored her, jumping up into his favorite chair and digging his claws into the red velvet. Mary Catherine took out her cell phone and tried to call Colin. There was still no answer. She called Danny to see if he was on his way back from the airport. She was going to have to find some way to get Bruno, Bubba, and Candy into the backseat of the taxi. Maybe it would be easier to simply admit, despite her beliefs to the contrary, that Meaty Boy dog food was all right for pets.

But she knew that wouldn't do. She winced as she squared her shoulders, pushed her lavender hat a little farther down on her head, and painfully crept down the stairs.

———

The Meaty Boy dog food plant was outside the downtown area, near the airport. It was a sturdy, red brick box with silos on one side to bring in the grain trucks that delivered on a regular basis. The green grass that fronted the plant was smooth and emerald-colored, leading up to immaculate white fences that bordered the property.

"This looks like something from an old TV show," Danny said as he pulled the taxi into the long, tree-lined driveway that led to the plant. "I didn't even know it was out here."

131

Mary Catherine separated Bubba and Candy for the tenth time while Bruno snored in one corner of the backseat. It seemed Bubba wasn't bright enough to realize that Candy meant it when she said no. The little Pekinese wouldn't even look at the homely basset hound. She much preferred Bruno, who wasn't a bit interested.

Of course, Bruno was neutered and Bubba wasn't. Mary Catherine tried to explain the difference to Candy, but the dog didn't care. She just wanted the basset hound to get away from her.

"Thank goodness we're here." She told all the dogs to stay put as she and Danny got out of the car. She had leashes for Candy and Bruno, but Danny insisted Bubba would walk in with him. "I'm really glad I didn't bring Baylor."

"Yeah," Danny agreed. "He would've been jealous of all the attention the dogs are getting. Does Meaty Boy make cat food?"

"Not as far as I know. Maybe it's just as well with the way dogs complain about the dog food. Cats are much more particular about what they eat. Except for mice and bugs, but that's a whole other story that involves ritual and culture."

"There you are!" Buck was with a large group of followers who greeted them from the doorway. "I see you brought your taste testers. Are any of them yours?"

"Bruno is," she responded, "but only until we find a home for him. This is Danny Ruiz and his dog, Bubba. The St. Bernard is Bruno and the little one is Candy. She belongs to the vet at the clinic."

Buck, who'd swept his Stetson from his head when he'd encountered her, placed the large hat back on his thick hair. "That reminds me. I have a check from Meaty Boy for your clinic because it does such fine work for the community."

Mary Catherine grunted when Buck pulled her close to him as TV and newspaper media seemed to spring out of the very green grass that surrounded them.

Buck held the check for two thousand dollars out in front of them and gave her a little squeeze. "I'm proud to present this money to you, Mary Catherine. Thank you for being here today."

She wasn't sure what to say. He was giving money to the clinic, which surely entitled him to at least a thank you. On the other hand, he'd maneuvered this whole situation to get her off guard so she'd help make him look good. The man was in a class by himself as far as grandstanding was concerned.

She realized everyone was looking at her, expecting some response. She smiled and held her side of the check as Buck presented it to her. "Thank you, Mr. Maybelle."

He laughed. "My daddy was Mr. Maybelle, Miz Mary Catherine. I've never liked titles much. I hope you'll call me Buck."

She agreed to call him by his first name and hoped that part of the ordeal would be over. He looked down at her and winked before giving her a final squeeze. Mary Catherine's heart beat a little faster for a moment. He *was* a very attractive, wealthy man.

She knew Baylor would laugh at her for thinking that—another reason she was glad the cat wasn't there. It wasn't like she was planning on running off with the dog food king. She reminded herself that Buck stood for all that was bad as far as taking care of animals. By doing that, she was able to look at him from a less attractive perspective.

"Now, we'll be moving to the taste evaluation room where we've had several of our employees bring their dogs to join in the Meaty Boy taste challenge." Buck was still hamming it up for the press, who were busy writing and recording every word he said as well as taking pictures every few seconds.

"Are you going to talk to the animals to see which dog food they prefer?" One reporter stepped forward. "You're the pet psychic, right?"

"I am Mary Catherine Roberts, the Pet Psychic on Lite 102.5." If Buck could play it up for the press, so could she. "I'll be monitoring what the dogs are saying about the food."

A hundred questions came up at once as the reporters all rushed to understand how her "powers" worked. "Can you talk to every animal? What about whales?" one reporter asked.

"I can't say I've ever had a conversation with a whale," she replied, "but I'm sure if they can think like we do, I could talk to one."

"What about the turtle who saw Ferndelle Jamison's killer?"

Mary Catherine recognized that voice but couldn't see the face of the man asking the question from the back of the group. "I can talk to him, but they don't see things like we do. It's not that easy."

"Getting back to our Meaty Boy taste challenge." Buck steered the conversation back to him. "If you'll follow me, we should find out quickly who the winner is in this contest."

He allowed Mary Catherine to go in the door before him, every inch the Southern gentleman. He blocked the door after her so that Danny had to come in with the reporters, Bubba trailing behind them all. Bruno yawned, wondering when they were going home and Candy strained at the leash Danny held, trying to get away from the crowd. She was a very nervous little dog; unlike most Pekinese Mary Catherine had known. Mostly they were small but extremely courageous.

The taste test was set up in a spotless white room. It looked as though there would normally be a table in the middle of the room, but now the shiny white floor was empty except for six numbered spaces where Mary Catherine presumed dog food bowls would go.

"I'll put my three challengers on this side," Buck told her. "You'll put your three over there. Each challenger will be served three different types of dog food. One of them will be my new and improved Meaty Boy Deluxe Dog Food. The other two will be top name brands. The winner will be the one the dogs prefer, according to what they tell you and how much they eat."

Mary Catherine agreed to the rules and explained to her dogs what was expected of them. Buck's white-coated assistant brought in their three dogs: one collie, one Great Dane, and one German Shepherd. The dogs were placed at their particular eating stations and the first dog food bowls were brought out.

"How do you know which is which?" a reporter asked Buck.

"It's a blind taste test. We won't know until it's over." He smiled for the reporter and graciously allowed a photographer to take his picture.

The dogs all put their heads into the bowls and tasted the food. Bruno was the first one to turn up his nose. He told Mary Catherine it tasted like bad meat and the other dogs soon followed his lead.

"I guess that says it all." Danny shrugged and looked at Buck. "Next course, please."

The second dog food was brought out. The dogs ate most of it, but told Mary Catherine they were hungry or they would've left it too. Candy wanted to know when they were bringing out the good stuff. This was worse than when she was living on the street stealing from trash cans.

"They aren't crazy about this stuff either," Mary Catherine told everyone. She was having some trouble communicating with the three strange dogs. They were so busy thinking about being in a room with so many people that they had trouble focusing their thoughts.

"We'll move on to the third and final dog food," Buck's assistant announced dramatically.

They brought out the last variety and set the bowls in front of the dogs. Immediately, all six dogs buried their noses in the food and swallowed it as fast as they could. Candy said it was the best food she'd ever had, with visions of steak in her head. Bruno and Bubba agreed. They didn't know what it was but they wanted more of it. The other three dogs agreed. All of them looked up when they'd finished and whined for more.

"I'd say the third brand is the winner." Buck smiled at Mary Catherine. "What did the dogs tell you?"

At that moment, the three strange dogs were telling her they had been brought from the pound, shampooed, and set here for the taste test. They all expected to be returned to the pound and die within the next few days. They'd all seen it happen before. This was like some dream of a home for them. They wished it would go on and were fearful it was coming to an end too quickly.

The fear and anguish in their minds almost took her breath away. That any creature should feel that way broke her heart. She knew she couldn't take every dog and cat from the pound. She'd done that before and ended up with an unmanageable situation.

But she could help these three even though she didn't want to think what Jenny would say when she came back with them.

She looked up, disturbed and tearful. Everyone was staring at her. With an effort, she brought herself back to the human world and realized everyone was waiting for her answer. Buck's three dogs had no preference; they were too worried about dying. Bubba, Bruno and Candy, all orphans from the street but no longer afraid of what was going to happen to them, related that the third variety was definitely the best.

Mary Catherine told Buck and the reporters what her dogs said. Buck's smile was huge. She knew the last brand was Meaty Boy even though it was *supposed* to be a blind taste test.

Buck ripped the front panels covering the labels on the dog food bags. The third brand was Meaty Boy. "I guess you'll be doing commercials for me now, my little psychic angel."

Hi, Mary Catherine!

This is Dawn from Delaware. I have a hurt seagull I've been taking care of for two months. He can't fly. I'm beginning to worry he may never fly again and he won't be able to survive on his own.

What should I do?

TWELVE

"So MEATY BOY WON?" Jenny put down her habitual cup of coffee and stared at her dog. "Candy ate Meaty Boy? We've tried it before. She's always hated it."

Danny shrugged. "Maybe it's the new and improved part. Bubba hated it too. But not today. Even Bruno wolfed it down. You know how finicky he is."

"I think there may be something more involved," Mary Catherine told them. She took out a handful of dog food from her pocket. "Maybe we could run some tests on this and see what it was the dogs liked so much."

"Do I look like a research scientist?" Jenny stared at her as she put Candy on the floor. "It's all I can do to keep up with this place. I wouldn't know one kind of dog food from another."

"Maybe you know someone who could do the work," Mary Catherine suggested. "The dogs have been asking for it constantly since we left the Meaty Boy plant. When have you ever known of dogs who were well fed thinking about the food they just ate? They're always thinking about the next meal."

Jenny scratched her head. "Oh I don't know. Maybe the last time *I* talked to dogs, they were all about the food. I think they told me I was beautiful too. Of course that may be the new dogs you brought back with you. Do we have shot records for them or am I supposed to research *that* too?"

Mary Catherine ignored Jenny's ill humor the way she always did. "I'll find someone to check it out. But I'm assuming, since the three new dogs were headed for the gas chamber, that they don't have shot records. In order to get them adopted, we'll have to vaccinate them."

"I think we should wait a few weeks to make sure none of them have rabies too." Jenny glanced at the quarantine room where the three new dogs were located. "I'm surprised they aren't barking. If you locked me in a room, I'd bark."

Danny snickered. "Come on, Bubba. It must be time for us to go. I'm beginning to think about locking people in rooms by themselves."

"You always think everything is so funny," Jenny fumed. "If you were a dog, you'd be a hyena."

"I don't think that's a *perro*," Danny said. "But don't mind me. I'm just the taxi driver."

"Thanks for letting me use Bubba as a lab rat," Mary Catherine said. "The dogs aren't barking because they know they're safe. They'll be fine."

"What about Bruno?" Jenny asked around the St. Bernard's deep-throated bark.

"He's barking for a whole other reason," Mary Catherine said. "We have to find someone to adopt him."

"You're never going to find someone who wants that big monster." Jenny took off her lab coat. "I'm going home now. Please tell Baylor I hope he feels better."

"I will. I'm feeling better too, if that interests you at all."

Jenny waved as she led Candy out the door.

"Apparently, it wasn't all that interesting." Mary Catherine picked up the clinic's mail—mostly bills—and started upstairs. Her cell phone rang. It was Detective Angellus. He told her that Colin's emergency had been a package delivery from UPS.

"Is that all?" she asked. "Did you at least have the package checked out?"

"The officers I sent over scared the poor driver so bad that he had to be rushed to the emergency room with an asthma attack. Will that do it? Or would you like me to go question him in the hospital?"

"No need to get nasty about it. I was just concerned for Colin."

"I think your friend is taking advantage of you." He reminded her about his hermit crab. She told him she'd be right over, closed her cell phone, then realized she didn't have her car and Danny had just left.

She didn't want to bother him again that day; he'd already made several trips to the airport. She decided to call another taxi company for a ride, but her cell phone was getting poor reception. She walked outside to get a better signal and found Charlie standing outside her door, his Suburban parked at the curb. "What are *you* doing here?"

"I thought I'd offer you a ride somewhere in case you need to go out."

It was very annoying, this habit of his turning up right when she needed him. She supposed it would be a good trait in someone she trusted. But in Charlie, where she was trying hard to stay objective in case he wasn't all that he seemed, it was difficult.

Was he somehow tuned into her frequency? She was psychic and had known many other people who were as well. It wasn't too far a stretch for her to imagine the possibilities. Part of that was where her problem lay. "No, thanks. I'm going to call a taxi."

"Why? I'm right here. I'll take you where you want to go."

She glared at him, wishing he'd go away. It was better when she could question his motives, like being there when her car wouldn't start. *That* was a physical thing. But she was beginning to feel he was going to be there when she needed him, like last night with Baylor. There were heavenly guardian angels, and then there was Charlie. "I'd rather call a taxi."

"What is there about me that you don't like?" He continued to badger her. "I don't think it has anything to do with my calling Elmore when I found Colin."

"You're right," she admitted. "Now go away. I'm trying to call a ride."

Charlie put his hand on her cell phone, grasping her hand beneath it. "I'm very attracted to you, Mary Catherine. I would've thought that was obvious."

"Of course you are. It's been a curse all of my life. I think it has something to do with talking to animals."

He stared at her for a long minute, then burst out laughing. "Are you telling me I like you because you can talk to dogs?"

"No. Not exactly. I think it has to do with being psychic. People who don't use their gifts are attracted to people who do. You seem to use your psychic abilities somewhat. I'm sure you know what I mean. Women are probably attracted to you as well. That's why you find it hard to believe I could reject you."

"Is that what this is?"

She nodded, averting her eyes, trembling. It was a terrible thing to want someone and turn him down. When she was younger, she'd never tried. If someone she found attractive found her attractive as well, she gave in. But the loss of her last husband was devastating. She didn't know if she could go through that again.

"Okay. If that's the way you want it." Charlie shrugged. "I can do that too. That doesn't mean I don't want to help with your investigation and that I can't drive you where you need to go."

She took a deep breath that included a whiff of his spicy aftershave. She wasn't strong enough to completely cut him out of her life. She realized it could be the mutual attraction due to the psychic bond they were developing. "All right. Just friends." She turned her hand in his and gave it a hearty shake.

He solemnly shook back. "Just friends." He released her hand. "So where to?"

"I have a date with a hermit crab."

Charlie opened the truck door. "Is there a hermit crab with answers about what's happening to Colin?"

"Not exactly. I'll fill you in on the way."

———

They got out at Detective Angellus' modest brick home a little after six PM. Two cars were in the drive. Mary Catherine knew Angellus was home too. He opened the door when he saw them pull up and glanced at his watch. "I was wondering if you were going to show."

"I *was* in an accident today," she told him. "There are a few too many of those in my life right now."

A fragile blond woman appeared at his side. "I hope it wasn't anything serious?"

"Not so you could tell, but I think I'm bruised all over." Mary Catherine put out her hand and introduced herself.

"I'm Sallie Angellus. You know, you could've come over some other time if you were in pain."

"That's all right." Mary Catherine smiled as she walked into the house. "I'll be fine. I'm just a little stiff. I hope you have some sweet tea. I'm dying for a glass of tea."

Charlie introduced himself to Sallie. Detective Angellus shook his hand warily. "Are you traveling with the psychic circus now, Dowd?"

Sallie nudged him with her elbow. "*John!*" She turned to Charlie and Mary Catherine. "Don't mind him. His mother told me he never believed in Santa Claus or the Easter Bunny when he was a kid. He doesn't believe in anything now either."

Angellus looked uncomfortable. "Honey, maybe we shouldn't say things like that to these people we hardly know."

"I don't know what difference that makes," Sallie retorted. "I'm sure they could tell from meeting you what kind of person you are."

Mary Catherine smiled, but didn't get involved. There was a little Yorkie who wagged his tail and pushed his head up under her hand. He was telling her more about this family than most people

143

would know in a lifetime. His thoughts were so fast she couldn't keep up with them. But everything he said was something nice about the man and woman he lived with. He had a good life and the people were kind to him.

"I'm sorry." Sallie shook her head. She was barely five feet tall, with delicate proportions. The cloud of silver-blond hair made her blue eyes startling and almost seemed too heavy to hold up on her thin neck. "I didn't mean to drag you into this argument. You might as well know, if you don't already, that John is a skeptic. I'm sure it makes him a great cop, but it makes it hard for me since I was raised to believe in things we couldn't see."

"You're from near Charleston, aren't you?"

Sallie, Charlie, and Angellus all stared at Mary Catherine. Sallie recovered first. "Yes. How did you know?" She glanced at her husband.

"Moose told me." Mary Catherine scratched the Yorkie's head again. "He likes living here with you. He told me you took him to visit some people by a place that sounded like Charleston to me. I probably wouldn't have known, but I was down there staying with some friends who own a very nice bed and breakfast."

Sallie was astounded. "I can't believe it." She tugged at Angellus' coat. "See? I told you she was real. How else would she know we named him Moose, or where my parents live?"

Angellus bent down to look at the dog's collar. "His name is on his collar, Sallie. I'm sure she could have read it."

"How about the connection to my family?" his wife demanded.

The detective didn't have an answer for that. "The hermit crab is this way."

"I'm so sorry." Sallie glared at her husband. "Let me get you some sweet tea. I have some shortbread cookies too."

"Thank you, dear." Mary Catherine followed Angellus to the sun porch in the back of the house. "I'm used to skepticism. It takes some people a while to believe."

While Sallie was gone, Angellus turned to Charlie. "You investigated my wife, didn't you, Dowd? I don't appreciate scams in my own house."

Charlie smiled. "I didn't do anything. This is all Mary Catherine. You might not want to believe it. I didn't. But I think she *really* talks to animals."

Angellus glared at Mary Catherine. "I was beginning to trust you. As long as you're hanging around with this jerk, no one will take you seriously."

Charlie pushed up against him. "Now I take offense to *that*, Detective."

Mary Catherine slid her ample form between the two men, who looked like pit bulls getting ready to spar. Only pit bulls would've been easier to reason with. "Excuse me. I'm sure neither one of you *really* want to do this. Let's talk to the crab and drink some tea. I know you can both act like gentlemen for a few minutes."

The two men glared a few minutes longer, but finally separated. Charlie sat down on a red-flowered wicker sofa and Angellus showed Mary Catherine where the hermit crab lived. "She calls him Bo-Bo. It's after some clown she remembers from when she was a kid. Don't bother trying to impress me."

Angellus took a moment to give Charlie a hard stare, as though he could make him disappear by looking at him.

"Believe me; I have no reason to bother impressing you. *You* may not believe, but there are millions who do," Mary Catherine said.

She turned her back on him and focused on the little crab, whom she could barely make out in the shell. His habitat was a large aquarium filled with sand, rocks, a water puddle, and a few extra shells. It seemed nice and spacious for him.

Because he was still a wild creature, his thoughts were unclear. Being a crustacean, he was even more difficult than a mammal would have been. There was no ego like the poodle, but Bo-Bo had a hard time forming thoughts she could comprehend. Unlike the Yorkie who was sitting patiently by her feet, there were no thoughts of the people who lived with him being kind or good. It was more like disjointed memories of his life, first at the pet store, then at the Angellus home.

Sallie brought in tea and cookies. Mary Catherine thanked her and took a few sips before focusing on the crab again. Angellus paced the room impatiently, refusing tea or cookies. Sallie stood and watched Mary Catherine. Charlie helped himself to cookies and tea, not bothering to hide his amusement with the situation.

"How much longer?" Angellus demanded.

"Shh! It takes as long as it takes." Mary Catherine bit into a shortbread cookie. "These are excellent, Sallie! You have to give me the recipe."

"I'll be glad to. It's been handed down for four generations in my family."

"Oh, for God's sake—" Angellus picked up a glass of sweet tea and sat down in one of the red-flowered wicker chairs to wait.

Two hours later, they were all still waiting. Sallie had scooted a chair close to the aquarium so Mary Catherine could sit down. Angellus had gone into another room to make a phone call. Charlie was asleep, his head thrown back, mouth open slightly, faint snoring noises coming from his throat.

Mary Catherine was beginning to understand the way the crab thought. It was random, almost making no sense at all, but there were certain images that kept repeating. Like deciphering some ancient text, she began putting those repeat images together to form a sort of pattern she felt sure would provide the answers she was looking for.

This wasn't the first time she'd tried to communicate with a creature even less easy to understand than the pelican trapped in the mesh. At least in that case, she could see what was wrong and what needed to be done to help the poor animal.

When she'd lived in Los Angeles with her second late husband, George Wilson, she'd run into the same thing with a snake. A friend of theirs had bought the ten-foot boa constrictor as a joke, parading the creature for his friends and allowing them to throw things into the snake's habitat. In that case, the snake just wanted to be left alone to finish a meal in peace, since it took him several days to digest what was given him. Mary Catherine persuaded their friend to donate the snake to the zoo. After that, he was fine.

"I think I understand some of the problem," she finally told Sallie.

Angellus had come back in the room a moment before. "Thank goodness! Please tell us why the crab won't come out of his shell."

Sallie frowned at him, giving him the look all wives know how to give. When she turned back to Mary Catherine, she smiled. "Thank you so much for taking the time to do this."

"You're very welcome. I hope it makes a difference."

Angellus deliberately slammed the door into the sun room and opened it up again. Charlie shot straight up on the sofa, blinking his eyes and wondering what was going on. "I didn't want you to miss the big moment, Dowd. Then you can get out of here."

"You're such a sweetheart, Angellus." Charlie straightened his shirt and ran his fingers through his hair.

Mary Catherine ignored them. "I think Bo-Bo's problem, which by the way, Detective Angellus, the crab is unaware that you've named him, so thank you for telling me his name. It didn't matter to him, but it was nice to have. Anyway, I think his problem is that his shell is too big for him."

"And how did you glean that tidbit of information?" Angellus hovered over the aquarium.

"It seems hermit crabs have a habit of grabbing the biggest shell they can find on the beach in case they can't find another shell for a while. Bo-Bo grabbed this shell, but it's far too heavy for his little body. Now normally he would've used the water coming in from the tide to get himself out. In this case, the only water is over there and he can't reach it. That's really all he needs. Then he can pick up a smaller shell. I'd advise not putting in shells that are too big for him."

"That's amazing!" Sallie said. "Thank you, Mary Catherine."

Angellus was still skeptical. "Let's just see about that, shall we?" He picked up the shell that held the crab and dropped it into the little pool of water. "Come out, Bo-Bo."

"John! You are the rudest man I've ever met!" Sallie reached for the little crab, but Mary Catherine stopped her.

"Wait! You see? Here he comes now."

The crab was slowly emerging from the shell, using the water to free himself. He finally pushed completely out, then scuttled out of the water to pick out another shell.

"Well, I'll be damned!" Angellus stared at the crab.

Charlie laughed. "No doubt."

"Look!" Sallie pointed. "He's better now."

Mary Catherine nodded. "He should be fine. You might want to consider a little more water in his environment. And the smaller shells, of course."

"Thank you so much," Sallie gushed, glancing significantly at her husband, who cleared his throat and thanked her as well.

"I was glad to do it. It's my gift, really the only one I was given. Helping animals is my life." Mary Catherine stood up and asked for the powder room. Sallie showed her the way, leaving Angellus and Charlie alone in the sun room.

"You believe she talks to animals?" Angellus stared at Charlie.

Charlie shrugged. "I've seen some wild things since I met her. She's doing *something*. I don't know how she does it, but it seems to work."

"What about you, man? What happened to you?"

"I don't know. I got tired of it." Charlie stood up. "You will too someday. I just wasn't worried enough about the pension and the gold watch to stay there. If that makes me crazy, I guess I'm crazy."

"They say you could find things you shouldn't have been able to find. Some people think you planted them."

"I can't explain that either and I don't care what they think." Charlie turned toward the door that led out of the sun room. "Nice talking to you, Angellus."

"Stay out of my case, Dowd, and keep her out of it too. I'd hate to see you lose your PI license."

Charlie didn't turn back or answer him. Mary Catherine and Sallie came out of the back of the house and met him in the hall. "Are you ready to go now?"

"Please come back anytime," Sallie urged. "It was wonderful meeting you. I love your talk show."

"Thank you, dear." Mary Catherine hugged her. "Don't worry. Angellus is a good man. He'll catch on in time. It's so difficult when one doesn't believe as a child."

Sallie laughed. "Don't worry. I'm not giving up on him just yet."

Mary Catherine walked out the front door into the damp heat that seemed stifling after the cool of the air conditioning. Charlie opened the truck door for her as her cell phone rang.

It was Jenny. "I hope you're on your way back. I think I've found out why all the dogs liked Meaty Boy best."

THIRTEEN

DANNY WAS ALREADY AT the clinic with Bubba when Charlie and Mary Catherine arrived. "I don't know what happened," he said. "Bubba and I were out for a walk when he started heaving. He wouldn't stop so I brought him back here."

"Jenny said all the dogs were sick." Mary Catherine tried to see what was going on in the back of the clinic. "It's weird not hearing Bruno barking."

"So you think that guy from Meaty Boy did something to the dogs?" Charlie asked.

Danny stared at him like he hadn't noticed him before. He asked Mary Catherine, "What's *he* doing here?"

"He took me to talk to the hermit crab. He wants to help with the investigation."

"I want a million bucks, but you can't always get what you want, you know what I'm talking about? He's a *traidor*. I don't think he should be here."

"Look, I'm sorry about that thing with Colin," Charlie started. "I did what I was paid to do."

Danny pushed him against the wall. "Like you were paid to make our dogs sick?"

"Don't be silly," Mary Catherine said. "He wasn't even there. Stop acting like an idiot, Danny. That was basically Colin's mistake. I'm not saying I liked Charlie letting Elmore know where Colin was, but I think he means well. Baylor likes him anyway."

"He's been sneaking around here," Danny argued. "Maybe he sneaked in here and put something in the dogs' food when we weren't looking."

"Why would I do that?" Charlie demanded. "I could just punch you in the face and get a lot more satisfaction."

Mary Catherine was trying to separate the two men (this was getting to be an annoying habit) when Jenny came out and asked them what was going on. "I can hear you out here over the sounds of six sick dogs. I don't think that says anything about my hearing."

"How are they?" Mary Catherine asked.

"I think they'll be okay. I gave them something for indigestion. That's all that's wrong with them. I think it was the food they ate at Meaty Boy today. It was heavily coated with lard and some meat byproducts."

Danny and Charlie glared at each other one last time before they moved away. "You think that guy at Meaty Boy knew it would make Bubba sick?" Danny punched one fist into the palm of the other hand. "I don't like the way he hangs around MC as it is. But making my *perro* sick is enough to take him out."

"That's just it," Jenny told him. "They were trying to make the food irresistible, not make the dogs sick. He cheated. Maybelle was a fool to do it. He had to know it would come right back on him."

"Let's go find out how stupid he is!" Danny started toward the door.

"Is that your plan?" Charlie stopped him. "We try to get into Maybelle's place, which is armed like a fortress and has more security than the White House, and punch him?"

"That's what I've got." Danny snorted. "You got something better?"

"Maybe. We won't get close enough to Maybelle to do anything to him if we drive up accusing him of making the dogs sick." Charlie turned to Mary Catherine. "Call him. Tell him what happened. Get him to come here, if you can."

Danny nodded. "*Si*! That makes sense!"

Mary Catherine agreed. "I don't think Buck would knowingly make the dogs sick. His image means too much to him. This event was on TV. The bad publicity could really hurt him. He was just desperate to have the dogs like his food."

"I think we should still tell him we know he cheated and it made the dogs sick," Charlie said. "Give him a call, MC."

Mary Catherine stared at him, her blue eyes like sapphire daggers. "Danny is the *only* one who has ever called me something other than my name. Except for my first late husband, Andrew Smith, and *that's* another matter entirely. You're on probation as it is. Watch it!"

Charlie laughed, but didn't press the point. Mary Catherine took out her cell phone and called Buck. Her phone performance of being distraught and worried was only slightly magnified from how she really felt.

In the back of her mind, she kept thinking about Baylor's close call the night before. She knew there was nothing seriously wrong with Bruno and the other dogs, but coming on the heels of everything else that had happened, it was scary.

After talking to Buck, who panicked and told her he was coming down to the clinic, Mary Catherine closed her cell phone and went into the back of the clinic to talk to Jenny. She found the surly vet poring over some dog food. "I'm sorry I left you alone to figure this out."

"I'm not on *CSI*, but it wasn't all that difficult. It's really not a bad solution but it was too heavy. Some dogs might not have had a problem with it. It could be modified to work, making the dog food better without causing the indigestion."

"You're sure it's not like some dog stomach flu thing, right?" Mary Catherine looked at all the samples and slides on the table.

"Don't touch anything!" Jenny slapped her hand. "I'm working!"

Mary Catherine wondered for the hundredth time why she put up with Jenny's rudeness. She reminded herself it had everything to do with finding a vet who'd work for what the clinic could pay. There wasn't much chance of finding a volunteer vet who'd do everything Jenny did. She was grateful to the other woman, but wished she'd change a few of her ways.

Fred, the toucan, told Mary Catherine he was afraid to eat his food. What if it made him sick like the dogs? He wanted new food that was safe. He babbled on about his cage not being big enough and not having enough water.

She asked him to quit complaining or please be quiet. She was stressed enough as it was, without him giving her a hard time. She asked him if he'd seen anyone sneaking into the clinic when she or Jenny weren't there.

Fred told her the only person he'd seen sneaking around was Charlie. He complained about Charlie holding his cell phone up a lot, not talking to him as he walked by.

Mary Catherine thought she understood the reference to the cell phone. Apparently, Charlie had been taking pictures of the clinic as he had of Colin. Despite his proclamations of innocence, he was still working for her cousin. It was clear to her that he'd do whatever he had to do to make his clients happy.

Of course she couldn't be sure he was still spying on her or if Fred was talking about the first time Charlie was in the clinic. The toucan didn't have a very good sense of time. It could go either way. But she'd confront Charlie at the first available opportunity. He might be more of a problem than she'd realized. And his heart-felt request to help with the investigation into Ferndelle's death might only be a chance to keep spying on her.

It was only a few minutes later that Buck was driven to the clinic in his long, white limousine. He wasn't dressed up to his usual Marlboro Man standards. His shirt was half unbuttoned and his hair was messed up. The jeans he was wearing were dirty and wrinkled.

"Have you called the police yet?" he asked Mary Catherine as he strode into the clinic.

With all of them in the tiny space, the limited size of the clinic stood out even more. Mary Catherine was aware of the bad paint job and bare floors. She'd spent so much money on the care and feeding of the animals, she'd forgotten about what the place looked like. She had to find some way to raise funds to remodel. That was number 292 on her to-do list for that month.

"Not yet," she said. "I wanted to talk to you first. My vet thinks the food the dogs ate during the taste test today made them sick."

"What? That's ridiculous! I hope you're not thinking *I* had anything to do with it."

Danny jumped on him, pushing him against the wall. "That's exactly what we think, *idiota*! We think you wanted to hurt our dogs."

"I don't have any reason to want to hurt your dogs," Buck argued, not even trying to get away from Danny. "In fact, I have every reason to want your dogs to stay healthy. Imagine the field day the press will have with this! It would ruin me."

"Maybe that's what needs to happen." Danny grabbed Buck's shirt collar. "I should punch your lights out right now for hurting Bubba."

Buck appealed to Mary Catherine. "Will you call off this lunatic? I know you know I didn't do this. It wouldn't make any sense. If it happened at my factory, something else must be involved. I'll pay for testing."

"Like we'd trust your testing," Danny said.

"I think that's a good idea." Jenny pulled off her gloves as she walked out of the lab. "I can only do so much here with the equipment I have to work with. It's all we can do to feed the animals and keep the roof on this old place over our heads every day. I'm sure we can find an independent lab that could help us out with this."

"Exactly!" Buck smiled at Jenny. "Mary Catherine, you should promote this woman! I like the way she thinks."

"This isn't exactly a corporation like Meaty Boy," Mary Catherine said.

Jenny snorted. "Or like anything else that's up and running."

Mary Catherine started again. "We're a nonprofit organization. We exist on donations and whatever I can spare to keep the place going. There's nowhere to be promoted. Jenny is our only veterinarian."

"What about him making our dogs sick?" Danny demanded. "We don't trust him too, do we, MC? We can't trust every *idiota* who walks in off the streets."

"No we can't," Mary Catherine agreed, tactfully moving Danny away from Buck's throat. "And we don't have to trust him if Jenny picks out an independent lab and Buck pays for the testing."

"Sure! I knew there was something I'd have to do with it." Jenny shook her head. "It's not enough I single-handedly run this place. Now I'm the Yellow Pages."

"I think it sounds like a plan," Charlie added. "We hold off telling the press about this while Buck pays for the tests. Sounds fair to me."

"Don't I know you?" Buck walked toward Charlie as he straightened his shirt. "I'm sure I've met you before."

"Charlie Dowd." He held out his hand. "I installed the security system at your house."

"That's right! I remember now. Great job! Not even a seagull can get through."

Mary Catherine smiled, thinking there were too many layers to Charlie. "You could've told us how you knew about the security at Buck's home."

Charlie shrugged. "What would be the point? Danny already hates me. I can't imagine that makes you trust me any more."

"It doesn't matter," Mary Catherine lied. "Tomorrow morning we'll find an independent lab that can do this testing for us. Charlie's right. We'll hold off talking to the press until we know what happened."

"What about the police?" Danny asked. "Whoever did this should be locked up."

"Look, all I did was add some meat flavoring to the food," Buck said. "I'm sorry it made the dogs sick. But maybe we can find a happy medium here. The dogs really liked the food. If we add a little less, maybe that would work and not make them sick. I'd be happy to give the clinic a sizable donation for your help."

Danny got in Buck's face again. "Not if you're *entre rejas*, Mr. Meaty Boy. We'll just see."

———

Mary Catherine woke up late the next morning. She'd been up helping Jenny with the dogs until almost one AM. She flew through her morning ritual, found a gold and sapphire caftan to wear, and waited downstairs for Danny to come.

Jenny had slept on a cot in the sick room with the dogs. She was already up and checking them when Mary Catherine got there. "Are they any better this morning?"

"They're fine. It wasn't anything really serious."

"I'm so glad. I was worried about them."

"Candy has a very sensitive system. I hope we've made Buck feel bad. But I think he may be on to something. It will take some development, of course."

"Are you sure? I'd hate to make any other dogs sick."

"It was a stupid thing for Buck to do." Jenny sighed. "But probably good for your talk show ratings. It's been all over the news."

"Which is ultimately good for the dogs and all the other creatures we take in here. Good ratings mean more money at contract time."

Jenny snorted. "Not if they're all sick."

Mary Catherine was glad when Danny honked his horn. Even with her natural optimism, Jenny could be enough to ruin her day. "Call me if you need anything. I'm going to the station."

"While you're there, pick up an extra fifty thousand dollars to remodel this old place. I could use another exam table and some supplies."

"I'll see what I can do," Mary Catherine said. "Talk to you later."

There was no sign of Charlie outside the clinic this morning. It was just as well. How could she feel secure about his ability to be there when she was in trouble if he was the one causing the trouble?

"Morning, MC." Danny turned back to pull out into the road. "It was an awful night last night without Bubba. Is he looking any better this morning?"

"I think so. You know Jenny. It's hard to say."

"Yeah. I'd just as soon ask the toucan."

"Hopefully, Jenny will be able to sort through all this with some of Buck's resources."

"Are you sure we shouldn't call the cops on this? I mean, it's one thing to get that dirt bag Maybelle to cough up some money to help out. It's another to let him get away with this."

"I know you think Buck did this on purpose," she argued. "But I don't think he'd do anything to ruin Meaty Boy's reputation."

"Unless he thought we wouldn't find out or suspect him."

"Which would be saying we were complete morons. Even Buck can't think that."

Danny stopped at the radio station. "I hope you're right. I just want Bubba back home. I really miss that little dude."

Mary Catherine said goodbye and went into the building. A black man in an expensive gray suit was waiting for her. He obviously knew who she was. When he saw her, he got up and held out his hand. "Mary Catherine Roberts?"

"Of course. And you are?"

"Bartholomew Jesup. I'm your cousin's attorney. Do you have a moment?"

"Not really. My show starts in just a few minutes. I have to check in upstairs. Can you wait an hour?"

"No. I'll make this brief." He reached into his expensive leather briefcase that made Mary Catherine shudder to look at it and produced a handful of photographs. They were taken inside and outside the clinic and her apartment. "Your cousin is concerned about the condition of his mother's building. He's not an ungenerous man, however. He's prepared to offer you double what it's worth."

"I'm not interested, Mr. Jesup." Mary Catherine knew Charlie had taken those pictures. Danny was right about him. He wasn't to be trusted. It was a pity; she knew she could grow to be very attached to him.

"My client is very persistent. He won't give up easily."

Mary Catherine lost her temper. She'd look back and see it as a combination of stress and lack of sleep. It didn't help she'd allowed herself to run out of her favorite perfume. "Mr. Jesup, the mayor himself knows about the clinic. He was there for our grand opening. Half the city council has contributed money to us. I don't think you'll find a receptive audience there. Tell my cousin I'm not selling or giving the property back to him. My aunt obviously knew what she was doing when she left him out of her will. Good day, sir!"

She stamped into the elevator and refused to look at the man before the doors closed, shutting out his face. Of all the nerve! The man wouldn't take no for an answer. She didn't know what it would take to make him leave her alone. She knew she could cut Charlie out of her life and at least her cousin wouldn't have inside information.

Colin was in the studio that morning. Mindy was there too, but not with her usual smiling face. "I told her about Charlene," Colin said when he was alone with Mary Catherine. "I hope you're happy. She's not speaking to me."

"I've had just about enough of you whining about this thing happening to you," she told him. "You chose to sleep with Charlene. Everything else has been part of that. Mindy is a great girl. You chose to ignore that. If she never speaks to you again, I wouldn't blame her."

"Don't say that, Mary Catherine! I can't live without her."

"Then you better start acting like it. We all have to be responsible for what we do with our lives, Colin. Grow up!" She put Baylor down on the floor and he jumped on the closest chair before she closed the door to the sound booth and put on her headphones. "I don't know what's wrong with the world today, Baylor. It's like somebody opened the door and all the crazy people ran out."

Corey and Mindy gave her the high sign to let her know they were on the air. "This is Mary Catherine Roberts, the Pet Psychic, on Lite 102.5, WRSC. I'll be here for an hour, answering your questions about animals."

A call came in almost immediately. "Good morning, Mary Catherine. I have a question for you about my hamster, Zack. He doesn't like for me to pick him up. He's started nipping at me when I put my hand down close to him. What can I do?"

"Well, first of all, did he *ever* like for you to pick him up?"

"When I first got him, he didn't seem to mind. We had an accident and I dropped him. It wasn't far. He didn't get hurt. I don't think that's the problem."

"You might if you were as small as a hamster and some giant came along and picked you up and dropped you," she said. "Are you *sure* he wasn't hurt? Did you take him to the vet?"

"No. But he was up and running right away."

"But he bites you when you come close now." She sighed. "You're going to have to be patient and work to regain his trust. *You* were the one who dropped him. You have to prove it won't happen again. It might take some time. Believe it or not, the hamsters I've known had very long memories of any slights against them."

"But he's *just* a hamster."

"And you're *just* a human. You made a mistake. Have you apologized to Zack? That might go a long way toward him trusting you again. After that, take your time when you approach him. Show him you aren't in a hurry and are willing to be very gentle with him."

"It might be easier to get a new hamster!"

Mary Catherine held on to her temper by a slender thread. *Why was he even calling her about the poor hamster if he was ready to chuck him down the toilet and get a new one?* "That may be true, but you would probably face the same issues with another hamster. They're small, fragile creatures. If you want to be careless and not take the time to get to know your hamster, I suggest you get a bigger pet."

"Thanks, Mary Catherine. I wouldn't really get rid of Zack. I'll try what you said."

Mindy pointed in her direction and Mary Catherine took her second call. "This is the Pet Psychic. What can I do for you?"

"Sorry about your dogs," the voice said. "I guess the Meaty Boy taste test failed. I hope nothing else happens to them."

This is Devon from Boston.

If you can really talk to animals, tell a bird to fly over our congressman's house and drop a bomb on his head.

'nuff said.

FOURTEEN

"Why don't you tell me what you know about that," Mary Catherine encouraged the caller.

"I think I've said enough for now. I think you know why this happened. I don't need to spell it out for you."

"You're wrong. I have no idea what you're talking about. If you were a dog, we might be on the same wavelength, but as a human—"

Corey made the cut sign, telling her the phone line was dead. Mary Catherine nodded and pressed the button for the second phone line. The caller was a teenager worried about her Lab puppy who didn't want to play. Shaken, but determined not to let the psycho caller ruin her show, Mary Catherine continued through that call and five more before the show was over.

She picked up Baylor and took him out of the sound booth with her. She was trembling with anger, but not willing to give the psycho caller the satisfaction of knowing it.

Angellus was already there. "Why didn't you tell me about all of the things happening around the clinic?"

"Because I couldn't see where they had anything to do with Ferndelle's death and that's what you're investigating."

Colin joined them. "We're getting slammed with phone calls about Meaty Boy dog food. What's going on, Mary Catherine? I know the station owner is going to call and want to know too."

"I don't know what to tell you. The dogs Buck brought in and the three dogs I brought for the taste test were all sick last night. Jenny said it was the Meaty Boy food, but it was just some extra fat he put on the food to make the dogs like it. Of course he cheated to make himself look better."

"That's just great." Colin threw up his hands.

"All of the dogs are fine this morning. Jenny thinks they can come up with a formula using that idea to make the food better. Buck is paying for testing and giving us a nice donation for the clinic. Or at least he was going to if we kept this quiet."

Angellus shook his head. "I think we've gone beyond the Jamison murder case. I don't know what's happening yet, but between finding your cat in a cage, and your threatening caller, something's wrong. I didn't even know about the dog food."

"Don't forget somebody cut the brake line on her car yesterday," Charlie added as he got off the elevator.

"*You!*" Mary Catherine flew at him. "You have a lot of nerve showing your face here. You sent my cousin pictures of my home and the clinic."

"I took pictures." Charlie defended himself. "But I haven't talked to him since I got to know you."

"So you quit the case?" Angellus asked.

"Not yet," Charlie admitted. "But I was getting around to it. Since I was spending time with her, it was a conflict of interest."

165

"Like I believe that!" Mary Catherine turned her back on him. "He's probably my psycho caller. Ask him where he was when that man called my show a few minutes ago."

"That's easy," Charlie said. "I was downstairs getting coffee, listening to your show. I knew you'd need a ride home."

"You bet that's easy," Angellus told him. "Let me see your cell phone."

"My cell phone? There are sensitive client numbers on my phone. I can't just hand it over to you."

"That sounds suspicious to me," Colin pointed out.

She raised her chin, conscious of all the men in the room looking at her. "He was there. He was there when Baylor ended up in the cage too. He was right there when my brakes failed."

Angellus nodded. "That sounds suspicious to me too. Dowd, I think you and I need to have a talk at the station."

Charlie spun Mary Catherine around to face him and held her arms. "I thought we had an understanding about all this." He kept his voice low, his eyes focused on hers. "I thought you understood the other part of me that knows when there's trouble. You don't really believe I had anything to do with what's happened, do you?"

She refused to look at him. "I don't know what to believe right now. All I know is that you've told me you were working for my cousin who wants the building I inherited. His lawyer showed me the pictures you took. What else can I think?"

"Come on," Angellus urged him toward the elevator. "I think you've become an unwanted member of this group now and we'd like you to be a member of our ongoing party at the station. Move, Dowd!"

Charlie tried to shake Angellus off. The detective threatened to put him in handcuffs if he didn't cooperate. With a last look at Mary Catherine, Charlie left with Angellus.

"Wow!" Colin sat down on one of the green plastic chairs. "That was intense. I don't know why he'd want to hurt you, Mary Catherine. It doesn't make sense."

Mindy came out of the engineer's booth and put her hands on Colin's shoulders. "I think Corey got a fix on the number that called you, Mary Catherine. We could try calling it back again and see who answers."

The three of them, with Baylor looking over Mary Catherine's shoulder, looked at the cell phone screen as she dialed the number. The person who answered was Teddy, who said he was working first shift at a local convenience store in Landfall Park, about twenty minutes from downtown.

Teddy didn't sound anything like the psycho caller. After twenty years of taking phone calls, one thing Mary Catherine knew was voices. "Was there anyone else using the phone at the store?"

"I'm the only one here until noon every day," Teddy responded. "I went to the bathroom for a few minutes but the store was empty when I left."

Mary Catherine thanked him and hung up. "I don't know who it was, but it couldn't have been Charlie. It would take him too long to get back here."

"Who else would want to do something like this?" Colin asked. "Not that I'm complaining. Your ratings are gonna go through the roof."

"I'm sure that's not what the caller had in mind," Mary Catherine said. "The question is: how does this person know so much?

Charlie, Buck, Jenny, Danny, and I were the only ones who knew about the dogs being sick."

"Maybe Charlie is keeping someone posted on this," Mindy added. "He's a private detective. Maybe someone hired him to do these things."

"And the psycho caller is the one who hired him," Colin added. "That makes sense."

"I feel so stupid letting him into my life," Mary Catherine told them. "You'd think I'd know better by now."

"*You?*" Colin laughed. "At least no one is trying to frame you for murder."

"One thing I'm curious about," Mary Catherine said. "What made you come to Ferndelle's house the morning I found her? Was that a routine thing?"

Colin shrugged. "Not really. I visited her once in awhile. We weren't especially close, even before my parents died. After the thing with the money, we only saw each other occasionally. Believe it or not, she was angrier about the money than I was. I went there that morning because someone called me and told me there was a problem. I thought it was the police when I found out she was dead."

"Did you tell the police about this?"

"I think so." He played with his glasses. "I'm pretty sure I did. I might've forgotten. It's hard to think when you're worried about someone beating the information out of you."

Mary Catherine thought for a minute. "Did he call you on your cell phone?"

"Of course! I don't have a land line. Those are so passé." He smiled at Mindy. "Only old folks have those now."

"What are you thinking?" Mindy wondered.

"I'm thinking if someone called Colin that morning to lure him to his aunt's house, we should be able to find out who it is."

"How would we do that?" Mindy held Colin's hand. "I thought you couldn't trace a cell phone call."

"Of course you can," Mary Catherine told her. "Even us old folks know you can look at calls made to your cell phone from your online account. Let's find a computer."

Colin logged into his cell phone account, recalling about what time the call had come in telling him he needed to go to his aunt's house. "I just got off my treadmill after the *Pet Psychic* show was over and Buck had finally stopped complaining and left the studio. I think that must've been around 10:15 or 10:30."

"There it is!" Mary Catherine pointed to the incoming phone call on his account. "Let me write that down."

"You don't need to." Corey was watching from behind them. "That's the same number of the convenience store where the call to the *Pet Psychic* originated today."

"Are you sure?" Mindy asked. "That would mean the two things are related."

"That might mean I'm off the hook." Colin stood up and did a little dance. He stopped, red-faced, when he realized what he'd done. "I guess we should call the police."

"I don't know about that," Mary Catherine disagreed. "I think we should pay Teddy at the convenience store a visit. Then if we find something important, we can call Detective Angellus. Otherwise I'm afraid he might ignore it."

"I'm for anything that proves I'm not a killer," Colin said. "We can take the station van."

"One of us has to stay here," Mindy said. "I'll stay, honey. You go out and prove you're innocent."

Colin kissed her. "You're the best, sweetie. I'll call you if we find anything."

Mary Catherine waited until she and Colin were on the elevator alone going downstairs. "You lied to me. You haven't told her yet, have you?"

Colin squirmed. "I was all ready to tell her. Then I started thinking: is this the kind of thing I'd want to know about Mindy? I decided it wasn't. She's better off not feeling guilty about me turning to another woman."

"Are you serious? Why would *she* feel guilty?"

"Because women are like that, Mary Catherine. They don't always want to know the truth. Sometimes, they want to be coddled and protected from the harsh realities of the world."

"If you were worth it, I'd kick you in the butt! You can't put this off, Colin. If you don't tell her the truth, I will. Every woman deserves to know the truth about the man she's going to marry. You might be telling yourself all that other hogwash, but don't ask me to buy it."

"She'll leave me. I might even lose my job."

"You should've thought of that before you started running around with Charlene and her egotistical poodle." Mary Catherine walked out of the elevator as the doors opened.

"You don't understand." Colin followed her. "I don't think Mindy can take the truth. She might go off the deep end. She really loves me, you know."

"And obviously she's a fool to do it." She looked down the street to find where the station van was parked. "I'm not kidding. If you don't tell her by this time tomorrow, I will."

Colin pulled the keys out of his pocket as they located the van parked near the corner. "Okay. I'll tell her. But it's on your head if something bad happens."

"I'm afraid not, my friend." Mary Catherine boosted herself up into the passenger seat after putting Baylor on the floor. "It's about time you grew up and took some responsibility. I suppose that's why your aunt kept the family money."

"No, that was bad planning on my parent's part. They probably hadn't changed their will since I was a baby. As for being responsible, I graduated from Duke University the youngest in my class. I've worked at WRSC since I graduated and you don't even want me to go into how many charitable organizations I belong to."

"None of that makes you emotionally responsible, Colin. That's what I'm talking about. What possessed you to sleep with another man's wife in the first place?"

"She was hot." He shrugged with a half smile. "And she wanted me, too."

"That makes *all* the difference."

"You don't get it!" Colin pulled the van smoothly away from the curb into traffic. "Women like that *never* want me."

"Please stop or I won't care if someone charges you with murder."

"How was I supposed to know Aunt Ferndelle would be murdered? Of all the people in the world to die a violent death, she would have been last on my list."

"Did you know your aunt was dying from cancer?"

"No!" Colin stared at her. "She never mentioned it. Did the police tell you that?"

"Yes. I suppose it would be better for you if you'd known about it. There wouldn't be any reason for you to kill her if you knew she was going to die anyway." Mary Catherine looked out the window, too disgusted to talk to Colin for a few minutes. Baylor agreed that the boy had some growing up to do.

They drove up Market Street toward the Landfall area of the city, which was booming with growth. Hotels and shops were crowded along the highway between the Cape Fear River and the Atlantic Ocean. Expensive houses joined them for a few miles, their multi-tiered roofs set behind palmetto and oak trees.

Mary Catherine was glad they hadn't built any of that along the river. She liked the old downtown area with its distinct flavor. She never attended town council meetings, but she hoped the town planners had enough good sense to keep it that way. The old brick buildings and narrow streets might not be good for Wal-Mart or some other big-box store, but it was perfect for everything else.

"Here we are." Colin pulled the van into the convenience store parking lot. "There might be a phone inside. I don't see one out here."

"If not, maybe Teddy has noticed someone suspicious looking hanging around." She got out of the van, telling Baylor to wait for her.

The cat told her not to go without him. She'd never be able to tell if some human was lying to her the way he could. And he was sure he could identify his attacker.

"I don't care. There's too much traffic and you aren't familiar with this area. I don't want anything else to happen to you. I'll be back in a few minutes." She patted him on the head, then locked and closed the door.

Colin looked around at the swarm of people pumping gas and buying diet Pepsi. "How are we supposed to tell the person who called me from any of these other people?"

"That's not the plan," she said. "The plan is to enlist Teddy's aid. I'm sure you can manage to make friends with him. We just called from the radio station. Tell him you're an FCC official looking for the psycho caller. He'll cooperate."

"Great." Colin looked at her. "What are you going to do?"

"I'm going to look around a little and see if anyone else has seen or heard anything suspicious."

"You mean animals, right? Have we *truly* established that you can talk to animals?"

"We could establish it by me asking that bird over there to poop on your head." Mary Catherine smiled at him. "Would that take care of it?"

"I'm going in! You don't have to threaten me!"

"You know, Colin, if I'd ever had a son," she sighed, "I hope he wouldn't be anything like you."

He grumbled, but finally went into the store. Mary Catherine watched him talking to the store clerk, probably the same one who answered the phone after the psycho killer. She walked around the exterior of the building. There were plenty of birds on the rooftop and the power lines, but she was hoping to find an animal who knew humans a little better.

There was a half-starved, multicolored cat in the alley who was scavenging in the trash cans for food. She ran off as soon as she felt Mary Catherine's presence. Too bad. The poor thing probably needed help. She could've taken her back to the shelter.

There were hundreds of rats around the dumpster and scurrying along the edge of the building. She could question them if she got desperate. The problem with rats was that they knew human beings *too* well and had taken on their unpleasant characteristic of lying. You could hardly believe a word from them.

There was a single tree growing to the right of the convenience store. Mary Catherine heard some scratching sounds near it and was surprised to see a raccoon pop his head out. Raccoons were wild but had affiliated with humans long enough to converse easily. This one had lived in the cottonwood tree for several years. He was waiting for the forest to come back, but it had been cut down to build the houses and shopping centers. In the meantime, he foraged what he could from the dumpster and the occasional handout from a kind stranger who was amazed to see a raccoon in an urban setting.

Mary Catherine greeted the old raccoon. He acknowledged her and asked what she was looking for. If it was fish, the stream had long since gone with the trees and the other animals. This was good and bad in the raccoon's opinion, since being alone meant he didn't have to share his meager food source and had no natural predators.

On the other hand, he was lonely and wished he could find a place to live where there was more than one tree.

"I'd be glad to help you with that," she whispered to him. "I know some fabulous places with lots of trees and probably other raccoons. Would you like me to take you there?"

The old raccoon was beside himself with joy. He gladly allowed her to pick him up and walk away from the tree. He confessed a moment of sorrow at leaving his home but was happy about the idea of spending his last days with others of his kind.

"I know this may not make much sense to you, but I'm looking for a man who might have stood out here using a phone, like this one." She showed the raccoon her cell phone. She knew it was a long shot. Even if the raccoon had seen someone back there talking on the phone, how would she ever find him?

But the raccoon, Cheetos, whose name was taken from some trash he fancied, had seen one man in particular in the back of the store talking on the phone many times. He believed the man worked there, since he was at the store for long periods of time. Cheetos was only there at night, like any normal creature would be, instead of the insanity of being out during the day as they were.

Mary Catherine pointed him toward the clerk in the store, who was still talking to Colin. "Is that the man?"

Cheetos answered that it was the man, though he wasn't sure why he was there now. The raccoon asked again about the forest and the other animals, then snuggled into Mary Catherine's arms to take a nap.

Colin came out of the store. "I think we might have something. Teddy was scared when I told him I was with the FBI."

"I thought you were going to say FCC?"

"FBI sounded better." Colin grinned. "You know; Colin Jamison, FBI."

"Anyway…"

"He said a man came in here and paid him to use the phone." Colin took out a scrap of paper with a little chili on it. "He wrote down what he should say. And this isn't the first time it happened. The clerk said the man paid him one hundred dollars each time. He's the one who called me when Aunt Ferndelle was killed."

"Excellent! Does he think he can identify the man who paid him the money?"

"He says he can and also knows what kind of car he drives; a red '80s Honda."

"Does he have any way to get in touch with him?"

"I don't think so. It sounds like he just shows up."

"I think we need more before we can call Detective Angellus." Mary Catherine smiled as the raccoon in her arms woke up and looked around.

Colin jumped back two feet from her, his eyes comically large. "What the hell is that thing?"

FIFTEEN

COLIN REFUSED TO GET in the van with the raccoon. Mary Catherine reluctantly returned the old animal to his tree with a promise that she'd come back for him. Because he was a wild animal, he trusted and believed her. A dog or cat would've been less trusting, having lived with humans for so long.

"I'm sorry," Colin apologized as they drove to the clinic. "Those things carry diseases that can kill you. I'm too young to die because of a raccoon."

"Never mind. I'm sure that poor, old animal doesn't mind waiting to find someplace to die. I'll go back out later and get him."

"So, who do you think the man is who paid to have the store clerk call the radio station? I'd say Cousin Bob, if Angellus hadn't said he wasn't capable of getting out of bed."

"It has to be someone who knows you and would profit from you losing the family fortune because you were in prison."

"There's no one like that except Cousin Bob. Maybe he tricked Angellus someway. Maybe he's really behind all this. Maybe he ran back home and pretended he had a stroke."

"I'm sure Detective Angellus would've researched that," she said as Colin parked the van beside her building. "Is Cousin Bob the last member of your family?"

"The last one who can inherit except for myself and my children, which are still in the planning stages."

"Not for long, unless you tell Mindy the truth." Mary Catherine got out of the van. She looked up to see the handyman on the roof nailing down shingles. "I hope he doesn't fall."

Colin looked up too. "Who is that guy?"

"He's the handyman Danny hired for me to do odd jobs around the building. He's been a big help so far."

"He kind of creeps me out. Why not hire a service where the workers don't look like walking corpses?"

"You have a vivid imagination." Mary Catherine put Baylor on the ground to follow her inside. The cat objected immediately, springing back into her arms, complaining that she wanted him to be lured into another trap. She told him he was being ridiculous, but carried him into the building anyway.

Inside, several independent (she assumed they were independent) dog food testers were working with Jenny on the new Meaty Boy formula.

Jenny looked up as she was speaking to one of them, saw Mary Catherine, and stalked toward her. "Where have you been? Was I supposed to handle all of this by myself? You could at least find me some volunteers. I have enough to do without testing dog food."

"Have you found anything yet?" Colin made the mistake of asking.

"What do you think? Would we be here testing if we had?"

Mary Catherine intervened, as she frequently had to do in Jenny's relationships with other people. It was a good thing animals loved her so much, because most people couldn't stand her. "Of course not. Colin was trying to be pleasant."

Jenny snorted, her long, curly gray hair held back from her face with a bulldog clip. Her clear blue eyes narrowed. "Is that what it was?"

Mary Catherine turned to Colin. "I'm sure you need to get back to the station and talk to Mindy."

His cell phone rang. "You must be right. I'll talk to you later. I'm going to visit Cousin Bob myself and make sure he's not faking."

"That sounds fine." She was already walking into the back of the clinic. Bruno was demanding attention with his deep barking. "Be sure to take someone with you in case he jumps up and hits you with his cane."

Colin agreed and turned to leave. He groaned as he opened the front door. "Oh no. It's Buck! Is there a back way out?"

"Through the clinic." She stood back and let him go through. She knew she might as well wait for Buck anyway. He was bound to have something to say about this morning's show.

"What happened?" Buck didn't wait to get inside before he started talking. "It's all over the media. The USDA is going to shut me down until they run a complete examination of all my facilities. I thought we had an agreement that you wouldn't tell anyone about what happened."

"Go back and listen to the show," Mary Catherine recommended. "It wasn't me. The psycho caller who's been plaguing the show called in again. Somehow he knew what happened."

Buck closed the front door behind him. For once he wasn't wearing his Stetson and his usual air of self-confidence and bravado was missing. "This could ruin me. I may never recover from it. I could sell the houses, I suppose, and the race car. But my life is over."

"Don't be so melodramatic, at least not yet. Let's continue the testing here and offer our results to the USDA. Maybe that will help." Mary Catherine started upstairs to her apartment. "Come up and have some tea. I have a few questions I'd like to ask you."

"All right. But no cracks about Meaty Boy."

She smiled, but didn't answer. There was no reason to gloat over her victory. The dogs only wolfed down the food because he'd cheated. That meant no commercials for her.

Mary Catherine made some lemon balm and chamomile tea to help soothe Buck's nerves. He wandered through her living room and library while the water boiled and she put out the honey bear and cups.

"Who's this guy with the swordfish?" Buck looked at the pictures on her mantel.

"That was my third late husband, Per Van Eppen. He loved to fish. He never kept any of them because he knew I wouldn't like it. I didn't like him catching them either, but there's only so much you can do to educate a person."

"What happened to him?"

"His helicopter pilot landed on top of him." She sighed as she poured tea for both of them. "It was heartbreaking."

Buck sat down at the table and grinned. "You don't have much luck with men, darlin'. I think you and I would be good together. I don't have much luck with women."

"What happened to your last wife?"

"She managed to shoot herself when she fell off her horse." He sipped his tea and made a face. "Do you ride, Mary Catherine?"

"No. Horses tolerate us because they think we don't know any better. They're a very old race, you know. They're very wise and tend to think of us like children. That doesn't mean we should enslave them to our bidding."

Buck laughed a full, hearty belly laugh that shook his shoulders and turned his already pink face red. "Honey, you have the craziest ideas! That must be what I love about you."

She smiled, feeling a little like a horse must feel about a human. "That and my market share. I'm sure that's an unbeatable combination."

There was the sound of footsteps stomping up the stairs. It was Jenny, of course. She had to be part horse herself. "I think we found it!"

"Can it be safely duplicated?" Buck seemed to stop breathing while he waited for an answer.

"Duh! There wouldn't be much point if we couldn't use it to make money."

"Is this a new partnership?" Mary Catherine asked.

"Fifty-fifty," Jenny said. "I think that's fair, don't you, Buck?"

"Whatever you say. I'm glad you made it work. Like I said before, you have talent, ma'am. Maybe you should come work for me."

Jenny laughed. "I'd like to, but this place would fall apart without me. We do a lot of good here, despite Mary Catherine always trying to undermine us."

Baylor shuddered and pushed his head under the pink chenille throw on the sofa. He'd heard enough about dogs being sick and dog food. Maybe they shouldn't worry so much about the dogs and more about who caged him. *That* was the important question.

Mary Catherine ignored him. "I guess congratulations are in order."

"What's even better is a family came in this morning who wants Bruno. I told them they had to wait a few days to make sure everything is fine. But imagine! No more bellowing."

"And my new and improved Meaty Boy is safe, right?" Buck demanded, taking out his cell phone.

"Yes. It was only the additional meat fat that upset the dogs' stomachs."

Mary Catherine didn't know how she felt about losing Bruno. It was for the dog's own good, but she'd miss him. "That's good news about the dog food, and Bruno."

"Don't forget your promise to talk to those vultures at the USDA," Buck reminded Jenny. "They'll still have to do their own tests, but it can't hurt to have a professional recommendation."

Buck and Jenny had already gone downstairs when Mary Catherine heard a noise in her bedroom. Baylor's head popped out of the blanket. His ears perked up and he stared at the bedroom door. "Is that a mouse?" she asked him.

Baylor didn't think so. There was no mouse smell (she should know he couldn't tolerate that scent) and the sound was too loud for a mouse to make, in his opinion. He felt sure it was human.

Mary Catherine took out a small, pearl-handled revolver given to her as a gift by her fourth late husband. She didn't hesitate to approach the room, despite Baylor's warning that she should wait for help. "I think I'm capable of dealing with an intruder. You sit here and wait for me."

She tried to walk quietly across the squeaky wood floor until she was at the door. She could hear muffled moving sounds in the room. It sounded like someone was looking for something. There was a large window with a rusted metal stairway leading down from it, but she thought anyone would have the common sense to ignore it, even if they were bent on stealing from her. The stairway was a deathtrap she'd meant to have removed but had forgotten in her hectic life.

The revolver was firmly in her grasp as she opened the bedroom door. It was dark thanks to her heavy purple velvet drapes. She liked to sleep late sometimes.

The movement sounds stopped but she knew someone was in there. "It would be a good idea for you to come out now," she said to the room at large. "No one's going to hurt you, but you need to leave."

In answer, the chair from her antique vanity came up from the darkness and hit her in the face. She fell back to the floor, the revolver clattering on the wood. Baylor screeched and hissed, leaping at her attacker.

———

Mary Catherine was dazed and confused for a few moments. Baylor was hissing and she could hear muffled swearing. She tried to see what was going on, not able to communicate with her cat, but there was something in her eyes. She couldn't see anything until she wiped her hand across her face. The bright blood stained her hand. She was bleeding from a deep gash on her forehead.

Strong hands helped her to her feet and found her a kitchen chair to sit down. She assumed, even in her weakened state, that it wasn't her attacker. At least until she heard his voice. "Here, hold this wet paper towel on your head," Charlie said. "You might need some stitches in that."

"What are you doing here?"

"Isn't it obvious?" He crouched down beside her. "Every time you're in trouble, I show up. I can't help it. I know when things will happen. It's like you talking to animals, I guess, except less scary."

"For you, maybe." She winced as she tried to clean some of the blood from her face.

"I'm not kidding." He stopped her by putting his hand on hers. "That's a really deep cut. What happened?"

"You were sneaking around in my bedroom and hit me in the face with a chair."

He laughed. "There wasn't much point in sneaking around in there if *you* were out here."

"Don't try to sweet talk me. I *know* what happened."

"Not if you think I hit you with something." He glanced around the room. "Where's Baylor? He'll clear me on this."

She squinted, trying to look past the blood and her hair hanging in her face. "I don't know. I heard him attack whoever hit me with the chair."

"What makes you think it was a man?"

Mary Catherine stared at him. "I don't know. I guess a chair seems to be more a man's weapon. But I guess it wasn't you. I'm sure whoever it was has a face full of scratches."

"I came up the stairs from the clinic." Charlie got to his feet. "Did you leave this outside door open?"

"No." She stood up beside him, swayed dizzily, then sat back down. "Please see if Baylor's out there. I can't hear him."

Charlie checked the door and walked outside on the rickety landing. "I don't see anyone out here, including Baylor. But I think you're right—there's some blood out here on the stairs. I think your assailant came out this way."

Mary Catherine made herself walk to the door. She had to find Baylor. What if the man who hit her took him? It might be the same man who'd tried to cage him before.

"I think you better sit down before you fall down." Charlie eased her back into the apartment. "I'll get Jenny and whoever else we can round up to look for Baylor. We should call an ambulance for you."

"No thanks. I'm fine. Head wounds bleed, you know. I'm sure it's not as bad as it looks."

"Well it looks awful, so maybe you could at least clean up a little and let us look for Baylor."

Her head throbbed painfully and her stomach threatened to heave. She wanted to trust her instincts about this man. "How do I know I can trust you?"

He shrugged. "We're a lot the same, you and me. I think we have to trust each other. And you said Baylor trusts me. I know that counts for something."

Mary Catherine acknowledged that it counted for a lot but she didn't tell him. "All right. I guess Detective Angellus couldn't find anything against you or he wouldn't have let you go."

"Angellus couldn't find his way out of a paper bag, but if it makes you feel better to trust him instead of me, okay. I'll go look for Baylor. You take it easy."

There wasn't much else she could do. It was taking every bit of will power she possessed to stand upright. She knew she wasn't affected that way by the sight of blood. It had to be the wound and shock.

She went into the bathroom, skirting the mess her attacker had made in her bedroom. *What on earth was he looking for?* It didn't make any sense.

This couldn't involve Colin. She'd thought for a while it did, but this was personal. Whoever broke into her home had ransacked every drawer in her bedroom. She checked her jewelry (her fourth late husband had been very generous), but nothing was missing, and she didn't keep any cash lying around. She couldn't figure it out.

Giving up, she turned on the bathroom light and looked at her face. Moaning, she realized she'd probably be horribly disfigured by the attack. Stitches might make the wound smaller, but she'd certainly need plastic surgery to ever look normal again.

Fortunately, most of the scar would be hidden by her hair. She cleaned her face and washed the blood from her hair. The cut was still bleeding, but not as badly. She found a large square bandage left over from an injury she'd received last year from one of Tommy's wild cousins, and covered the clean wound.

She didn't feel strong enough to take a shower so she washed up with a wet sponge and changed her clothes. That action made her feel a little better. She took the bloody clothes and put them in the trash can. She'd never wear them again anyway.

Mary Catherine wished she could walk downstairs, but her head was spinning. She wished she would hear something from Baylor, but right now, she couldn't even hear Bruno downstairs. She couldn't hear anything except the cars passing by in the street outside and the beating of her heart.

She sat down hard on the bed and realized she couldn't hear any animal voices. No crickets, no mice scurrying in the basement. For the first time in her life, she couldn't hear what any animal was thinking.

The realization took her breath away; or she was having a heart attack, she wasn't sure which. The terrible silence was worse than anything she could imagine. Even if Baylor was at her feet, she might not be able to hear more than the purr everyone else could hear.

It was like suddenly being blind or truly deaf. What would she do if she wasn't able to communicate with animals?

She probably wouldn't have to worry about money. Her husbands' money that she'd stashed away would no doubt see her through. How long could a person live this way? She didn't want to think about it.

The outside door to her apartment opened. She glanced around, but her revolver was still on the floor in the living room. She'd seen someone use a can of hairspray as a weapon once but she was sure he also had a cigarette lighter. She'd given up smoking too long ago to even have matches. She wasn't sure if a candle lighter would do.

She started to pick up a piece of her broken vanity bench to defend herself when the bedroom door opened and Charlie walked in. "Are you all right?" he asked.

Mary Catherine threw the piece of wood at him. "I can't believe you walked in here without knocking! Suppose I'd been dressing?"

He grinned, then checked himself. "I was only thinking you might need some help. The thought never occurred to me that you might be half naked."

She wished her head didn't hurt so much. She enjoyed the little thrill of excitement his words brought. But in this case, it only made her want to vomit. "Did you find Baylor?"

"No. I'm sorry. I called Angellus. I can't figure how this all fits together, but I thought he should know. How's your head?"

"Not as bad as my heart right now." She knitted her fingers together in front of her. "I can't hear Baylor or any other animal."

"Wow! That must be scary. I don't always like what my gift brings me, but I'd hate to lose it. I'm probably the only man in the world who never has to look for his TV remote."

She smiled. "I guess you do understand."

"Jenny, Danny, and that weird cowboy from the dog food company are still out looking for Baylor. He'll turn up. And you'll get your gift back again."

"Are you guessing, or do you have a new gift for telling the future?"

"Let's call it a gut feeling."

Mary Catherine started to walk toward the door and the room tilted. She would've fallen except for Charlie's quick action. He caught her close to him and her arms went around him like they were meant to be there. "Thanks," she whispered.

"Not a problem." He smiled. "I told you that you needed me."

"You might be right." She allowed her eyelids to flutter closed as he leaned his head down to hers. She hoped there wasn't any blood left on her face. She hadn't been kissed by an attractive man in more than two years. Despite the headache and the queasiness, she didn't want to screw it up.

Charlie's lips had barely touched hers when the outside door to the apartment flew open and Danny yelled for her.

"Maybe next time," Charlie muttered.

"Maybe," she agreed.

"MC! You gotta come quick! I was afraid to move him. I think he's hurt really bad. There's blood everywhere." Danny looked from Charlie to Mary Catherine and blinked. "Did I interrupt something?"

Dear Mary Catherine,

 I am a four-year-old girl. I have a dog named Lucky and a cat named BBQ. My mom says I can have a goldfish too if you say it's okay.

 Is it okay?

SIXTEEN

EVERYONE HURRIED DOWN TO the street with Danny. Baylor lay still on the sidewalk, covered with blood that gleamed on his shiny tabby fur. Danny stood to one side with Charlie stopping short behind Mary Catherine.

Jenny ran out of the clinic with Buck, her medical kit in her hand. She looked at Baylor, then at Mary Catherine. "What did you do to him now?"

"I didn't do anything." Mary Catherine explained the situation. "Whoever attacked me must have left him here to die."

"We'll see about that." Jenny rolled up her sleeves, pulled her hair back from her face and shoved a pencil in it to hold it up. "I'll see to Baylor first, then take a few stitches in your stubborn head. Ask him where he's hurt."

Mary Catherine didn't plan on the vet doing *anything* medical to her. And she wasn't sure about Baylor. "Let me talk to him."

Jenny sighed. "For heaven's sake, I thought you'd already done *that*."

Charlie and Danny helped Mary Catherine get down on her knees beside the prostrate cat. She wished she could hear something from him, *anything*. But there was nothing. "Baylor," she crooned near his ear. "Can you hear me?"

The cat didn't move. His small pink tongue dangled out of the left side of his mouth. His eyes were wide and glassy, staring off into the street.

There was a pop in her ears, like water being released after swimming and suddenly, Mary Catherine could hear the robin in the tree above them who was worried about finding more worms. And she could hear Baylor. It was such a welcome relief to be normal, at least for *her*, she almost fainted. As she swayed, Charlie came to her left side and Buck came to take her right arm. *Life was good.*

"Will you help me up, please?"

The two men helped her get back on her feet and stood on either side of her, glaring at each other across her tabby-colored hair.

"I might need some help getting back upstairs." Mary Catherine smiled and blinked her eyes at both men.

"What about Baylor?" Jenny demanded. "Is he in shock?"

"He's faking," Mary Catherine told her. "This is his new trick. It's art, I grant you. I think the blood must belong to my attacker."

Jenny knelt down beside Baylor on the sidewalk. "That dent in your head must've reached your brain. No cat, no *animal*, plays dead like this. I'll take a look at him. But you better not go upstairs. You might have a concussion."

"Trust me, I'm the injured party here." Mary Catherine leaned heavily on her rescuers. "If we had some idea who we were looking for, he'd be easy to spot. All you'd have to do is find the man whose face looks like a scratching post."

Jenny put her latex gloves on and leaned close to Baylor. As she was set to examine him, Baylor jumped up and began to follow Mary Catherine back into the building. "I can't believe it!"

Danny laughed. "Yeah, he's some *loco gato*."

Baylor trotted behind Mary Catherine, who forbade him from going upstairs until he'd had a bath. She was so glad he was unhurt and she could hear him again, she almost let him go upstairs anyway when he complained about being hungry.

She sat down in one of the plastic chairs in the clinic waiting room. Baylor jumped on her lap and she didn't shoo him down off her clean clothes. "Have you seen him before?"

Baylor meowed and shook his head. Whoever attacked Mary Catherine was wearing a mask. He'd managed to scratch the person's arms; that's about all. He admitted to going into the fray blinded by rage. It could've been anyone, even someone he knew. He didn't remember. Of course, it wouldn't matter because Mary Catherine's attacker would be scarred for life after his self-confessed, lethal strike.

Buck shook his head. "That beats all. I don't know how she talks to them, but I think she really does."

Charlie ignored him. "We should get a blood sample before Baylor gets cleaned up."

The cat jumped down and hissed, daring Charlie to try and take a blood sample without losing some of his own.

Mary Catherine laughed. "Not *that* kind of blood sample." She looked at Charlie. "He was afraid you meant *out* of him. I'm afraid he's had too many blood tests. He doesn't like needles. But you mean a sample of the blood on his fur."

"We can take it to an independent lab." Charlie reached over to get a long cotton swab from a jar behind the counter.

"Or you could let the professionals handle it." Jenny and Danny were followed into the building by Detective Angellus.

Angellus looked at the cat and at Mary Catherine. "What have you got yourself into this time?"

The several variations of the story came out at once, causing Angellus to shout, "All right! One at a time! Mary Catherine first, since she looks like she saw the most action, and I can't talk to the cat."

Mary Catherine was happy to tell him what happened—with a little embellishment that Baylor called her on. She ignored him, but made sure Angellus knew how important Baylor's role was in saving her life.

"So you think this guy was here to hurt you?"

She shook her head, immediately sorry. "I don't think so. I think he broke in and was trapped. I believe he was looking for something in my bedroom."

Angellus wrote down what she said. "Was anything missing?"

"Not that I could tell. And that's the funny part. It must've been something very specific because he left my Cartier watch and a diamond necklace behind. He wasn't interested in robbing me."

"And where were *you* while this was going on?" Angellus asked Charlie.

"I was going home after you let me go. I thought I should stop in here."

"You *thought* you should stop in?" Angellus raised one dark brow. "I would've *thought,* after this morning, you'd know the lady didn't want you here."

Baylor was absolutely certain Charlie came in after the attacker. Mary Catherine couldn't argue with him. "I called him," she lied. "I wanted to apologize for what happened this morning. I was lucky Charlie got here when he did. Who knows what might've happened."

"Fine. I guess that means you're off the hook. *Again.* But don't go too far." Angellus glared at Buck. "What about *you?*"

Surprisingly, Jenny spoke up in his defense. "We've all been down here today working on this Meaty Boy thing. Buck was here the whole time."

Buck smiled and thanked her. Jenny blushed a deeper red than any of Mary Catherine's scarlet scarves. "We have an answer to the dog food problem," Buck said. "I wasn't involved in what happened to Mary Catherine, if that's what you're thinking."

"Let's leave that paranormal stuff to her, huh?" Angellus turned to Danny, who raised his hands and swore he was driving his taxi all day until he got to the apartment and found Baylor on the sidewalk.

The group was silent after that. Angellus put away his notebook. "I won't lie to you. I don't have any idea what's going on. If all of this ties together, it's beyond me. I think Dowd is right, much as it pains me to admit it. If we test a sample of blood on Baylor's fur, we'll at least have a comparison to go by if we find a suspect."

"What about the crazy guy who keeps calling MC on the radio?" Danny asked.

"I think Colin and I have the beginning of an answer for that." Mary Catherine explained about the convenience store clerk and the raccoon. "All we have to do is wait for the man to come around again and pay Teddy to call the station. He thinks Colin is with the FBI, so I'm sure he'll call."

Angellus had a pained expression on his lean, dark face. "And how does Cheetos the raccoon fit into all of that?"

"He saw the man on the phone in back of the store," she explained. "He may not be the *same* man, but it's something to go on."

When Mary Catherine put her hand to the painful gash in her head, Jenny stepped forward and demanded the inquisition come to an end. "I think she needs stitches. Maybe even a brain transplant. I mean, some rest."

Everyone turned to look at her and Mary Catherine fainted dead away on the clinic floor.

———

When she woke up again it was night. She wasn't in pain and her brain felt normal. She thought she was in the hospital until she saw the huge picture of dogs playing poker on the wall across from the bed. Surely no hospital could be so tacky.

It hurt a little when she moved. Between the car accident and being attacked in her apartment, her whole body was in agony. She definitely needed a massage. But if she wasn't in the hospital and she wasn't at her home, where was she?

Baylor jumped up on the bed and answered her question the best he could. It seemed she wasn't hurt badly enough to stay at the hospital but Detective Angellus (Baylor referred to him as the crab man) thought she shouldn't go home yet. The police were collecting evidence from her apartment and she might be in danger of being attacked again.

"Thank you for saving me." She stroked the cat's clean fur. "You're my hero."

He acknowledged her thanks with the sometimes graceless tact only a cat can have. He went on to tell her one of the two men who went with her to the hospital decided she should spend the night at his house. Baylor couldn't really tell her which man it was, but she assumed from the size of the room it wasn't Danny.

Her slippers and robe were on the bed. She put them on and walked out of the bedroom, Baylor immediately behind her, claws partially extended and senses heightened.

Mary Catherine knew where she was before she descended the elegant stairway. She had no doubt Charlie lived in a small apartment. This had to be Buck's home.

Her head didn't hurt anymore, but she took her time getting downstairs. The furnishings were typically masculine—a suit of armor on the landing and paintings of scantily clad young women hanging on the walls. The carpet on the stairs was new. It reflected the expense of her surroundings, if not the good taste.

But men were like that—especially if they spent too much time alone. With the proper incentive, she could have this crusty old bachelor's pad in decent shape in no time. Of course, that would mean taking on the crusty old bachelor who would come as a package deal. She didn't think she was ready for that yet.

She saw Charlie, Danny, and Buck in the study at the bottom of the stairs before they saw her. Buck and Danny were playing cards while, from the sidelines, Charlie nursed what looked like bourbon. She was flattered they'd all stuck around to see how she was. Buck and Charlie had ulterior motives; they both wanted to sleep with her. Danny, on the other hand, was simply a good friend.

Baylor sat down beside her on the bottom step, wondering what she was doing. He supposed she was choosing a mate from among the three men, and was quick to point out that none of them were worthy.

"I suppose you're the only one who's truly worthy." She stroked his fur and he purred in agreement. "I don't think that would work out, but I appreciate the offer."

Taking a deep breath, she pushed the double doors into the study completely open and swept into the room. All three men got to their feet, Buck knocking over a cup of coffee in the process.

"MC! It's good to see you vertical," Danny said. "How are you feeling?"

"Like I was hit by a chair." She caught the image of herself in the mirror that hung between the two large sets of deer antlers above the bar. A large white bandage covered most of her head and the top of her face. She grimaced but found a place to sit down anyway. It wouldn't be worth falling down again to get away from that image.

"Is there anything I can get you?" Buck offered. "I told Mrs. Chambers, my housekeeper, to keep the kitchen open."

"No, thanks. I'm not hungry. Maybe just some water."

Buck tried to summon his housekeeper but the intercom seemed to be dead. "I'll go get it myself. You just sit right there."

When he was gone, Charlie swallowed the last of his bourbon and got to his feet. "I guess I'll be going. I wanted to make sure you were okay. I'll talk to you later."

"Where are you going?" Mary Catherine hated to lose even a small part of her audience. It wasn't every day a woman got to be admired this way. "We haven't solved the problem yet."

"Listen, MC," Danny butted in. "I think this guy is part of the problem. Maybe you should let him go."

Baylor hissed at Danny, assuring Mary Catherine that Charlie was *not* part of the problem. He was sure the man could help end all the trouble so he could go home and flex on his favorite sofa.

"What'd I say?" Danny patted Baylor's head. "We're *amigos*, right?"

Baylor walked away from Danny with a swish of his tail.

"Thanks." Charlie smiled at Mary Catherine and touched her cheek with a long finger. "But I don't think you're up to solving anything tonight and I think Buck has been on the verge of kicking me out ever since we got here. I don't want to get into that. Call me when you get home."

"Tell me what really happened with my cousin." The words came out of her mouth before she knew what she was saying. "I don't know why yet, but I think it has something to do with all this."

"When you're better," Charlie promised as Buck came back with water in a crystal goblet. "We'll talk."

Mary Catherine knew there was nothing else she could say. Men weren't particularly social creatures in the first place—adding rivalry for a female only made matters worse. She'd have to follow her sudden hunch about her cousin tomorrow or the next day; whenever she was on her feet again.

It made sense now that she thought about it. The man who'd attacked her was looking for something without monetary value, at least at first glance. Maybe he was looking for something that could help her cousin take the building from her.

The deed was in a safety deposit box and her aunt's will was finalized two years ago. Nothing he could find in her bedroom could help him, but he couldn't know that. Was it possible her cousin would stoop so low as to try and steal the building from her?

Mary Catherine's mind was filled with images from the last few days. There was the car accident, Baylor's accident, and now the man in her room. That sounded like a pattern to her. Maybe her cousin thought he could get rid of her.

There was no way to prove any of this, at least none she could see. She could tell Angellus her theory in the morning, she yawned. Despite being unconscious for several hours, she was exhausted.

"Maybe I should go too." Danny got up and put on his ball cap. "Give me a call when you're ready to go, MC. You know I'll be here."

"Thanks, Danny. I'm sure I'll be fine tomorrow. Thank you for staying."

"Sure. I hope we can figure out what's going on with all this. Things have just gotten kind of crazy."

Buck walked Danny to the front door, obviously not threatened by the younger man. Mary Catherine sat back in her chair and tried not to think about the mess she was in. It was hard not to think about it since it involved her well being, but she tried to clear her mind. A good night's sleep would help this situation.

She was glad when Buck was polite and unassuming, walking her back upstairs to her room without complaint. She could've handled him if he'd gotten out of line, but she was relieved that she didn't have to.

"I hope this will clear things up between us," Buck said before he left her at the bedroom door. "I've always had the greatest admiration for you, Mary Catherine. I hope we'll be closer when this is over."

"I hope so too." She didn't want to commit to any kind of relationship with him. Right now her thoughts were with Charlie. She wasn't sure what it was about him that she found so intriguing. She'd been kissed many times and that peck he gave her couldn't even be considered passionate.

Maybe it was that odd psychic sense about him. She'd met many men and married many men. None of them had been psychic. She believed Charlie had a gift for finding things and being there when there was trouble. It put him in a bad light; she could see that now.

Baylor yawned and meowed from the bed, taunting her that it had taken her long enough.

"Are you okay, Mary Catherine?"

She glanced up, surprised to find Buck still standing in the doorway. "I'm so sorry. I'm not myself. I hope you understand. Maybe we can talk tomorrow." She shooed him out of the room. "Good night. Thank you for letting me stay here."

She closed the door and stood against it for a few minutes. She was really feeling very well now that she'd been up and moved around. Some of that was the pain medication for the gash in her head, no doubt, but most of it was her. Life was too interesting to lie around for long.

"Baylor, I think we owe Charlie an apology and we need to straighten out this rivalry between him and Buck. Buck is a good man, I'm sure. He certainly has a nice house and plenty of money. Normally he'd be my first choice."

The cat rolled over and started preening himself. He was unimpressed with her thought processes. None of them actively pertained to him.

"But I'm older now and I can take care of myself. I don't need a man to support me. I like Charlie and I can see a place for him in our lives. I know you like him too. Don't pretend you haven't stood up for him all this time."

Baylor responded it was only his place to make sure Mary Catherine knew what was going on. If she chose to have Charlie in her life, that was up to her. She could certainly do worse for a mate, in his estimation.

"I appreciate that." She turned out the light and got into bed. "We'll call him first thing in the morning. There's something he knows about my cousin he's not telling. We'll see."

She stroked the cat's fur as he climbed up near her chest and put both front paws on her arm. He purred as he buried his nose in her side and flexed his claws into the down comforter. "It's all right. I know you were worried about me. I was worried about you too the other night." She laughed. "No, not when you were playing dead. You know I can tell the difference."

The cat fell asleep beside her, but Mary Catherine had a hard time closing her eyes. It had been a traumatic week, not the least of which had been those few moments when she thought she might never hear another animal's thoughts.

The sounds were so ingrained in her; it was frightening simply to think about it. It had been over quickly, but what if it hadn't? What if she never heard Baylor's thoughts again? Her mind almost shut down at the idea.

She couldn't imagine what she'd do or how she'd continue with her life. Many times, she'd wondered how people lived without hearing those things. Sometimes she thought it was more a curse than a blessing. As she got older, she realized it was truly a gift to be able to share herself with Baylor and Bruno and Cheetos, for that matter. She couldn't always help them, but she did the best she could and it was very satisfying, but not in the same way it had been when she was younger and looking for attention to highlight her gift. Now it was something more personal and spiritual.

Her cell phone rang and she stubbed her toe in the unfamiliar room trying to get to her purse. "Hello?"

"Mary Catherine," Colin's whispered voice was barely audible. "I'm out at the convenience store in Landfall Park. Teddy called me. The psycho caller is on his way out here. I need backup!"

SEVENTEEN

DESPITE BUCK'S PLEAS FOR her to ignore Colin's call for help, Mary Catherine dragged herself out of bed, called Danny, and headed to the convenience store. Buck tagged along, grumbling about being out so late at night.

Baylor, who sat next to Mary Catherine, agreed with her feelings that Buck was definitely the wrong man for her. Imagine being so put out by a little jaunt at night! She and Jenny had gone out much later to pick up stray animals along the waterfront.

"How much farther is it?" Buck asked for the third time.

"Not much," Danny said. "But you don't get an Icee when we get there since you've been so *impaciente*."

Buck was quiet after that; he wasn't so thickheaded he didn't get the childish insult. Mary Catherine tried to plot their strategy, but without knowing the circumstances, it was difficult. "Maybe you should wait by the car," she said to Danny. "Keep your eyes open and be ready to move as quickly as possible."

"No way! I'm not staying with the car. I want to be where the action is. *You* stay with the car. You were injured earlier. Let me and Colin handle this."

"All right." She could see the logic in that strategy, even though she didn't like it. "We'll get there, park on the far left side, then look for Colin. I hope he hasn't done anything stupid."

Danny shrugged. "He's Colin. He doesn't have much choice."

But when they got to the convenience store, there was no sign of Colin. Danny got out of the taxi and walked around the building, but couldn't find Colin. "His car is in back but I didn't see him. I told you," he reported back to Mary Catherine. "What were the chances of him not doing something stupido?"

Mary Catherine considered the possibilities. She was afraid to try and call Colin—what if he were in a vulnerable position when his phone went off? On the other hand, they couldn't wait here all night not knowing what was going on.

"I'll go in and talk to Teddy," she volunteered. "Maybe he's already talked to the psycho caller and Colin is going after him."

"Can I just say one thing?" Buck held a finger in the air.

"No!" Mary Catherine and Danny said it at the same time. Buck sat back and drummed his fingers on the car seat beside him.

"Okay." Danny took Mary Catherine's arm. "Don't take any chances. If anything looks weird, you come back out and we call the police. Okay?"

"All right." She took a deep breath and began limping to the door. The outside of the store looked as empty as the inside. No one was there pumping gas or buying snacks and lottery tickets. She looked for Teddy before she got to the door but didn't see him behind the register.

She pushed open the door and a chime rang loudly. She called out for Teddy but there was no response. She was about to use her cell phone to call 911 when a back door opened and a man ran into the shop. "Where's Teddy?"

He glanced at her and started running toward the front door. She fumbled with her cell phone, trying to alert Danny and Buck. She limped after him, but there was no way she could keep up. She couldn't speed dial fast enough and reached the door, certain the man had gotten away.

She was about to yell for Danny when she saw him sitting on top of the man who'd run out of the store. "You got him!"

Danny grinned. "*Si!* I'm hoping he was someone I was supposed to get. He *looked* suspicious."

Mary Catherine finally reached them and said to the man under Danny, "Have you seen Colin Jamison?"

"Who?"

"The man you're trying to frame for his aunt's murder. Where is he?" She searched his face, but as far as she could tell in the dim lighting, there were no scratches on his face.

"I don't know what you're talking about."

Buck went into the convenience store and came out yelling for help. "He's in here with the store clerk."

Mary Catherine rushed in (as fast as she could) and looked behind the counter. Colin and Teddy were both tied up on the floor. "Are you all right, Colin?" she asked. "Do you know what happened?"

Buck untied both men and rudely pulled the duct tape from their mouths.

"It was the psycho caller," Colin replied when he could move his lips. "That's what happened. I saw him talking on Teddy's phone in the back. He had a gun and tied us up here. He's probably gone by now."

"I don't think so. I think Danny has him in the parking lot." Mary Catherine explained even as she started back outside to warn Danny that the man he captured could be armed.

Colin and Teddy followed Buck and Mary Catherine out of the store. By that time, Baylor had joined Danny, sitting on the man and hissing at him.

"We better search him," Buck said. "He might be armed."

"I don't have a gun," the man protested. "I ain't done nothin'. Get these two off of me."

"Is this the guy who tied you up?" Mary Catherine asked Teddy and Colin.

"Yeah. He's got a gun somewhere on him." Colin didn't make a move to search him.

Buck and Danny did the dirty work, but couldn't find a weapon. "He's clean," Danny said. "Are you *sure* he had a gun?"

Colin looked at Teddy who shrugged. "It looked like a gun in his pocket to me."

The man Danny had captured laughed. "I didn't need the real thing for you jokers. What's wrong with making a few phone calls anyway? The pay's good and it don't hurt no one."

"We'll let the police make that decision, my friend." Colin puffed out his chest and jabbed his finger in the man's face.

"Yeah," Teddy said. "This guy's with the FBI. You're going away for a long time."

No one disabused the psycho caller about Colin's status with the FBI. Mary Catherine called the police, but there was an emergency on Martin Luther King Junior Parkway and their response time was questionable.

"Let's take him in ourselves," Danny suggested. "MC, you know where Angellus lives. We'll take him there."

Mary Catherine wasn't so sure that was a good idea, but by that time Buck and Teddy were tying the man's hands with plastic garbage ties and escorting him to Colin's car. The men decided that Teddy, Buck, and Colin would take the caller to Angellus' home, with Mary Catherine and Danny leading the way.

"Great." Colin grimaced as Teddy locked up the store. "Buck's gonna be talking about Meaty Boy advertising all the way."

———

Angellus opened his front door a little after one AM to find all of them on his doorstep. "What are you doing here?"

Mary Catherine smiled at his orange tropical shorts. "We captured the psycho caller for you, Detective Angellus. I think we might be able to find out what's going on now."

"I'll tell you what's going on," he replied. "You're all going home until a decent hour or I'll put you in jail overnight."

He started to close his front door when Sallie came up behind him with Moose running and barking behind her. "What's going on, John?" Sallie saw Mary Catherine and immediately opened the door wider for all of them to come inside. "I can't believe you left them standing outside all that time," she scolded her husband. "Would you all like some coffee? I think I have some cookies too."

"I have to pee," the psycho caller said. "And I think these bread ties have cut off the circulation to my hands. I want a lawyer!"

Angellus groaned as they all walked into his house. "Coffee, maybe. But no cookies!"

Mary Catherine appointed herself as spokesperson for the group. She told Angellus everything that had happened from the time she left Buck's house until they all left the convenience store. "He confessed to calling the radio station," she explained about the man they'd taken into custody.

Angellus shook his head. "You got me up at two in the morning to tell me you've arrested someone? You can't arrest people. You're civilians!"

"It's a citizen's arrest," Buck said. "We're allowed to do that."

"Did you witness him committing a crime?" Angellus looked up at the man as Danny escorted him back from the bathroom. "Nothing he told you can be used as evidence. Take the bread ties off him."

"You can't just let him go," Colin protested. "He pretended he had a gun, and tied me and Teddy up. That must be some kind of offense."

Angellus frowned. "Did he rob you?"

"No," Teddy replied. "But it really hurt when that guy took off the duct tape."

"I rest my case." Angellus looked at the psycho caller. "I apologize for this mix-up, sir. If you'd like to file a complaint against these people, I'll take your statement."

"Yeah." The man chafed his wrists with his hands. "I'd like to file something against them. They're all a bunch of loons!"

"But you called the radio station and threatened Mary Catherine, didn't you?" Colin accused him with all the fervor of a rampaging DA.

"What if I did? There's no law against that."

"Technically, that's not true," Angellus added. "Are you confessing to those phone calls at the radio station?"

The man shrugged. "I didn't mean no harm. Someone called me; offered me a couple hundred bucks for each call. I didn't see what difference it made. No one got hurt until this guy," he pointed at Colin, "got all up in my face. And then that other guy with the ball cap and the cat jumped me."

Angellus took a deep breath. "All right. Maybe we can work something out. If you come into the station and talk to us about this person who offered you money to call the talk show, I'm sure you won't be charged with anything and we can keep to ourselves what happened at the convenience store tonight."

The man shrugged. "I just wanted to make some extra money. I don't want no trouble."

Angellus got dressed and took the psycho caller to the station with a promise to talk to all of them later about the incident.

"I think it was really brave of all of you to catch this man." Sallie smiled at them when her husband was gone. "More cookies?"

"No, thank you." Mary Catherine struggled to her feet. "I have to go home and get some sleep. I appreciate you being so gracious with us popping in like this."

"Yeah." Danny yawned. "Some of us have to work tomorrow."

After saying good night to Sallie, Danny offered to take Teddy back to the convenience store.

Buck and Mary Catherine got in Colin's car. "Maybe we should think about what we have in common." Colin pulled the car out into the road and turned back down toward the river.

"Obviously you have the radio station in common," Buck replied. "But I don't see where that matters."

"No, maybe you're onto something here," Colin said. "Maybe whoever is doing these things wants to get Mary Catherine off the air. Or close down the radio station."

"That's stupid," Buck said. "Even if they hated Mary Catherine, not that anyone could ever hate her, why would they want to hurt the station?"

"For obvious reasons," Colin pointed out. "I manage the radio station that produces her show. Anyone can see the correlation."

"We aren't going to accomplish anything arguing about it," Mary Catherine said. "Buck may have a point, but so did Angellus. We aren't going to get anything done tonight. We'll have to take it up again tomorrow."

The group was silent after that as they rode through the nearly deserted downtown area. Colin dropped Mary Catherine and Buck back at Buck's home.

Mary Catherine's cell phone rang as she struggled out of the car. "MC!" Danny said. "If you need me to come get you before morning, call me. I didn't like the look on that guy's face."

She laughed. "Thank you for worrying about me, but I'll be fine. You know what Baylor did to whoever was in my apartment. He wouldn't let anyone paw me but him."

"Okay. I'll be there by eight thirty. Take care."

Mary Catherine was almost too exhausted to walk inside. She focused on finding the stairs that led to her bedroom when Buck stopped her. "What was that about?"

"Nothing. Just lining up my day tomorrow."

"You could have my limo driver for the day, if you need him," Buck offered.

"Thank you, but I wouldn't hurt Danny's feelings that way. And thanks again for letting me stay here. Good night."

"You're entirely welcome." He smiled and started up the stairs. "Say, is that little vet at your place seeing anyone?"

"No one she doesn't have to see. She's not really a people person."

"Neither am I. Thanks."

Baylor wanted to know everything that had happened while he'd been trapped in the car. Mary Catherine undressed and laid her head on her pillow. "We'll talk about it in the morning." She fell asleep listening to the cat complain about being left behind.

———

Mary Catherine was in high spirits the next morning. Her head didn't feel stuffed with cotton, and it didn't hurt either. She was a little stiff and sore—nothing the whirlpool tub in Buck's guest room couldn't help.

She lamented Danny's choice of outfits: a bright orange and yellow pant suit that had seen better days. She hadn't worn it since husband #2, George Wilson, had died. The incandescent colors seemed inappropriate. That was a different time in her life.

The questionable part of Danny's decision (not that she didn't appreciate a clean outfit) was where he'd looked in her closet to find it. There were dozens of outfits in front of it. She only kept the outfit to remember those long-ago days with George.

In the end, she had no choice but to wear it. Fortunately, it wasn't too tight. Angellus had called her earlier and left a message on her cell phone that the crime scene team would be finished in her apartment by noon. She supposed that meant it would be safe for her to go home and change clothes. That would be followed immediately by the installation of an alarm system and any other security device she could afford. She wouldn't let someone sneak up on her again if she could help it.

Baylor complained he was all the alarm system she'd ever need ... if she'd just pay attention to him. Hadn't he warned her that something was wrong in the bedroom?

"Yes you did and I got a chair in my face for it," she reminded him as she brushed her hair.

He meowed and rolled over on the bed, showing his back to her. If she didn't need him, he might as well stay with Buck.

She realized his cat pride was hurt and sat down beside him, stroking his tawny fur. "You know I need you, sweetie. But we'll both be safer with an alarm system. Don't forget; he tried to trap you. We don't want that to happen again."

The cat agreed with that and started purring and flexing on her leg. Mary Catherine got up carefully, mindful of the effect of claws on polyester. "I have to go to work now. Are you coming with me?"

Baylor was at the door before she was. She smiled as she let him out into the hall. She knew he wouldn't leave her any more than she'd leave him. They were together until something happened to one of them. Mary Catherine didn't want to think about that.

"Good morning!" Buck greeted them. "How about some breakfast?"

She shuddered. "I try to avoid that meal, thank you. I'm more of a night person usually, but I appreciate you offering and your hospitality."

"You're certainly welcome, darlin'. I hope that means we'll be talking Meaty Boy commercials by the end of the month."

"I don't think so. You rigged the taste test. You didn't win the challenge."

He frowned. "But Mary Catherine, the dogs ate all of it and told you they liked it. That must count for something."

She patted his cheek. "Until the dogs *like* the food, without additions, I can't endorse it personally. I'm sorry. Even though WRSC thinks our major audience is people, it's really all the animals out there that trust me to be honest with them and their people. I hope you understand."

Buck shook his head. "I can't say that I do, but I respect you for it."

"Talk to Jenny about it. Maybe she'll agree to endorse it. Then you could say veterinarian approved."

He considered that and his face lightened. "Say! That's not a bad idea. I might do that."

Anything to take his mind off having her endorse Meaty Boy. "Good. Come on, Baylor. I think Danny's here."

Mary Catherine picked Baylor up at the doorway and slowly went down the steps. Danny was pulling in to the long circle drive. He jumped out of the taxi before she could reach it and opened the door. "*Buenos dias*! That's the best outfit I've ever seen you wear, MC! It brightens up your whole face."

"You mean I look like I'm seasick." She carefully got in the car and let him shut the door behind her. "I look like a giant jar of juice."

He laughed. "No! You are *mila bella*! I don't know why you had that outfit stuffed in the back of your closet. You should wear it."

"Thanks anyway." She glanced at her watch. "We've got some extra time this morning. They pushed my show forward an hour. I'd like to go out to Wrightsville Beach, if you don't mind."

"That's cool with me." He started back down the drive. "Any special reason for the beach trip? Is there a whale washed up or a dolphin headed for the tuna factory?"

"Nothing that dramatic. I want to get a little perspective, that's all."

"The beach it is."

Mary Catherine was quiet as they crossed town and headed toward the beach. Danny talked, and when she didn't talk back, he turned on the radio and started singing. He was a good-hearted soul, but she needed some time to herself. If she were an animal, she supposed she'd find a secluded place to lick her wounds. Going to the beach was her way of finding solace.

When they finally reached the crowded beach area outside of Wilmington, she wasn't sure she'd be able to find an area that wasn't occupied by girls in bikinis and guys in Speedos. Colorful towels littered the beach, while teenagers in ragged jean shorts tried to surf the small waves coming into the shore.

It was a colorful sight—planes with banners flew through puffy white clouds while seagulls wheeled across the sky. Hot dog, juice, and pizza venders peddled their wares as beach goers fought for places to park and walk to the oceanfront.

"Where do you want to go on the beach?" Danny pulled out of the steady stream of traffic to the side of US Highway 74 and looked back at her in the rearview mirror.

"This will do fine." She got out of the car, Baylor at her heels. "I'll meet you back here in forty-five minutes."

"Hey! Wait! Where are you going? What am I supposed to do?"

"Check out the good-looking girls," she advised. "I'm sure you can find someone to talk to."

"But what are *you* gonna do out here?"

"Find the answers to what's been going on. I'll meet you back here in forty-five minutes."

Good morning, Mary Catherine!

I love your show! I was wondering if you could tell me what kind of cat food Baylor likes to eat. I have three cats who love to listen to your show. They'd all like to know what Baylor eats.

Thanks. Say hi to Baylor for us.

EIGHTEEN

MARY CATHERINE HAD FOUND in her life that standing beside the ocean was one of the most rejuvenating things she could do. Being in tune with the infinite life force given out by the creatures of the sea was like a shot of adrenaline. Their minds were too random, too wild for her to understand most of them, but the swell of their thoughts and emotions centered her.

She stood in the shadow of one of the large hotels, arms outstretched, sea grass waving frantically in the breeze. Her eyes were closed as she listened to the song of the whales and the laughter of the dolphins. There were no judgments here; no petty grievances like the ones shared by humans on the land. She was glad she wasn't privy to human minds most of the time. Although she admitted it would be easier sometimes, it would also, she suspected, be more frightening.

She could lose herself in the vast depths of the sea that stretched out before her. The millions of creatures that inhabited all parts of it slipped into her mind and she floated with them in the cool, briny deep.

There was always something that called her back. She wondered if one day she'd simply follow that siren song, appealing and seductive. That day, they'd find her lifeless body on the shore, never dreaming of the wonderful melodies that had carried her away.

But today, Baylor was playing with a crab who didn't appreciate his attention. He slapped at the crustacean, which pinched his nose and sent him howling. A group of gulls called out as they spotted a meal left by humans that was ripe for plunder. A small boy squinted up at her. "Whatcha doin'?"

Mary Catherine opened her eyes and brought herself back to her frail, human body that was sometimes so limiting. "I'm talking to the whales."

"Nobody can *really* talk to whales."

"I can. I've been doing it all my life."

"Really? That's so cool! Can I try?"

"Of course. Anyone can talk to them."

"Where are they?" He looked out at the deep gray water. "I can't see them."

"They're out there. Close your eyes and concentrate. Can you hear them?"

He nodded, his eyes tightly closed. "I hear them! I can hear them singing."

It wouldn't surprise her if he could. Children were closer to the source and could hear and see things adults had trained themselves not to. She remembered people, especially her mother, telling her she couldn't really understand animals when she was a child. Luckily, she'd ignored them.

"Allen?" a woman's voice called from behind the sand dunes. "Are you over there?"

"I'm here, Mom," he answered. "I'm listening to the whales."

A sunburned face with straw-like brown hair looked around the sea grass. "I'm sorry. I hope he's not bothering you."

"Not at all. He's a wonderful little boy." Mary Catherine picked Baylor up when the cat refused to leave the crab alone.

"I can hear the whales," Allen said. "Close your eyes, Mom. Maybe you can hear them too."

Allen's mother smiled at Mary Catherine and walked over to take her son by the hand. "He's got an awful imagination. I talk to him about it all the time."

"Imagination is never bad." Mary Catherine turned to go. "Keep listening for those whales, Allen. Say hello to them for me."

The mother frowned and insisted the little boy stop playing games. They walked in the opposite direction that Mary Catherine took, past the hotel and along the street to meet Danny.

"You're late," Danny said when he saw her. "We'll never make it back in time."

She took a deep breath of the salty air. "It doesn't matter. I feel much better now."

"And you know who killed Aunt Ferndelle and who hit you with a chair, right?"

"Not exactly. But I know it'll all clear up. We just have to be patient."

He got in the taxi and started the engine. "*Dio*! Who are you and what did you do with MC?"

"I'm the whales," she replied. "And the sea turtles."

"Okay. You're *really* scaring me now. Can we talk about something else?"

"If it makes you feel better."

"Colin called while you were doing whatever you were doing out there. He wanted to talk to you, but he said there was no answer on your cell phone."

"I had it turned off. It'll wait until we get there."

"It might be important."

"Maybe. But it can still wait."

They drove back through town the way they'd come. Mary Catherine used the time to get back in tune with her world. Danny practiced his country music ballads. Baylor complained about the noise and the painful nip on his nose. "It was your own fault," she told him. "How many times does that have to happen for you to learn not to chasc crabs?"

"You talkin' to me?" Danny looked at her in the rearview mirror.

She laughed. "If you were chasing crabs like Baylor, I was. I hope you got a sore nose for your trouble too."

"Crabs are good eating. Even the little ones. We can't all live on rabbit food like you do."

"And a shark would eat you."

"Let's not talk about that."

The taxi bumped up next to the curb in front of the radio station. Mary Catherine thanked Danny for the ride. "Could you come back for me in an hour? I hate to ask but I haven't heard anything about my car. I guess I better give my insurance agent a call."

"You've been busy. And I never mind coming back for you, you know that. See you in an hour."

Mary Catherine let Baylor follow her into Port City Java where she bought a large mocha before she went upstairs. The cat flirted with the pretty young girl behind the counter. "Come on. She's not going to give you any milk. You know it makes you gassy."

The girl giggled and stroked Baylor's fur. "He's such a cute kitty."

"At least *he* thinks so." Mary Catherine sighed.

Colin was pacing the floor upstairs, pulling his hair, when he saw her and Baylor get out of the elevator. "Where have you been? Do you know what time it is? I was worried about you. You could've called me."

"I'm sorry." She smiled at him. "I knew I'd be here on time. Jimmy isn't even out of the booth yet. There's plenty of time."

She stepped into the sound booth as Jimmy, the food critic, walked out and saluted her. Baylor sat down in his usual chair. Mary Catherine put on her headphones and got behind the microphone. "This is Mary Catherine Roberts on WRSC, Lite 102.5. I'm the Pet Psychic, here to answer your questions about the animals we all know and love."

Corey cued her to let her know he was ready and a caller was on the line. "Good morning, Mary Catherine. I'd like to ask you a question about my goat, Orpheus. He won't eat grass anymore. He walks around with a sad expression on his face and will only eat dog food."

"Have there been any changes in his life recently?"

"Not really. We've had him a couple of years. We got him because our backyard is so hard to mow."

She thought about the problem for a few seconds. "How old is Orpheus?"

"We got him when he was a few months old so I guess about two and a half. Do you think he's sick?"

"Not sick exactly. I think he might be lonely."

"You mean he needs another goat to play with?"

"No, I think he's looking for romance. You might think about seeing if someone you know has a nice girl goat. I think that would make Orpheus feel better."

"Really? I never thought of that! Thank you. We'll try that."

Corey went to commercial, and Mindy popped her head in the door. "Are you okay? Need some water or anything?"

"I'm fine, thanks." Mary Catherine looked at the girl's pale face and the dark circles under her eyes. Colin looked much the same way. She didn't want to pry, but asked, "Are you feeling all right?"

Mindy laughed and played with her hair. "Better than all right, actually. Did Colin tell you?"

Corey signaled that the commercial was over and Mindy closed the door. Mary Catherine took the next call from a woman who wanted her to come and speak to the fire ants who'd taken up residence in her yard. Mary Catherine told her insects were difficult and she might have to call an exterminator.

"I tried that, and it didn't work," the woman said. "Maybe you could project your thoughts to them. You're in North Carolina, right? I'm in South Carolina. Maybe if you tell them to leave, they will."

Mary Catherine was burning with curiosity about Mindy and Colin and didn't want to argue with the woman. "All right. I'll do that. Call me back and let me know how it works."

"Thanks. We always listen to your show. You have such inner knowledge."

They went to commercial again (Meaty Boy, this time) and Colin opened the door to the sound booth before Mary Catherine could get up to look for Mindy. "I'm sorry. I would've called you if I could. Don't worry. We'll have a reception everyone can come to."

"What are you talking about?"

"I thought Mindy told you." Colin grinned like a small child and held up his left hand. "We drove to Myrtle Beach this morning and got married. I've never been so happy."

"Did you tell her?" Mary Catherine demanded as Corey started signaling her to get ready for the next caller.

"I told her. Everything's okay. I think that's why she wanted us to go ahead and do the deed. It's gonna be great. You're on!"

Mary Catherine was stunned. She had thought Colin and Mindy would eventually get married, but it was surprising the girl got over Colin's betrayal that quickly. It was possible he'd lied to her. Colin might not have told Mindy the truth. She knew she was going to have to find some way to ask Mindy about what happened.

She took three more phone calls during her hour program. Two of them were very long, and involved more than one segment to answer questions about animals that were dying. Mary Catherine was crying with the two families who had called for help in dealing with the trauma of losing a member of the family.

It was a difficult decision for one family, whose vet insisted they should put their beloved golden retriever down. They said the animal wasn't in pain now, but they were worried she would be at some point.

Mary Catherine didn't like to see suffering in people or animals. On the other hand, she believed animals had their road to follow as well as the people who loved them. Since the animal wasn't in pain, she disagreed with the vet. She knew that would bring her a ton of mail from other veterinarians, but she could only speak from her heart. It was difficult for any family to lose a loved one. Euthanizing the dog right away wouldn't soften that blow.

By the time the show was over, there wasn't a dry eye in the station. As she walked out of the sound booth, everyone was either blowing their nose or wiping their eyes. Baylor wondered at all the fuss over losing a dog. In his cat wisdom, dogs were meant to be subservient to cats. He would only miss a dog who'd served him well.

"Dogs are wonderful companions," Mary Catherine agreed as she rummaged through her purse for a tissue. "People are just as sad to lose them as they are to lose cats."

Baylor didn't understand. His nose was still hurting from their beach outing and he wanted to go home. She told him he'd have to wait and his nose wouldn't feel any better at home.

When the next talk show host was in the sound booth, Colin and Mindy came to talk with Mary Catherine. She held both their hands and smiled at them, all the while wondering how she could get Mindy away by herself. It would be better to break up the marriage now by telling her what had happened between Colin and Charlene than to wait until there was a child and a mortgage.

"You both look terrible," Mary Catherine said. "But it's a good kind of terrible. Congratulations! You'd better be planning on having a reception here. I feel cheated by missing the wedding."

"I'm sorry." Colin's face turned red. "It was so spur of the moment, but it was perfect. We'll get something set up in the next week or so. Don't worry; we want your wedding gift."

Mindy was blushing and smiling too. "Be happy for us. It's taken us all this time to work up to it. I don't know if we'd have done it now, except for everything Colin has been through recently. I needed to be close to him, since it's not over yet. This way, as his wife, I can share in his difficulties."

"Without anyone asking you if we're related." Colin kissed her and Corey called him for something.

Mary Catherine knew she'd never get a better opportunity. Before they needed Mindy for the next show, she pulled the girl into a corner already occupied by a plastic plant that needed dusting. "I'm sorry to have to ask you this, but did Colin tell you something?"

"Something like what?"

"Something important that could affect your relationship and might have changed your mind about marrying him."

Mindy smiled, and patted her hand. "If you're talking about what I think you're talking about, I know all about it. But thank you for sticking up for me. Colin told me you threatened to tell me yourself."

Mary Catherine felt like a weight was lifted from her heart. "I'm so glad. I just wanted you to start out fresh. And if women can't stick together over these things, the world would certainly be a bad place."

"I think knowing about that woman who lured Colin away from me will make us stronger. He won't be alone again for anything like that to happen."

"You're a wonderful, forgiving woman with a big heart." Mary Catherine hugged Mindy. "I don't think I could be as forgiving. I hope the two of you are very happy together. If not, I'll know who to blame and it won't be you!"

Mindy kissed her cheek. "You've been such a wonderful friend the last two years. I don't know what I would've done without you."

Colin and Corey called Mindy for a new show setup. Mary Catherine was glad she'd had the opportunity to talk to the girl. If Mindy was okay with Colin's unfaithfulness, it certainly wasn't a problem for her. And she loved to go wedding gift shopping. But first she had to find out what was going on with her car.

She waited for Danny on the street in front of the radio station, cell phone against her ear, as she tried to maneuver through the maze of people who didn't know if repairs were being made to her car. Baylor sat beside her on the bench watching traffic go by on Water Street. He loved colorful cars; one of the reasons she'd chosen the red Mini Cooper.

By the time Danny got there, Mary Catherine had learned her car was in the shop and insurance funding had been released for repairs. Her agent said her insurance rates would go up, even though the wreck wasn't her fault. They were calling it a malfunction and checking to see if the same thing had been happening to other cars like hers.

She'd argued with her insurance man for five minutes about the rate hike, but in the end, she knew she couldn't beat that system. She'd be more likely to understand a snail on her doorstep.

She got in the car with Danny and told him about Colin and Mindy. He was surprised too. "Colin's lucky to have someone like her. Not everyone would forgive something like that."

She agreed as her cell phone rang. It was Detective Angellus. "Not that I'm encouraging the stunt you guys pulled last night, but I wanted you to know the man confessed at the station too. He called you after being paid for each call."

"Who paid him?" she asked, thinking about her cousin.

"He never met the person. After the initial contact, there was money left on his doorstep. We're following up. Leave it alone and let us do our job."

"What about my apartment?"

"You're clear there. We picked up some prints and some partials. I'll let you know if any of them turn out to be anything. In the meantime, in light of what's happened, we'll have a police car sit out there for a while. We'll hope whoever it is doesn't come back again."

"Thank you, Detective Angellus. How is Bo-Bo doing?"

"He's fine, I guess. I'll talk to you later."

Mary Catherine changed her mind about going home. She took out Charlie's business card. "If you don't mind, will you take me to this address? I think it's down by St. James Episcopal Church in the historic district."

"You got it." Danny turned the taxi around in the Cotton Exchange parking lot. "I thought we hated him?"

"I think he's right and I might need him, unless I want to live with Buck for the rest of my life, which I don't."

"I could protect you." He glanced at her in the rearview mirror. "You know I'm here for you. After all we've been through together; I wouldn't let anything happen to you."

"That's very sweet and I appreciate it, but we need to resolve this. Angellus is a good man and probably a good detective. But I need someone to work outside the system. I don't want anyone to protect me for the rest of my life. We have to find out what's happening and why."

"Okay. I didn't want you to feel like you had to ask that scumball for help. You have *amigos*, MC. You know that, right?"

"Yes, thank you." She squeezed his shoulder. She couldn't find the words to tell him that Charlie might end up being more than a friend. She knew the signs were there but she was resisting this time. Maybe she wasn't ready for another romance yet. Or it was just the circumstance of their meeting.

Charlie lived in an old house that had been made over into what looked like four apartments. His name was on one of the top floor mailboxes when they checked the door. Mary Catherine had insisted she'd be fine, but Danny had come with her anyway. She pressed the buzzer by Charlie's name and they waited.

After another two tries on the buzzer, Charlie's voice called out, "What do you want?"

"It's Mary Catherine. You said I could call on you. Can I come up?"

There was no response for a long moment. Finally his voice rasped, "Come on. I'll buzz you in."

Danny opened the door as the buzzer sounded. Mary Catherine put one hand on his shoulder. "I think I should go up alone."

"That's *loco*! I should go up with you. You don't even have Baylor to claw his eyes out if he messes with you."

Baylor's sentiments echoed his from the taxi where she'd left him. "I'll be fine. I'm a good judge of people. You and Baylor wait down here, please."

He shrugged. "All right. But I don't like it. What if he's the guy who attacked you at your apartment and Baylor is wrong?"

"I don't think he is. But I think he can help solve what's going on. I haven't treated him very well and I want to talk to him alone." Mary Catherine smiled and walked into the old house, the ornate stained glass door closing lightly behind her.

NINETEEN

Mary Catherine started up the steep stairway, looking at the crisscross network of stairs above her. She'd already looked for an elevator; there was none. By the time she'd reached the first landing, she wished she'd sent Baylor and Danny instead.

She was breathing hard by the time she reached Charlie's door. She pounded on it and the door came open. "Charlie?" She wasn't sure if she should go in.

"I'm here," he said in an unsteady voice.

The room was dark but Mary Catherine could see the outline of furniture and clothes strewn everywhere. It was nothing more than a large living room that was made into a sitting area, kitchen, and bedroom. She could fit all of it into her sitting room. There was a bad smell that reminded her of a cheap bar: whiskey and cigar smoke. Was she in the right place?

"Sorry the place is such a mess."

She tried to tell from the direction of the voice where Charlie was located. It was definitely his voice but she didn't believe he lived here. Something seemed wrong—or maybe she thought she knew him better than she did. Lucky thing for her she was taking her time and being cautious at this stage of her life. "Where are you?"

"Actually, I think I made a mistake. You should go."

"Charlie, I made it up the stairs, I think I can handle seeing you. What's wrong?"

"I think I know who hurt you; who was looking through your apartment."

She tried again to peer through the darkness. It was no use. She could see the outline of a window behind a large blind. She walked over and lifted it, sunlight streaming into the room.

"What the hell did you do that for?"

Mary Catherine pulled the blind open all the way and made sure it was secure. "I think you need to take a shower and I'll make some coffee. Then we'll talk."

"I can take care of myself. I've been doing it for a long time now. I'm not a rescue animal you can understand."

"We'll talk about that when you get out of the shower." She ignored him and started cleaning her way through the room. She wasn't much of a housekeeper herself and understood a certain amount of disorder, but this was ridiculous. There were week-old pizza boxes heaped on top of two-week-old Chinese carry-out. No wonder the place reeked.

Charlie's puppy whined from the corner of the kitchen area. She bent down to stroke him and see if he had any idea what was going on. Baxter was sad and confused. His relationship with Charlie was good, but the man was unhappy. Was there anything Mary Catherine could do to make him happy?

She wasn't sure. When she looked up, Charlie was standing beside her. He hadn't shaved and his eyes were bloodshot. From her wilder days, she knew he was hung over. Empty Jim Beam bottles on the counter told their own story.

"Why are you here?"

"I'm here because you said you'd help me." She stood up straight and stared back at him. Baxter was right. He was a mess. She'd seen worse, but not in a long time.

"Didn't you hear me? I think I know who hurt you and I'm pretty sure I led him to you."

She bustled away from him, giving herself the excuse of looking for coffee. "I'm sure you didn't mean to. You've been very kind to me. I know you wouldn't hurt me."

"I'm not so sure." He ran his hand across the dark stubble on his face. "These days I'd do anything for money. It wasn't always like that. This damn curse of knowing things ahead of time has ruined my life."

"Maybe. But I know you can help me. The police can't. I need you to pull yourself together, Charlie. I know what it's like to know things other people don't know. I know what it's like to be ridiculed for it. I wasn't always a world-famous talk show host, you know. I've had some dark days. There have been whole years I didn't see daylight. I know what blackness looks like inside."

His eyes assessed her face. "So I was right. You're here to save me from myself. I knew it the first time I saw you."

She laughed. "I've never tried to save a human being. I don't know for sure that you need saving. But I know I need your expertise and I'm sorry I doubted you. Will you help me?"

He stood there for so long, not moving or speaking, she didn't know if he was going to agree to help her. Finally, he nodded. "All right. I'll get dressed. But you don't have to clean up while I'm gone. It might not be much of a life, but it's the only one I have. Save me some dignity at least."

"I'll make some coffee."

"I think the pot's over there." He pointed toward a pile of clothes and food containers that seemed to be on a tiny stove. "Coffee is above it in the cabinet."

Mary Catherine didn't move until she heard the water running in the shower. She really hated that she wasn't as drawn to Buck with his big house and fat bank account as she was to Charlie with his messy apartment and obvious issues with society. She'd always made the right choices with the men in her life. They were wealthy and good to her. She loved every one of them and felt they'd enriched her life. She wasn't sure if she could be the guiding light in the darkness for a man like Charlie.

She fed Baxter and made a pot of coffee. She wasn't sure about that either, since she never made coffee at home. She wished there was a coffee shop she could pop out to and come back with a cup, but she did her best with what she had.

Danny called and she assured him and Baylor that everything was all right. She might still be a while so if he had any pressing engagements or wanted to take a fare or two, that would be fine. "With the cat?" Danny asked. "I don't think my fares would like that. When are you coming down?"

"As soon as I can. Charlie is ... sick."

"Okay. I'm supposed to run a package out to the airport. I'll do that and come back for you."

"Thank you. You're the best. Baylor, behave yourself or no extra tuna tonight."

The cat meowed loudly, unhappy with her threat and not afraid to give her one of his own; it was very unpleasant trying to sleep with a cat jumping up on you.

Mary Catherine ignored him and closed her cell phone. She looked in the tiny refrigerator but there was nothing to eat. Charlie looked like he needed food as much as he needed coffee. She finally found a box of Rice-a-Roni in the cabinet and while that wasn't what she had in mind, it was better than nothing. She found a dirty pan and washed it. By the time Charlie emerged from the bathroom, it was nearly cooked.

He sniffed appreciatively. "You found food?"

"I'm pretty good at that." She brushed an angry spider out of a coffee cup she found hanging on the wall. "That and talking to animals. And marrying well. Those seem to be my gifts."

She poured him a cup of coffee and found a plate for the rice. Charlie looked and smelled better as he sat down at the table she'd uncovered. "You know, I wouldn't have taken you for a domestic kind of woman."

"Oh? What kind of woman do you think I am?"

"From your background, I would've thought an opportunist. Self-centered, egotistical."

"I'm glad I don't have to use that personality profile at Match. com. It might make it hard to get a date." She scooped the rice onto the plate and set it down in front of him with a little unnecessary force. *Opportunist indeed!*

He sipped his coffee and made a face. "Who taught you how to make coffee?"

"I'm really a tea maker, along with being self-centered and egotistical," she said. "But I guess you couldn't tell that from my profile."

"Profiles can be wrong." He shrugged. "I'm sorry. Would you rather me be honest or tell you what you want to hear?"

She was tempted to ask for the latter but she knew it wouldn't be true. The conversation was too personal. She needed to get it back on track. "I want to hire you to help me."

"You don't have to. I owe you. Like I said, I think I led this guy to you. I think your cousin is responsible for what happened to you."

"I spoke to his attorney. Why do you think he's responsible for what happened?"

"It all makes sense. I think he was looking for the deed to the property when you caught him there. He was probably the one who called your show and trapped Baylor. I don't know about your car, but that could've been him too."

Mary Catherine explained about capturing the psycho caller at the convenience store. "I suppose my cousin could've hired him. Is there pirate gold hidden in the basement or something? Why would anyone go to those kinds of lengths to get that old building? Obviously he's never paid an electric bill there."

"Some people get a bug about doing things. I think he's angry about not inheriting the building. He wants it. That's enough if you have the right personality."

"But we can't prove any of that." She tapped her fingernail on the tabletop impatiently. "Do you think I'm in danger if I go back?" She told him about Angellus' offer of police protection for the next few days.

"If it helps any, I don't think he set out to kill you or anything. Like any other thief, he reacted badly when you caught him."

"What do you suggest?"

"I think you should call his lawyer and set up an appointment. If he believes you're suddenly willing to negotiate about the building, I think the other stuff will stop. We can meet with him and if he's all scratched up, we'll know he's responsible. Angellus can get his fingerprints and tie him to the break-in."

"Good plan," she complimented. "Any theories on who killed Ferndelle Jamison?"

"Maybe. But they all involve your friend Colin. I know you don't like it, but he looks guilty from where I'm sitting. He had everything to gain from her death. I don't know how much money is involved, but their feud over it has been pretty public."

"What about it being the result of a thief she caught?"

"It's always possible, but most thieves will do what they have to and run away. Whoever did this stuck around and killed her. I think her death was the intent."

"What about the person who called Colin to have him show up at the crime scene and put him in the middle of the investigation?"

"The truth?" He looked at her over the rim of his cup. "I don't think there was a call. Killers like to come back and take a look at what they've done. Firebugs are the same way."

"I can't believe Colin did this. I know everything is against him right now, but there has to be another answer."

Charlie ate the last of his rice. "If there is, we'll find it."

Mary Catherine wasn't sure if he was serious about that commitment until she looked into his eyes. She knew what she saw there. He might be down on his luck right now but he was a man of his word. She knew she could trust him. She should've believed Baylor. "I'll never hear the end of it."

"Excuse me?"

"Baylor told me from the first that I should trust you. I hate when he's right. You have no idea how obnoxious that cat can be when he's right and I'm wrong."

He laughed. "I'll have to remember to thank him. Where is he? Usually he's wherever you are. They had a heck of a time with him in the hospital."

"I made him stay outside with Danny. Neither one of them were too happy about it."

"You seem to attract a devoted following. No wonder you're so popular on the air."

There was a moment or two of awkward silence until her cell phone rang, startling them both. Danny and Baylor were back and threatening to come upstairs. She calmed them down and hung up. "I guess that's my ride."

"I'll set up a meeting with your cousin. His name is Bernard Caldwell, by the way. I'd rather go it alone but I'm afraid at this point we'll need your validation for Angellus to investigate anything we find."

"I'd rather be there and face Cousin Bernard anyway. I might bring Baylor along. He'd like a chance to get even with the person who tried to trap him."

"That could work." He smiled at her. "Thanks for coming up. I'll let you know when I've talked to him and his lawyer."

Mary Catherine knew she was weak when she looked at him, freshly shaved and smelling of soap and aftershave. Her knees quivered. She didn't know why she was so attracted to him. Maybe this was the bad-boy stage of her life.

"Thanks." She leaned forward and touched her lips to his. "Never mind the dark parts, Charlie. I think we could find some light together."

"I should warn you I'm not any good at relationships." He pulled her closer.

"At least your past efforts are probably still alive," she whispered in a husky voice. "I can't promise you won't die in some horrible accident if you're with me too long."

"Not a problem. My longest try so far has been about two weeks. Maybe I can stay alive that long."

Mary Catherine put her arms around him and welcomed his kiss. There would be nothing else between them then, at least. She was past the kind of passion that could ignore old Chinese food on the table. She had a perfectly good, reasonably clean apartment that would be much better. But that would be later.

"You're unbelievable, Ms. Pet Psychic." He opened his eyes as they parted and smiled at her. "Can you read my mind?"

"Yes I can, Mr. PI. And it's not gonna happen." She winked at him. "At least not right now."

She left him there, finding Baylor and Danny on the front steps of the building as they tried to figure out a way in.

"What took you so long?" Danny asked when he saw her.

Baylor didn't need to ask. He meowed at her, then ran back to the taxi. The cat told her he advocated trusting the man, not mating with him. She hushed him and lied to Danny about what had happened upstairs.

"And what happens now?" Danny opened the taxi door for her.

"Right now, we go home, take a nap, and wait for Charlie's call. I think you should work for a while. I don't want to be the cause of you getting in trouble."

"Okay. But you'll call me before this meeting, right? I don't want you going with this guy alone."

"I will if there's time. And Baylor has said all along that we should trust Charlie. I think we should take his advice."

———

Jenny and Buck were cozy in the back of the clinic when Mary Catherine stepped out of the foyer. Fred the toucan was graphic about what had been going on between the couple while she'd been gone. Waldo the goat didn't care about the couple; he just wanted to go outside.

"There you are." Jenny looked up, an attractive pink blush settling over her features. Her hair, usually drawn tightly back from her face, was a loose cloud of curls. She almost looked pretty. "I was wondering when you'd drag in."

Mary Catherine considered it might take more time with Buck to change Jenny's attitude. Then again, love could only do so much. She told them about her meeting with Charlie and the possibility of trapping the person responsible for what had been happening at the clinic. "If Charlie's right, we might have our thief and saboteur."

"That sounds good." Buck actually seemed nervous. "We've been working on the new Meaty Boy formula. Jenny's a whiz at this stuff.

She's going to be the Meaty Boy spokesperson once we finish. Imagine that!"

Bruno was barking from the back of the clinic. He was impatient to start his new life with the adoptive family who were picking him up today. He told Mary Catherine he'd miss her, but was anxious to be with children again. He'd stay if she asked him, but he hoped she wouldn't mind if he left.

She assured him he could visit and that she was happy he'd be with a family again. She didn't tell him she wouldn't miss his food bill. They might only be able to rescue small dogs for a while until they started receiving some larger donations for the clinic.

"Taste this." Jenny held out a morsel of dry dog food. "Too salty?"

"That's your job," Mary Catherine told her. "I'm sure you and Buck would rather feed each other dog food. Thanks anyway."

Jenny followed her back out into the foyer. "What's wrong with you? Are you mad because I took Buck away from you?"

"Took him away? Are you serious? I was hoping not to have to hurt his feelings."

"Whatever. You wanted him. I understand that. He wants me. I hope this won't affect our working relationship."

"Believe me, I *never* wanted him. You're welcome to him." Mary Catherine started up the stairs with Baylor at her heels.

"You're setting your cap for that private detective, aren't you?"

"If you're talking about Charlie, I guess you could say there's something between us."

Jenny laughed. "Bad choice, Mary Catherine. Buck is a much better catch."

"If you say so. I'm going up to take a nap. I hope you two can taste test Meaty Boy quietly down here."

Her apartment was in such a mess, she felt guilty calling Charlie's place bad. Of course, this wasn't her fault. Between getting hit in the head and the police looking though everything, there wasn't much left where it belonged. She sat down heavily on her red velvet sofa and called her housekeeper, who wasn't due for two more days. She convinced her to come early with the offer of a bonus.

"Well, that's done." She yawned and looked at Baylor who'd already settled down between the velvet and the chenille throw. "I need to feed Tommy."

She took out the turtle food and looked for the bowl on the kitchen table. It was gone. She tried to contact the turtle. There was no answer. She finally found the bowl on the floor but Tommy wasn't in it.

She looked around the room as much as she could with its war scene devastation. She couldn't find him anywhere. "I guess I'll put the food on the floor over here, Tommy. If you get hungry, I know you'll find it." She put a big platter with some water on it beside the food in case he started feeling too dry. She supposed she shouldn't be surprised that his bowl was overturned with everything that had happened.

Before she could get comfortable on the sofa (she wasn't going in her room again just yet) the phone rang. Charlie had already set up an appointment to meet with her cousin. "Can you be ready to go in twenty minutes? I'll swing by and pick you up."

She wanted to get this over with. She knew she needed to examine Cousin Bernard for Baylor's scratches as soon as possible. On the other hand, she really needed a nap and something to eat.

Putting an end to what was wrong in her life won out and she told him she'd be ready. There was bound to be a blueberry muffin left and she could eat lunch later.

Mary Catherine put on a flowing pink caftan and matching sandals. She was careful with her makeup, mindful of the marks on her face. The large gouge in her forehead she left under a bandage. It was too terrible looking to show the world.

If she was right and her cousin was responsible for her pain and possibly permanent disfiguration, the man deserved to see the worst. She wasn't happy going out like that, especially with the new understanding between her and Charlie. She smiled at herself in the mirror. "I guess you've still got it."

Baylor had something to say about that. His comment wasn't something she cared to dwell on. Naturally he was jealous. He'd been the only important male in her life for two years. He'd get over it. No matter how close she and Charlie became, they'd never have the bond she shared with Baylor.

The cat jumped up on the sink, rubbed up against her and meowed. She kissed his nose. "You have nothing to fear there. You and I are together forever."

Finally dressed, Mary Catherine waited outside for Charlie. He was right on time and helped her into the truck. "You look great," he said. "Are you ready for this?"

"Yes. You notice I left Baylor here. I don't want him howling and screeching like a mad thing. I don't know how he'll react when he sees my cousin."

Charlie agreed with her assessment. "I called Angellus to let him know what we're doing. He can't exactly offer backup, but he promised to be close by in case we need him. I've got him on speed dial."

They drove up Chestnut Street past the New Hanover Public Library. Her cousin lived on Third Street, about two miles from Thalian Hall. Mary Catherine and Charlie talked about visiting the hall, which was a favorite place for musical productions and other community events.

"It's haunted, you know." Mary Catherine recounted a visit with a medium who'd pointed out all the cold spots; places where ghosts walked.

Charlie laughed. "Finding things is about all the paranormal activity I can handle in one lifetime." He reached for her hand. "Or at least I thought it was until I met you."

She had goose bumps from the encounter and spent the rest of the trip thinking about the two of them together. Charlie wasn't as rich or successful as her other four husbands had been and she might not even marry him. But he was interesting and he made her feel alive again in a way she hadn't for years.

Bernard Caldwell lived in an old, gray stone two-story that had towering fir trees in front of it. Charlie parked on the street, squeezed her hand, and they walked up the sidewalk to the house.

After Charlie rang the doorbell, Mary Catherine almost walked away. She didn't know if she wanted to confront this man. She wished she'd brought her little pearl-handled revolver. Maybe then she'd feel safe. That might've ensured he would never hurt her or Baylor again.

The door opened and she was surprised to see her handyman, Bernie, who'd been working on the building. "*You!*"

"I can explain, Mary Catherine," he said. "Please come in."

He walked ahead of them and Charlie whispered to her, "No scratches."

"Maybe." She followed her cousin into an elegant sitting room. "We'll see."

Hello Mary Catherine!

You probably don't remember me, but we met in San Francisco years ago. I've called your show a few times. You always have good advice. I've talked to you before about my goldfish, Fergie. He's doing much better now with his new tank. We both wanted to say thanks and wish you a great day.

TWENTY

"You see, I've been more concerned with the structure of the building," Cousin Bernie said. "I knew it was in disrepair when my mother was alive."

"Why didn't you just say so?" Mary Catherine demanded. "Why all the sneaking around? And you had your lawyer offer to buy it!"

"I won't lie to you. I was hurt that she left the building to you. It's not a terribly valuable piece of property. The city will never allow much commercial building down there on the river. But she hadn't seen you in years. I didn't even know you existed. I'm sorry I didn't simply come by and introduce myself. It would've made things much easier."

"But you weren't in my bedroom rummaging through my things looking for the deed to the property?" she asked him.

"No, my dear." He laughed. "I could've, I suppose. But I had no need. I know that building inside and out. I wanted to have a look and see what was going on there and what kind of shape it was in.

I think the structure's sound. I'd like to have it checked out by a building expert."

Mary Catherine wasn't sure what to say. She'd been so sure this was the answer, only to have it turn around on her like a pleasant, well-meaning snake. A thought struck her. Baylor would never forgive her if she didn't check every contingency. "Would you mind if I look at your arms?"

Charlie and Cousin Bernie both stared at her. "What's up?" Charlie asked.

"It's a simple request," she continued, ignoring him. *Please don't let him be involved in this.* "May I look at your arms?"

"I suppose so." Cousin Bernie shrugged and looked at Charlie again.

She got up from her sunny window seat and approached her cousin. She had to know if Cousin Bernie's arms were scratched. He was wearing a long sleeve shirt so there was no way to tell unless he rolled up his sleeves. She hoped she wasn't right. If her cousin was concealing the scratches, he might get unexpectedly violent again. Charlie was right behind her if she needed help. She had to be brave enough to know the truth.

She stood close to him and reached out her free hand to slide up the sleeve on his blue knit shirt. There were no bandages and no sign of scratches.

"Mary Catherine?" Charlie asked. "What are you doing?"

She moved the sleeve all the way up Cousin Bernie's arm. Baylor would never forgive her if she wasn't thorough. There was still nothing. She did the same thing to the opposite arm. Still nothing.

If Baylor was right and he'd scratched her attacker's arms enough to generate all the blood they found on him, there would have to be some sign of it on Cousin Bernie. Or he wasn't the person in her apartment.

A long-haired calico cat scooted into the room, skidding to a stop behind the baby grand piano in the corner. She looked out from one leg of the piano and stared at her.

"Hello!" Mary Catherine turned her attention from the man to the cat. Obviously she was wrong about her cousin. Someone else had been in her apartment.

She walked over and scratched the cat behind the ears. The animal purred and immediately began telling her everything she knew about what went on in the house, at least from her point of view. It was a well-run house except for the occasional mix-up in her food. The cat adored the man who frequently gave her tuna and she allowed him to share her bed every night.

"Well there's no arguing with that." She turned away from the young cat and smiled at her cousin. "I'm sorry. I was wrong about you."

"That's really amazing!" Cousin Bernie said. "Suzy doesn't let anyone pet her except me."

Charlie laughed. "Didn't I tell you? She talks to animals. I thought it might run in the family."

Cousin Bernie furrowed his eyebrows. "What do you mean she talks to animals?"

"I mean she talks to animals. They understand her. She has a radio show. I'm sure this was all in my report."

Mary Catherine turned to him. "You did a report on me?"

"It was before we met. I didn't know you then. I haven't filed another report since then. Ask him."

Cousin Bernie nodded. "He's been lax in that regard. I thought he was slack. I guess he was smitten instead."

"I know it's hard to understand," Mary Catherine began. "I haven't known many people who could believe it without proof. I can ask Suzy something only you'd know, if you like. I'm not crazy about parlor tricks, but I'll do them when necessary."

"Please." Her cousin waved his hand. "There's no need. My mother had the same ability. She could communicate with all kinds of animals from cats to lizards. Everyone knew about her. She wasn't on the radio but she was well known in Wilmington. I think if you take a look in the archives of the Wilmington Star, you'll find an article about her."

Mary Catherine sat down abruptly in an upholstered chair. "But my mother wasn't that way. I remember trying to talk to her about it. She acted like she thought I was crazy."

"I'm afraid I can't have my mother do parlor tricks to prove it." Cousin Bernie smiled. "But I grew up knowing it was true. Maybe that was what caused the feud between our families. And possibly why my mother left you that building."

"I don't believe it." Mary Catherine got to her feet and paced the floor. "All these years. I could've spoken with her. We had so much in common. Somehow the gift missed my mother and came to me. This is wonderful!"

"I'm glad we had the opportunity to talk. And I'm sorry I approached this in such a bad way. I didn't know what you were like." Her cousin got to his feet. "I hope you'll consider me your family. I think the two of us are all we have left. Maybe we can have dinner together and look at family pictures."

She hugged him, crying. "Of course! That would be incredible! I never expected to find family here. Thank you."

"Nothing to thank me for." He hugged her back awkwardly. "I hope you'll consider my home as yours for as long as you live here. Suzy already loves you."

The little cat was nuzzling her ankle as the two cousins hugged. Not as mindful as she probably should've been about her make-up, Mary Catherine wiped the tears from her face and reached down to pet Suzy.

"This is great." Charlie interrupted the family reunion. "But it leaves us out in the cold as far as knowing what's going on."

"Why don't you start at the beginning, as you would have if you'd been sending me those reports I paid for," Cousin Bernie said. "Maybe I can help."

Over sweet tea and cheese biscuits (Mary Catherine was thrilled to find out there was food) they explained everything that had happened at the house and clinic. "I'm afraid Charlie's right," she mourned. "You were our only suspect."

"What about this other event you were involved with?" he asked, giving Mary Catherine the last cheese biscuit. "Could that have these repercussions?"

As though on cue, the front door burst open. Angellus came through the doorway, weapon drawn, looking for trouble. "Is everything all right?"

"It's fine." Mary Catherine paused with the cheese biscuit half-way to her mouth.

"You were supposed to call me," Angellus growled as he put away his gun.

"Sorry." Charlie shrugged. "I forgot."

"So no attacker here?" Angellus looked at the cousin.

"I'm sorry." She introduced the detective to Cousin Bernie. "Thank you for checking on us. Everything seems to be under control."

"Except we lost our suspect," Charlie reminded her. "We're back to square one."

Her cell phone rang. It was Colin. "You have to come over here right away," he said. "Something terrible has happened."

He babbled for a few more minutes but she couldn't understand what he was talking about. When he finally paused for breath she asked, "Where are you?"

"I'm at Aunt Ferndelle's house. Come as fast as you can."

She closed her cell phone and smiled at the three men. "I'd like to stay but there seems to be another crisis in Colin's life." She went on to explain to her cousin who Colin was. "Here's my phone number," she told him with a last hug. "Let's be sure to keep in touch."

"Here's my phone number." He handed her a business card. "I plan to see you soon for that dinner. It was wonderful finally meeting you as myself."

"No more skulking around," she warned with a laugh. "If I need someone to work on the building, I'll hire someone."

Mary Catherine walked outside with Charlie and Angellus. She was amazed and grateful things had turned out so well.

Angellus walked toward his car, a plain, gray Chevy. "Sorry to break up the party but I was afraid you two were in over your heads when I didn't hear from Charlie."

"That's fine." She smiled. "Thanks for checking on us. I hope Bo-Bo is doing well."

He looked uncomfortable. He would never be *comfortable* with what happened that night. "Yeah, well, he's okay, I guess. Any more potentially lethal meetings you have planned?"

"Not unless you call Colin's weekly meltdown potentially lethal." Mary Catherine opened the passenger side Suburban door. "But I'll be sure to call you if something comes up."

Charlie helped her into the truck as his cell phone rang. "Damn. I forgot all about that. I hate to ask, but could I drop you off and swing back by after this appointment? I think I have a new client."

"Don't worry about it," she assured him. "I'll have Colin run me back home."

"I don't mind coming back."

"It's not a big deal. You can swing by the clinic later, if you have time."

"Okay. Thanks."

They talked about what had happened with her cousin and agreed he was a strange man to approach the problem as he did. "But strange sounds like it runs in my family. I'm really glad he told me about my aunt. I'll have to look up that article. I wish my mother would've been that way."

Ferndelle Jamison's home (soon to be Colin's home, Mary Catherine imagined) was only a short drive away. Charlie pulled the truck into the driveway just as Mindy was getting out of her car. "Looks like you have company," he said.

"It must be a *major* meltdown. Thanks for the lift."

He surprised her by leaning closer and kissing her lightly. "I'll see you later."

She slid down out of the truck, but her feet never touched the ground. She loved being in love. There was nothing else like it, despite what Baylor would have to say on the subject. "I see he called you too," she said to Mindy as Charlie left.

"Yeah. I had to find someone to cover for me at the station. I hope it's nothing serious. Colin sounded frantic on the phone. He was supposed to meet with his lawyer about finally inheriting the estate."

"But when doesn't Colin sound frantic?" Mary Catherine asked as they approached the house. She recalled her initial feelings about the mellow old manor and how wrong they'd been. It hadn't proven to be a safe haven for Ferndelle or Tommy. She hoped it would be better for Mindy and Colin.

She noticed her producer was wearing a long-sleeved green sweater. It was a sultry, 95-degree day. She'd never known Mindy to be cold natured. The question she and Charlie had been asking for the past week took center stage in her mind: *Who stands to benefit from Ferndelle's death?*

It suddenly occurred to Mary Catherine that Mindy stood to gain from Ferndelle's death as well as Colin's going to prison. Colin thought Mindy hadn't known he was fooling around with Charlene. *But what if she had?* What if all of this was payback for Colin's indiscretion?

"You must be roasting out here in that sweater," Mary Catherine commented, thinking about everything that had happened. *Was it possible Mindy could be responsible for all of it?* It was hard to look at her sweet face and imagine her cutting Ferndelle's throat. Surely she was overly suspicious. What difference did it make that Mindy was wearing a sweater?

"I was chilly in the office." Mindy played with the end of her sleeve. "You know they keep the air conditioning turned down really low all the time. I'm always a little cold."

Mary Catherine's eyes almost popped out of her head. Not only was Mindy wearing a sweater, there was a hint of white that looked like a bandage on her arm and a few scratches on her hands. *Why didn't I notice those scratches before?*

It was too terrible to contemplate, but all the pieces were starting to fall in place as Mary Catherine looked at Mindy. She wanted to turn away and pretend it wasn't happening but she couldn't. With a determined grasp on Mindy's wrist, she pulled back the sweater sleeve and exposed heavy bandaging on the younger woman's arm.

"What are you doing?" Mindy jerked her arm back. "Leave me alone."

"I can't believe it." Mary Catherine shook her head and stared at the bandages that covered Baylor's heroic efforts to save her. "You hit me with a chair. Did you kill Ferndelle too?"

Mindy pulled a small gun from her pocket and pointed it at Mary Catherine. "Shut up. Get in the house. You couldn't stay out of it, could you?"

Colin opened the door to the garage, not knowing what had happened between the two women. "We can't go in the house. The police still have that blocked off."

"What are you doing here then?" Mary Catherine tried to point to the gun Mindy was holding in her back. She had no illusions that the girl she thought she knew so well wouldn't pull the trigger. The image of Ferndelle lying in her own blood came to haunt her.

"I was just looking around. I guess dreaming about finally living in the family estate." He looked terrible; his hair spiked up on his head from constant frantic hand motions through it. His eyes had dark circles and he was paler than usual. "Something terrible has happened." He grabbed Mindy's free hand, still apparently not noticing the gun in her other hand. "Thank God you're here."

"What is it?" Mindy took his hand, pressing harder with the gun into Mary Catherine's back. "Breathe, Colin. Remember we talked about you forgetting to breathe when you get upset. You don't want to have a heart attack and die."

He kissed her. "You're so wonderful. I feel so bad about this."

Mary Catherine had enough of the drama. If Colin was too dense to notice that his wife was going to shoot her, she'd better point it out to him. "If you're not going to tell us what's wrong, I'm going home."

"Okay." He took a deep breath. "I talked to my lawyer. Aunt Ferndelle left everything—the house, the money, *everything*, to her favorite charity, the DAR."

Mindy let go of Colin's hand. The gun against Mary Catherine's back pushed harder. "*What? Is that legal?* Can we fight it?"

"I asked my lawyer that question. He said we could fight it, but Aunt Ferndelle's lawyer is tops in the state when it comes to wills. I'm sure she went there because she knew I'd try to contest it."

"You mean there's no money?" Mindy's voice was breathless.

Mary Catherine stepped away as she felt the gun drop from her back. She wished again that she'd brought her revolver to turn the tide at that moment. She looked around for a weapon of some sort, but without lifting a lawnmower or the car, the garage was clean.

Colin took Mindy's hand again. "It'll be okay. I still have my trust fund and a couple of properties. We both have good jobs. Everything will work out."

Mindy snatched her hand back with a look of pure hatred on her pretty face. She brought the gun to bear on Colin. "I can't believe this! After all this time. After all I've done. Two years of my life setting all this up. Spending time with *you*."

"What are you saying?" Colin looked even more pathetic.

"I'm saying I killed your stupid aunt for *nothing!*" Mindy began to pace back and forth, smoothing one hand across her hair. "But we're married. That has to count for something. I could still fight the will."

Mary Catherine edged to the side of the wall while Mindy confronted Colin. There was a broken rake leaning there. As weapons went, it was pitiful, but it was better than nothing. She kept backing closer, hoping Mindy wouldn't notice her movements.

"What are you saying?" Colin asked. "You killed Aunt Ferndelle?"

"You would too if some old lady was standing between you and ten million dollars. I killed her; that was always part of the plan after your parents died. I made it look like *you* did it after I found out you were cheating on me."

"Honey bee? What are you saying? The shock has affected you. You didn't even *know* I was cheating on you until right before we got married."

"I'm not a stupid moron like you." She noticed Mary Catherine's movements and waved the gun in her general direction. "Don't try to be clever. Both of you sit down over there until I have a chance to think about this."

"I can see why you'd want to kill Colin," Mary Catherine acknowledged, "but why me? And why break into my apartment? I don't understand how the two things go together."

"Not that I need to enlighten you," Mindy taunted. "But you almost screwed up everything talking to that slimy turtle. Good thing I got him out of there before he could say anything else. I mean, what are the chances that someone who talks to animals would find Ferndelle's body and talk to her turtle? Colin was supposed to find her. And I wish I'd killed your stupid cat the first night I had him."

"I hardly think that's a good reason to kill me," Mary Catherine objected.

"Shut up and sit down. I have to think."

Mary Catherine sat on the side of the covered riding lawn mower. Colin sat on the concrete floor beside her. Mindy paced the garage with short, frantic steps. Colin tried to speak twice and she leveled the gun at him. He subsided and watched her.

"This can still be made right," Mindy told them. "After all, I'm your wife. Even when you die, I inherit. I can fight the will. The police investigating the incidents at the clinic can blame Mary Catherine's death on something to do with that. It's a good thing I thought of those things as diversions. The police will be totally confused by all of it."

"You mean you're the one who paid the psycho caller?" Colin couldn't believe it. "This can't be you. You need help. Don't worry; I'll be here for you."

She advanced on him until the gun was at his head. "You mean the way you stood by me with Charlene? Don't say anything else."

She continued to pace until she finally stopped short in front of them. "That's it. We'll take a little drive down to Fort Fisher. I'll wait for the tide to come in and roll the car into the water. Even if they find your bodies, it'll be too late."

"I'm not comfortable with water, Mindy, you know that." Colin got to his feet.

"That's not a problem, *honey bee*, since you'll have a bullet in your head and you won't care about the water." She waved the gun at them. "Now both of you, out in front of me. Colin, open the garage door."

Mary Catherine needed a diversion. She knew they wouldn't have any hope of surviving if Mindy herded them into the van Colin had brought from the radio station. She'd lost her opportunity to use the broken rake on Mindy while she was arguing with Colin. She needed to distract Mindy long enough for one of them to try and disarm her. She hoped that person would be Colin so she could speed-dial 911, but she wouldn't bet any money on it.

There was some skittering across the roof of the garage. Squirrels, no doubt. They were busy finding the giant acorns that grew on the old oak trees that surrounded the house.

Squirrels were sometimes difficult to talk to. They'd been around man long enough to understand many things, but they were like directing two-year-olds. She concentrated on communicating with them. There might be something they could do to make Mindy look away long enough for Mary Catherine to go back in the garage and grab the broken rake.

She wasn't sure what she was going to do after that. She supposed she could hit Mindy in the head with it and hope she went down long enough to get the gun away from her. Somehow she had to get Colin in on the plot. That was even more unpredictable than talking to the squirrels.

But love could make a woman desperate enough to try anything. She hadn't had the opportunity to spend time with Charlie yet. She wasn't ready to die.

Colin opened the garage door and walked outside with Mary Catherine behind him and Mindy (with the gun) behind her. As soon as Colin's head appeared, the squirrels in the trees and on the roof of the garage started pelting them with acorns.

Mary Catherine shielded her head from the barrage and nudged Colin to the left as the hailstorm of acorns continued, smashing into Mindy as well as them. Mindy put up both hands to protect her face. "Is this your doing?" she demanded, turning on Mary Catherine.

Mary Catherine tried to protect herself from the painful acorn attack. She didn't realize there were so many squirrels and thousands of acorns. She was going to be black and blue in spots she'd missed, but she wasn't going to be able to go back into the garage with Mindy threatening her with the gun.

With a strange cry, Colin suddenly lunged against Mindy, pushing her to the concrete drive and wrestling with her for the gun. Mary Catherine ran back into the garage and brought the broken rake into the fray. The acorns continued to plummet like painful little meteors, slamming into them.

She wanted to hit Mindy with the rake, but there was no way to use it with Colin fighting with her. The couple was rolling over and over through plant bits and dirt left from the last storm that had hit the coast. Every time she saw Mindy's head on top, Mary Catherine lifted the rake to hit her only to find Colin's head instead.

Mindy and Colin rolled off the concrete and into the side of an oak tree. Mindy's gun went off harmlessly into the tree and Colin was able to jerk it away from her. He sat on top of her, pinning her to the ground, while Mary Catherine tried to get the squirrels to stop throwing acorns.

"You know, we can't go on after this," Colin breathlessly told his wife. "I'm afraid I'll have to ask you for a divorce, sweet feet."

EPILOGUE

On the morning of Mindy Evans-Jamison's first court appearance, the *Wilmington Star* carried an account of what had led to her arrest at Ferndelle's home. Mary Catherine read it while volunteers assembled to help paint and remodel the clinic.

Her cousin had donated some money and convinced his banker friends to help out as well. Buck brought a legion of Meaty Boy employees, complete with paint brushes, to speed up the work so he and Jenny could go out for dinner that night. The couple had become very close in the past few weeks.

"You think they ever got the squirrels to stop throwing acorns?" Charlie asked, reading the paper over Mary Catherine's shoulder.

"It says here the police officers who responded were mystified by the squirrels' actions. They called animal control, but the squirrels left when the van showed up." She smiled at him. *They* had become closer the last few weeks as well. "They're capricious little animals but they did a good job if you don't count the bumps and bruises I had."

"But they saved our lives," Colin added, his white overalls without a spot of color on them, despite the fact that he'd been painting. "I can't believe Mindy set everything up with me after my parents' died just to get the money." He sighed. "Oh well. Charlene called me last night. She's leaving her husband. I guess life goes on."

"What about Tommy?" Danny asked. "How's he doing?"

"He's fine," Mary Catherine said. "Despite Mindy killing humans, I guess she couldn't find it in her heart to kill that poor little creature. Charlie and I took him out to the swamp with Cheetos yesterday. He was still wild enough to survive. I hope he can get over everything that's happened to him."

"Quiet everyone!" Buck yelled out. "Here's the new Meaty Boy commercial."

Everyone paused to watch Jenny talk about Meaty Boy's new formula. Mary Catherine was impressed. "You looked great," she told the vet when it was over.

"As compared to what?" Jenny retorted. "I'm *never* doing anything like that again."

Buck hugged her. "Aw, come on, darlin'. You were fabulous! Now everyone will want to eat the new and improved Meaty Boy dog food we created."

Baylor meowed, a big swath of dark blue paint on his back that refused to come off, no matter how much he licked it. He told Mary Catherine he was glad he wasn't a dog.

"I think Buck mentioned something about creating Meaty Boy *cat* food," she told him.

Baylor hissed and ran upstairs.

MARY CATHERINE'S ANIMAL NEWS

I'M HAPPY TO BE here with news from the world of animals! For thousands of years, we've heard stories about smart animals—animals that can predict earthquakes or manage to communicate a threat to their owners and save their lives. Many people pretend the stories aren't true, but animal lovers know that pets can be amazing!

Animals are really much smarter than people think and here are some real-life stories to prove it:

- Kwanza is a male ape. His trainer, Dr. Sue Limbroke, says he is able to understand more than 3,000 words and a few simple sentences. Limbroke says he can even combine words to create some simple sentences of his own making.
- Tiki is a border collie being studied by Professor Anna Marsh, an animal behavior expert. Marsh says Tiki can bark and growl

his recognition of more than three hundred toys. He can also understand a telephone conversation and act on it. Scientists are currently working to understand how animals can understand human language but are not able to use it.

- An African parrot named Causa has a vocabulary of more than a thousand words. She uses the words in conversation with her trainer, Larry Rice. Causa is able to express her feelings by using the words Rice has taught her. She can recognize photographs and relate their content to Rice.

- A cat named Oscar saved the life of a man in Toronto by dialing 911 on the phone to summon police officers. The cat's owner said he had worked to teach the cat how to summon help because of his serious health problems. The owner was found in time when help was summoned and he was taken to the hospital. Of course, Oscar was cared for by friends and returned to his grateful owner.

- In 1964, a young boy was found surviving with wolves outside a small village in Tibet. According to newspaper reports, when he was taken back to civilization the wolves attacked to protect him. They were all killed. After years of learning to speak, the boy described hunting with the wolves, running on all fours, and eating raw meat. He said the wolves cared for him like their own pups. He couldn't recall his human parents.

- Goldfish enjoy music as much as people do, according to a new study in animal behavior. Scientists say that fish think and have definite tastes in music that they remember from one session to another. The study took place over a period of three years. Scientists played many different types of music for the fish. Each fish had its own preference between opera and bluegrass.

- Researchers say the blind mole rat uses crystals in its brain to orient itself on long journeys. They have discovered that mole rats always check where they are in relation to the Earth's magnetic field so they can tell which way they're going. The researchers say there are magnetic crystals in the moles' brains that line up with the Earth's magnetic field, acting like an internal compass.

- Cheeto, the hamster, has been trained to roll over and play dead, do back flips, and come when called. His owner, Danny Robinson, has been working with Cheeto for more than two years. The hamster can also dance to music and prefers carrots to hamster food.

Live animal cams are a great way to see what's really going on in the animal world. Check out these live websites:

www.hamsterific.com/CHEEZ.cfm
www.appaloosa.org/livefoal.html
www.kittycam.net/
http://topsail-island.info/wordpress/index.php/turtle-hospital/

MARY CATHERINE'S SECRET RECIPES FOR ANIMALS

BRUNO'S FAVORITE ICE CREAM TREAT

(for those dog days of summer)

32 oz. plain yogurt

1 banana, mashed

2 Tbsp. peanut butter

2 Tbsp. honey

Blend everything together until smooth. Freeze in ice cube trays. Microwave for a few seconds before serving.

BAYLOR'S EASY CAT TREATS

1 c. soy flour
1 c. wheat flour
1 tsp. catnip (optional)
⅓ c. lowfat milk
2 Tbsp. wheat germ
1 Tbsp. molasses
1 egg
2 Tbsp. butter or vegetable oil
⅓ c. powdered milk

Mix dry ingredients together, then add molasses, egg, oil, and milk.

Roll out flat and cut into small, bite-sized pieces. Place on greased cookie sheet and bake for 20 minutes in 350-degree oven. Let cool and store in tightly sealed container.

———

Don't forget to talk to your pets and listen for their responses.

Just because an animal doesn't speak our language doesn't mean it doesn't understand. There are many things we don't understand about animals, but we know they can be loving, compassionate, and caring.

Until next time,
Mary Catherine

If you enjoyed reading *The Telltale Turtle* by Joyce and Jim Lavene, read on for an excerpt from J. B. Stanley's

Chili Con Corpses

available from Midnight Ink

ONE

TURKEY BACON RANCH WRAP

Sodium
per
Serving:

2024 mg

"I'M SICK TO DEATH of being on a diet," Bennett complained as he curled two free weights up and down from his waist to his collarbone.

James heartily agreed. The lunch he had eaten composed of a turkey bacon wrap with lettuce, tomato, and fat-free ranch dressing, served on a whole-wheat tortilla seemed like a faint, unsatisfying memory.

"I know what you mean." James pushed himself backward on the leg press machine, his thighs and buttocks burning as he moved the grudging stack of weights into the air. "Thinking about the nutritional content of every item I put in my Food Lion shopping cart is killing me. And I used to really enjoy going to the grocery store."

As James got up from the leg press and selected a pair of twenty-five-pound free weights, Murphy Alistair, the editor and foremost reporter of *The Shenandoah Star Ledger*, entered the cardio/weight-training room. Even though this was the only YMCA within a hundred-mile radius, and was therefore always busy, Murphy was hard to miss. She was wearing black nylon sweats, a form-fitting yellow tank top, and a yellow headband. Waving hello to James in the mirror, she stepped onto a treadmill and began to jog. Murphy's chin-length brown hair, streaked with golden highlights, flapped up and down on the sides of her head like bird wings as she moved. She looked completely at ease as she ran, her hazel eyes glued to the early news program playing on the wall-mounted TV, a towel draped casually round her neck.

"Spot me while I bench, will you?" Bennett asked James a few minutes later while preparing to lift a heavy dumbbell above his torso.

James examined the size of the circular weights attached to each end of the bar over his friend's chest. "Two hundred pounds, huh?"

Bennett scowled. "Hey, man. I'm gonna do more than one set."

"No, I'm impressed. That's quite a load you're lifting," James quickly soothed his friend, noting how muscular Bennett's arms and legs had become over the past several months. "You meant it when you said you'd be spending the summer getting buff. Well, now you're buff."

"Thanks, but I'm still the short mailman with the big gut." Bennett took a deep breath and removed the weights from the stand. "*You're* the guy who needed all new belts and pants."

James stole a glance at himself in the wall-length mirror. It was true. After pursuing a low-carb diet with his supper club friends and then counting points and pursuing a regular exercise routine, James had lost over thirty pounds of unwanted flab and several inches from his doughy waist. Even his second chin, which had once given him a rather bullfrogish profile, was nearly gone. He still had slightly floppy jowls and was a long way from resembling the fit and toned specimens that paraded around the cardio room in tight biker shorts and T-shirts advertising the previous marathon they had run.

"Okay, James." Bennett lifted the barbell so that James could settle them gently back onto the stand straddling the padded bench. "Let me just catch my breath before the next set." Bennett closed his eyes and focused on his breathing. While he waited, James watched Murphy's trim figure as she ran with a seemingly effortless stride and the black rubber of the treadmill moved beneath her feet like a fast-flowing stream. As he stared, Murphy's attention was drawn to the reflection of two blonde-haired women entering the cardio room. Her face broke into a smile and she waved at the pair vigorously.

James did his best not to drool, nudge Bennett in the side, or blatantly ogle every square inch of the newcomers. He believed the women must be visitors because he would have certainly noticed the gorgeous blondes if they lived within the county, which was located in a rather isolated area of Virginia's Blue Ridge Mountains. His town, Quincy's Gap, did not have a shopping mall, trendy restaurants, or boutiques selling the latest in haute couture, but today, apparently, two movie stars were present in the middle of Shenandoah County. After all, James reasoned to himself, no one else but a starlet could have such shiny blonde hair, flawless skin, enormous blue eyes, and a body with more curves than a road on Skyline Drive. And what's more, there were two of them. Twins, it looked like!

The young women moved with languid grace as they crossed the room, seemingly unaware that all of the men had ceased their activities and stood like mute statues in front of weight machines, ellipticals, or stair climbers.

A squeaking noise below James's chest distracted him from the sight of the beautiful women. Bennett, who was slowly suffocating beneath the weight of the barbell resting on his chest, was desperately trying to get his friend's attention.

"Oh, sorry!" James grabbed the barbell and struggled to return it to its metal holder.

Bennett took in a great breath and then, his lungs recovered, hollered, "What kind of spotting is that? You almost killed me, man!" Bennett sat up, rubbing his sore pectorals. "Do I have to send you to Gillian for some of her hocus-pocus herbal remedies to improve your attention span? Jeez!"

"Hey, you can't blame me," James mumbled, poking Bennett and pointing in the mirror so that he'd see the two blondes who were standing next to Murphy's treadmill, beaming at her with two sets of blinding white teeth.

"Damn." Bennett stopped rubbing his chest. "Those girls are *not* from around here. You think Murphy's doing some kind of Miss America story or something?"

"Twins in the same pageant? Doubtful."

"They could be from two different states," Bennett argued. "The one on the left could be Miss Virginia and her sister could be Miss West Virginia."

"That's pretty unlikely, Bennett." James observed the women more closely for clues as to who they were. "Look, the one on the right is wearing shorts with the Blue Ridge High Red-Tailed Hawks logo."

Bennett cleared his throat as he gawked. "Those shorts never fit any high school girl like that! They're tight as a wetsuit. That sweet thang must have dug that pair out of the lost and found at the elementary school."

James laughed. "They're a bit snug, that's for sure."

"And those two are almost as dark as me," Bennett continued his appraisal. "Where'd they get color like that?"

"Probably from tanning."

"In the dead of fall?" Bennett asked in disbelief.

"Yep. There are salons where you can go just to get a tan." James smiled at his friend. "Some people spend their hard-earned money to look like they've been to the beach when really they've been sitting inside a claustrophobic capsule, frying beneath light bulbs supposedly free from ultraviolet rays, while they wear purple goggles and listen to relaxing music."

"Sounds like sitting in a coffin while your own cremation's going on." Bennett gave James a strange look. "And exactly *why* do you know so much about this tanning nonsense?"

"I'm a librarian, remember?" James said as they headed over to the water fountain. "I read lots of magazines. In this month's issue of *Time*, there was an article about 'tanorexia.' Fascinating stuff."

"Tan-a-what?"

"It's a new addiction, like alcoholism or being addicted to drugs, shopping, coffee…"

"Now, now. There's nothing wrong with coffee," Bennett interrupted defensively. "The caffeine in regular coffee speeds up the metabolism, reduces the risk of heart disease and certain types of cancer, and can even stop an asthma attack."

"Bennett, I've never met someone who knew as much trivia as you. You have *got* to try out for *Jeopardy!* some day."

"They're comin' to D.C. again this year," his friend said quietly. "You know, for a contestant search."

James took a long drink of cold water and then patted his dripping mouth with his sweat-soaked gym towel. "When?"

Bennett shrugged. "This winter."

"You've got to go! You always said it was your big dream to appear on *Jeopardy!*"

His friend looked forlorn. "I don't think I'm ready."

"Just go to the tryouts. What have you got to lose?"

Bennett brightened. "You're right! Besides," he opened the gym door, casting one last look over his shoulder at the three attractive women clustered by the Y's single treadmill, "I could use a bit of a shake-up. My life has gotten kind of dull these days. Same old routine, day in and day out."

"I know what you mean," James said, eyeing the beige parka he had worn for the last six winters with distaste. He looked at his watch. He didn't want to go home, as his father was repainting the dining room and would demand help, and he didn't feel like making a last-minute date with Lucy because their previous one had ended awkwardly. Still, he felt strangely restless and wanted to do something other than drop by Food Lion or rent another lackluster movie from the video store. Suddenly, he got an idea. "Feel like spoiling your dinner?" James asked Bennett once they were in the parking lot. "We could stop by Custard Cottage."

Bennett zipped his navy blue uniform coat provided by the United States Postal Service and shivered. "Frozen custard in November?"

"Willy's got a coffee-and-custard deal going on right now. We'll get Sweet Lucy Light custard and skim milk in our coffees. A no-guilt snack."

"Twist my arm, why don't you?" Bennett sniggered. "You're on."

———

"Well, well!" Willy beamed as James opened the canary-yellow door of the purple and pink Victorian abode known as the Custard Cottage. "It's good to see you, my friends!"

"What happened to your garbage cans?" James asked, pointing out the window where the trash cans shaped like giant ice cream cones were normally placed.

"Graffiti." The jolly proprietor issued a deep belly laugh. "Apparently, Billy loves Jamie and in ways I don't think Jamie's parents would appreciate."

"Ah," James and Bennett replied in unison.

"I've got the stuff to clean 'em up with, but I figure they can stay inside for the winter anyhow. No one's eatin' outside these days—not even the teenagers who like to act like they're too cool to feel cold." He tugged on his starched, pinstriped apron. "Now what can I get for the most eligible bachelors in Quincy's Gap? I've got the most delicious Pumpkin Nutmeg custard you'll ever get on your tongue. Wanna try some?"

"Better not, thanks." James gestured toward a nearby chalkboard. "We'll each take your Cup & Cone special. Decaf and Sweet Lucy for me, please."

"I'll have full octane and a Chocolate Mousse cone." Bennett shot a glance at James. "I burned enough calories today—I gotta give myself a reward sometimes."

"Nothin' wrong with that." Willy completed their orders and then came out from behind the counter to sit with them while they ate. He stirred a packet of sugar into his own coffee mug and then took a sip. All of a sudden, he looked out the front picture window and began spluttering and fighting for air. Bennett thumped him on the back while Willy gasped. During the commotion, the front door opened to the tinkle of merry bells.

"What a *darling* place!" stated an appealing but unfamiliar female voice. James turned to see what the speaker looked like and was surprised to see Murphy and the gorgeous blondes hustling through the doorway, rubbing their bare hands together against the chilly November evening air.

"Don't worry, I'm not stalking you guys," Murphy teased, winking at James. "I'd like you all to meet my friends, Parker and Kinsley Willis."

The twins said, "Hi, y'all," and smiled. James could feel his heart flutter.

"Aren't Parker and Kinsley names of towns in Kansas?" Bennett asked once he found his tongue.

"Wow! You're the only person who's ever known that without us saying something!" The twin named Parker exclaimed. "You must be a master of geography."

"Well . . ." Embarrassed, Bennett looked to Willy for help, but the proprietor seemed to have forgotten all about the notion of providing customer service.

"Can we interrupt you for some hot tea, Willy?" Murphy prompted kindly.

Willy leapt out of his chair while issuing apologies. "Forgive a man for staring, ladies, but are you two famous or something?"

Kinsley laughed. "Nope. Just tall, blonde American girls with big white teeth. And these teeth would like to sink into a double scoop of Chocolate Cookie Dough Chunk, if you please."

Her sister examined the ice cream flavors carefully. "They all look delicious, but I'll just have a Diet Coke."

"And for you, Ms. Alistair?" Willy handed the twins their orders. "The usual Peanut Butter Cup Perfection?"

"You got it, Willy." Murphy linked her arm with the blonde sipping Diet Coke through a straw. "Parker and I were roommates at Virginia Tech," she explained to the three men. "Can you imagine what it was like to share a room with someone who looked like a supermodel and had the brains of a neurosurgeon?" Murphy smiled fondly at her friend. "But Parker was so nice that I liked her despite the fact that boys only hung around me to get inside info on Parker. What was her favorite flower? Was she dating anyone, yada yada. Now she's a vet with her own practice in Luray and between our two crazy jobs, we don't get together nearly enough."

"But we're working on it," Parker chimed in. "I've got a wonderful partner at my office, so I can leave the animals in good hands and we can hang out some more."

"Don't leave me out! I'm hoping you give Mr. Perfect Partner Dwight lots of furry clients so that you can show me all the sights," Kinsley said to her sister.

Turning back to the men, Kinsley offered them a winsome smile. "See, I'm brand new to town—a transplant from the North." She then paused in order to devour her frozen custard with gusto. James was amazed at how fast she could eat. After she licked a stream of custard from the back of her hand, Kinsley added, "but don't hold being a former fast-paced New Yorker against me."

"I don't think I could hold much against you, sugar," Willy said in appreciation while watching the beautiful young woman polish off her frozen treat.

After downing a cup of water, Kinsley wiggled the fingers on her left hand in farewell and headed back outside with Murphy and Parker.

———

"Did you get a load of those blonde bimbos?" Lindy squawked as she entered Custard Cottage a few seconds later.

"They're kind of hard to miss," James said with admiration. "And I don't think they're bimbos."

Lindy chose to ignore James. "I saw your mail truck outside, Bennett, and thought I'd join you. I need some sugar to perk me up after finding out that Barbie Number One is going to be joining the staff at Blue Ridge High."

Bennett gave Lindy an odd look. "What's the problem with that?"

Lindy thumped her fist on the counter. "What's the problem? I finally decided that I'm going to ask Principal Chavez out ... well, by the first of the year anyway. And now how am I supposed to do that? I'd be competing with a Heidi Klum lookalike. Every man in this town is going to be licking his chops over that girl."

"Ask him out anyway, Lindy," James advised.

"It's about damn time you did," Bennett commented. "You've been dreaming about that man for over a year, so why wait until January?"

Lindy ordered a hot chocolate with extra whipped cream and caramel drizzles. "Because I want to lose just a few more pounds. Especially now, with that young Christie Brinkley on staff. I need a boost of confidence."

"You don't need to lose any more weight," James offered. "You look terrific." It was the truth. Lindy had had her long black hair cut just above her shoulders. Layers snipped at sharp angles softened Lindy's round face, and she wore subdued makeup that enhanced her latte-hued skin and enormous dark eyes. Though Lindy was still quite curvaceous, especially around the bosom and hips, she had lost enough weight that her new and improved hourglass figure was strikingly voluptuous. Lindy had gone from being pudgy all over to being soft in all the right places.

"I wouldn't kick you out of bed for eatin' pork rinds," Willy teased as Lindy blushed.

"That's two resolutions for the new year then." Bennett raised his coffee cup in the air. "Here's to you bagging your man, Lindy. Me? I'm trying out for *Jeopardy!*"

Willy looked at James. "And what about you, Professor? You five always do stuff together, so you must be planning something big, too."

James shook his head and stared fixedly at the light brown drips swimming around in the bottom of his mug. "Not me. I'm fine with the status quo."

But he was lying. There was something he would very much like to change, and for once it had nothing to do with his appearance.

Suddenly, James felt the beginnings of a major headache coming on. He never used to get headaches, but lately they had been plaguing him more and more frequently. Rubbing his temples, he said goodbye to his friends and climbed into his old white Bronco.

For a moment, he gazed at his own reflection in the rearview mirror and then answered Willy's question truthfully. "I'd certainly like to change something. Yes, indeed. I'd like to know what a guy's gotta do to score with his girlfriend."

Jennifer Chappelle

ABOUT THE AUTHORS

Bestselling authors and award-winning journalists, Joyce and Jim Lavene, are a husband and wife team who started out writing novels in 1999 and have had more than forty books published. They enjoy spending time with their family (three children, five grandchildren) and their cat, Quincy who 'helped' them write *The Telltale Turtle*. Other books for Midnight Ink include *Swapping Paint* and *Hooked Up*. Visit them at their website: www.joyceandjimlavene.com
<http://www.joyceandjimlavene.com>

WWW.MIDNIGHTINKBOOKS.COM

From the gritty streets of New York City to sacred tombs in the Middle East, it's always midnight somewhere. Join us online at any hour for fresh new voices in mystery fiction.

At midnightinkbooks.com you'll also find our author blog, new and upcoming books, events, book club questions, excerpts, mystery resources, and more.

MIDNIGHT INK ORDERING INFORMATION

 ### Order Online:

- Visit our website www.midnightinkbooks.com, select your books, and order them on our secure server.

 ### Order by Phone:

- Call toll-free within the U.S. and Canada at
  1-888-NITE-INK (1-888-648-3465)
- We accept VISA, MasterCard, and American Express

 ### Order by Mail:

Send the full price of your order (MN residents add 6.5% sales tax) in U.S. funds, plus postage & handling to:

> Midnight Ink
> 2143 Wooddale Drive, Dept. 978-0-7387-1226-0
> Woodbury, MN 55125-2989

Postage & Handling:

Standard (U.S., Mexico, & Canada). If your order is:
  $24.99 and under, add $3.00
  $25.00 and over, FREE STANDARD SHIPPING

AK, HI, PR: $15.00 for one book plus $1.00 for each additional book.

International Orders (airmail only):
  $16.00 for one book plus $3.00 for each additional book

Orders are processed within 2 business days. Please allow for normal shipping time.
Postage and handling rates subject to change.